P9-DFF-926

COMMAND AND CONTROL GHOST RAID

By

JAMES D. MITCHELL

BERKLEY BOOKS, NEW YORK

This book is dedicated to the men of SOA (Special Ops Assn) and to all Special Forces Decade members who still maintain the vigil and keep the spirit of our fallen comrades alive.

Grateful appreciation is conveyed to the combined membership of the Trinity Arts Writers Association, Jim Morris, Amelia Mitchell, and Naomi Scott, whose collective and thoughtful critique contributed significantly in shaping this story.

COMMAND AND CONTROL 3: GHOST RAID

A Berkley Book / published by arrangement with
the author

PRINTING HISTORY
Berkley edition / December 1990

All rights reserved.
Copyright © 1990 by James D. Mitchell.
This book may not be reproduced in whole or in part,
by mimeograph or any other means, without permission.
For information address: The Berkley Publishing Group,
200 Madison Avenue, New York, New York 10016.

ISBN: 0-425-12437-1

A BERKLEY BOOK® TM 757,375
Berkley Books are published by The Berkley Publishing Group,
200 Madison Avenue, New York, New York 10016.
The name "Berkley" and the "B" logo
are trademarks belonging to Berkley Publishing Corporation.

PRINTED IN THE UNITED STATES OF AMERICA

10 9 8 7 6 5 4 3 2 1

VIETNAM
PS
3563
.I7663
G56
1990
c.2

Prologue

Prior to 1966 the primary mission of Special Forces in Southeast Asia was limited to counterinsurgency operations within South Vietnam. In mid-September 1966, that mission was expanded with the creation of a separate top-secret entity called Command and Control.

Command and Control was tasked to conduct covert combat operations and reconnaissance into denied areas. Command and Control North was the staging base created for the planning and support of operations into Laos and North Vietnam.

There were two other Command and Control projects: C and C South and C and C Central. CCS, located in Ban Me Thuot, targeted Cambodia. CCC, based outside Kontum, worked both sides of the fence—Laos and northern Cambodia.

Every Special Forces soldier involved with the C and C projects was a volunteer. Not that all Special Forces personnel in Vietnam weren't volunteers—they were. However, duty with C and C was a step beyond that, and generally viewed as patriotic masochism. Command and Control had the highest mortality rate of any Special Forces project in the war.

Command and Control teams were small—six personnel. Two Americans, designated One-Zero and One-One, comprised the leadership positions. Four indigenous personnel, usually Montagnard tribesmen, Yards, made up the firepower augmentation for the team.

The seven primary missions of C and C teams were area reconnaissance, bomb-damage assessments, enemy prisoner snatches, friendly POW recoveries, wire taps, sensor plants, and assassinations.

Each volunteer, upon accepting the C and C assignment, was required to sign a statement that essentially acknowledged: "If in the conduct of covert combat operations into denied areas, you are killed or captured, the United States and its allies will disavow any knowledge of you."

CCN was positioned south of Da Nang on a flat sandy coastal area. It was one of the largest Special Forces camps in Vietnam—three hundred meters long and two hundred meters wide. The eastern boundary was the South China Sea. Sixty meters off the southeastern tip of the wire zone, there was a Vietnamese fishing village. The village was nestled at the base of a huge rocky geographical freak called Marble Mountain.

Although the camp was secured by mine fields, concertina wire, machine-gun bunkers, and guard towers, it was always a high-priority target for VC sapper attacks. On August 23, 1968, CCN was hit hard by sappers and sustained one of the largest personnel losses in Special Forces history—sixteen KIA, twenty-six WIA.

Chapter 1

The dark struts of an inbound chopper stretched through the hot rotor downdraft like the giant talons of a condor. A stinging wave of sand washed over my face while I stood hurriedly rigging a nylon rope around my waist and legs, forming an expedient Swiss rappel seat. Cinching it tighter, the cord bit into my buttocks and thighs. I held it taut and quickly tied a square knot alongside my left hip, then looped two half hitches off on the loose ends of the knotted rope.

I glanced westward at the fading embers of Asian sun, then turned and squinted up at the huddled figure stranded high on a cliff ledge of Marble Mountain.

"How long's he been up there, sir?" I shouted as the whining chopper came to rest on the LZ.

Colonel Ivan Kahn stood with binoculars fixed on the motionless figure. He jerked the glasses away and turned into the wind facing me. "About twenty minutes! He's not moving. Probably scared shitless," he shouted. "Looks like his leg's broken. You ready?"

I snapped a carabiner through the frontal vertex of the Swiss seat while running to the chopper. "Roger, sir. Let's do it." I hefted myself onto the open troop cabin floor facing outward.

3

Colonel Kahn jumped to a seated position near two coils of green nylon rappelling rope. The Huey revved and ascended slowly out of a swirling cloud of sand. The hooch-dotted landscape of Command and Control North fell sharply away from our feet dangling above the chopper struts as we lofted upward like a huge Ferris wheel box.

Base camp CCN was positioned on a flat coastal plain nine klicks south of Da Nang City. The geographical freak that loomed just one hundred meters off the south side of our concertina wire zone was my destination. It was called Marble Mountain—The Rock. The mountain was about four hundred meters in length and jutted over three hundred feet straight up out of the sand. It was catacombed with tunnels and caves that the VC used as escape routes and hiding areas. It was also a sanctuary for the local Buddhists.

Our outpost personnel, located on the summit, kept a close watch on our most vulnerable side—but on occasion, at night, Charlie would rain sniper rounds down on our camp from the mouth of a cave, then disappear before we could get a fix on him.

I glanced at my watch: 1840 hours. Only moments before Colonel Kahn had sent a runner to my team hooch telling me to get to the chopper pad ASAP. The Vietnamese runner had briefed me about the situation while we both sprinted toward the chopper. He'd told me that one of the Montagnards on Recon Team Dakota had slipped and fallen about eighty feet down the mountain from the outpost at the top.

The One-Zero of the outpost, Brandon Flintlock, had radioed the command bunker immediately. At this point all we knew was that the Yard had landed on a rocky lip and that he was alive.

"We'll circle and try and get as close as we can before dropping you off on top, Brett. We need to see if the man is conscious,'' the colonel yelled, leaning toward me. "I'm not sure what we're about to attempt is in the books. You ever done this type rescue before?''

Colonel Kahn knew I'd been on the 7th SFG rappelling demonstration team at Fort Bragg prior to volunteering for 'Nam. I figured that was the primary reason he'd put me in the driver's seat on this. I was trained and proficient in every type of rappel inherent to mountaineering. And although I'd conducted rescue demonstrations several times at Bragg, that was under optimum conditions on a sixty-foot wooden tower with a safety belay man on the ground. This one was a different ball game entirely.

Leaning nearer to the colonel I shouted, "Negative, sir! But I did read about it once in a training manual.''

He jerked away and studied my face with squinted eyes. Cracking a half grin he said, "Well, at least we know it's in the goddamn books." He winked. "Don't worry, Yancy. If you crash and burn on this I'll make sure we name a bar stool in the club after you.''

"That's fuckin' wonderful, sir! I feel better already.''

Colonel Ivan Kahn had been CCN camp commander for two back-to-back tours. Every man in camp respected him—not out of gratuitous military protocol, but because he never hesitated to get out on the same wobbly limb with his troops.

He knew the enemy inside out and he made it a point to know the capabilities and limitations of his men. Often, before assigning a team to a mission, he'd meet with the One-Zero and solicit his opinion on target assessment.

Ivan Kahn could easily be sitting back watching this rescue attempt from the front porch. Instead, he chose to be right up here in the hot downdraft with me.

As our chopper approached the rugged wall face of the mountain I could see the little Montagnard huddled precariously on what appeared to be a two- or three-foot-deep ledge. The ship attempted to hover about fifty feet away from the wall to give us a good visual, but the coastal winds kept us swaying dangerously close to the cliff.

Colonel Kahn handed me binoculars. "Looks like he's conscious, Brett. He's holding his leg."

I focused the field glasses quickly on the Yard. His fatigues were badly ripped from the sliding fall. The good news was that he still had his web gear on. All C and C team gear was rigged with a harness to facilitate rope exfiltration from a hot LZ. The harness, called Stabo rigging, is essentially two nylon leg and shoulder straps sewn into the gear webbing with two carabiners, snap links, attached to steel D-rings on the top of the shoulder straps. When prerigged Stabo ropes were dropped from a chopper to a team on the ground all they had to do was snap into it and up they'd go right up out of alligator alley. If the team dangling below the chopper was real lucky, the pilot might even clear the trees before heading forward.

I moved the field glasses to scan the area above and around the cliff edge. The jolting chopper blurred my observation. I pulled the binoculars away and narrowed my eyes inspecting the jagged scabrous terrain. I could see several spider hole cave mouths and larger tunnel entrances partially concealed by scrub brush. There was no sign of VC but I knew damn well they were in there. If we left the Yard on that ledge overnight, he'd be dead by morning.

The slick dipped its nose and moved forward. The sightseeing tour was over.

Initially I'd thought about using a sixty-foot flex ladder hanging off the chopper. But after learning that the man was some eighty feet down the cliff, I realized a slick couldn't get close enough to the cliff without the rotor hitting the wall.

The only method available right now was Stabo—that meant I had to rappel down the wall and hook him up to a 120-foot rope that Colonel Kahn would drop from the chopper after I got into position.

As we rounded the east end of the mountain and ascended toward the top I shouted to Colonel Kahn. "I'm going to have to come down that wall right near a few of those caves. How about posting a couple of sharpshooters on a hooch roof to try and keep Charlie out of my hair?"

I felt I could get down the cliff easily enough, tie off, then get the man into position to hook up once the chopper brought the Stabo rope in to us. My primary concern was coming face-to-face with an AK rifle muzzle as I descended past a cave entrance. It would be a short-lived brick fight—me without any bricks.

"Roger, Brett. Good idea. As soon as we drop you off on top I'll head back to camp and have Murphy and Romero cover you.

"We're getting short on daylight," he said, scanning the dimming sky. "You're going to have to hurry this a little."

Our chopper swooped over the naked windy summit and began a slow descent. I grabbed a coiled rope, lifted it over my head, then down diagonally across my chest. I turned to inspect the circled rope anchored in the center of the troop cabin.

"Brett, after I get Murphy and Romero posted I'll be airborne again. We'll move in when I get the 'ready signal' from you."

"Roger, sir," I shouted back. "But don't throw that rope down to me. It could get tangled in the brush. Feed it to me a little at a time."

"Roger!"

We were on final approach coming down into the out-

post. I peered out through the swirling cloud of dirt at
Flintlock. A pair of tanker goggles covered his eyes. His
outstretched arms waved in the downdraft, guiding our
ship's descent.

A sudden jerk of the chopper indicated this was as close
as he could get to the rocky summit. I grabbed a floor
strap and carefully shifted outside the chopper to stand on
the strut before taking the final six-foot leap.

Colonel Kahn yelled over the thunderous rotor noise:
"Good luck, Yancy!"

I jumped clear of the ship and hit the jarring stony earth.
A second later the chopper disappeared over the mountain
edge and silence reigned.

Brandon Flintlock hurried through the dust toward me,
cocking his goggles up on his forehead. "Thanks for gettin' here fast, Yancy. Come on, I'll show you what looks
like the best route down."

I followed him to the northern edge of the OP.

"Careful here," he said, approaching the jagged rim.
He knelt and pointed at a broken-off section of ground.
"See, this is what gave way with him. I think it's all this
fuckin' rain we've had lately. Weakened this ground."

Flint leaned out farther. "If it hadn't been for that section of gravel down there breaking his fall, he'd have been
a goner for sure. We can't see him from here but he yelled
up to us once. His left leg's broken."

I removed my rope and dropped to a prone position,
gazing over the edge. Cool wind rippled through my hair.
Twenty feet below the rim there was a wide mound of rock
chips that sloped gradually downward and obscured any
view of the lower area. I could see a trough in the gravel
where the Montagnard had evidently hit and slid helplessly
over the side.

Flint informed me that below the gravel there was a

straight thirty- to forty-foot section of sheer cliff, then more jagged surface before reaching the small ledge.

"What's his name?"

"Ong."

"Ong!" I yelled. "You okay?"

A weak reply ascended as though carried by the wind. "No okay. No okay."

"No sweat, I come, we go Stabo. Go *bac-si*," I yelled back. It was important for him to know what the plan was so he didn't get hit with any surprises when I finally got down to him. All recon teams were trained in Stabo, but up until now nobody had done it off the side of a damn cliff.

I waited for a reply. None. After yelling again a reluctant "okay" rose from the depths.

Standing, I grabbed my rope and glanced back to the center of the summit. "I'll use that tree to tie off on," I said, dividing half of the rope and handing it to Flint. "Take this and coil it out on the ground with no tangles. Be right back."

I hurried to the tree with the lead section of rope, tied a bowline knot to anchor it, and pulled it tight. I then fed the remaining cord back to Flint's position.

"Brett, it just hit me you're not going to have a belay man down there. You don't have to . . . I mean, I could—"

"No problem, Flint. You can buy me a shot of Jim Beam when we get this vertical miracle accomplished," I said, grabbing the thick coil of rope and bouncing it loosely in my palm. I heaved it in a wide arc out over the cliff.

"Shot, hell! I'll buy you a fuckin' case," he said, yanking the tanker goggles off his head. "Here, you'd better use these on the trip down." He wiped the lenses with a quick brush across his sleeve.

I pulled a pair of leather gloves from my pocket, jabbed

my hands into them, then slipped the goggles on. Grabbing the lead end of the rope I lapped two parallel turns through the snap link gate and straightened them.

I backed slowly to within a meter of the windy cliff edge, then turned to gaze downward at my intended route of descent. The spiraled green cord trailed straight off the rim, down over the gravel chips, then disappeared below the nose of the slope.

"Y'all get back!" Flint yelled to his Montagnard teammates gathered near me.

I began pulling the trail end of the rope upward to see if it had any gnarls that had formed during the toss. After checking about thirty feet of the cord I was satisfied that there was enough unobstructed length to get well below the gravel slope. After descending that far I'd have to keep a sharp watch on the remaining rope. If a tangle had occurred, I'd have to stop, tie off, and then pull the gnarled end up to untie it. If a knot got into my snap link it would be like a wad of mud in a carburetor.

Glancing toward camp I could see a crouched figure running toward the idling chopper. Within moments Colonel Kahn would be airborne. I scanned the hooch rooftops to see if the riflemen were in position. Several men were climbing onto the S-1 admin building.

I turned, took a good bit of rope in my right palm, and brought it over my hip. I kept my grip loose, feeding the cord easily through my brake hand while backing to the cliff edge.

"Here, Brett. This might come in handy," Flint said, holding a .45-caliber pistol out to me butt first. "You're gonna be comin' pretty close to a couple of those caves."

My elbow involuntarily drew inward to touch the holstered 380 Beretta hanging inside my shirt. "Keep it, Flint," I said, noticing the M-26 fragmentation grenades hanging off his web gear shoulder straps. "Pass me a couple of those grenades."

He quickly pulled two of the grenades free and handed them to me. I tucked one into each of my shirt pockets.

I placed a brake hand firmly on the small of my back. Adrenaline began to pump as I eased my boot heels out over the edge and leaned slowly backward, feeling the rope crawl through my fingers like a spiral snake. Strong wind blew the cravat wildly about my neck.

"I owe ya one for this, Yancy," Flint yelled.

I darted a wink back to him. "Shit, I haven't done anything yet, Flintlock!"

Looking back into the wind I took two quick steps downward onto the jagged cliff wall and committed myself to wits, muscle, and 3000-pound tensile-strength rope.

The rasp of my boot cleats against the cliff scattered a cloud of dirt through the wind. I dropped rapidly to the lower slope and kept moving steadily backward through the loose ankle-deep stone chips. My movement stirred gravel along my path, spilling it over the lower nose of the slope.

I halted. "Rock, Ong! Rock!" I yelled as the shale cascaded down the mountain.

My feet began to slide. I hurriedly leaned forward, yanking slack forward through the snap link, then jabbed my brake fist into my backside. With all my strength I sprang away from the slope and plunged over the edge in free ascent. A stinging shower of stones pelted me like a hailstorm.

The abrupt halting shock jarred my spine. My teeth gnashed as the Swiss seat bit into my crotch. My body swayed, suspended beneath the dark lip of the overhang. Releasing my forward guide hand, I quickly rubbed the dusty residue off my goggles and squinted down into the pendulous shadows.

Forty feet below I could see the little Montagnard huddled in a fetal position on the ledge. He moved one arm, waving to me while keeping the other shielding his face.

Flint's voice echoed high above me. "Yancy! How you doin' down there, buddy?"

I grimaced, trying to pull the rope away from my groin. "Okay, but I could sure use a steel-cup jockstrap right now!"

Whispers of cool wind rushed over me as I descended gradually while scanning the dim, craggy area for signs of cave openings. Above and to the left of Ong there was a large triangular opening concealed partially by low brush. The only other opening I could see was directly below him several meters.

As I dropped closer to Ong the cliff angled outward, allowing my feet to touch the rough surface. My boots knocked rocks loose from the wall. Ong quickly raised his arm over his head again.

I pulled my feet away from the wall and turned sideways using my left hand to steady myself while dropping to within three feet of the small ledge.

"You about ready to go home?" I said, stopping— dangling above him.

"Me ready!" he said with a gritty-faced smile.

"Where hurt?"

"Hur' here *beaucoup*," he replied, pointing to his left leg.

I peered out into the dimming sky and saw the distant silhouette of the chopper. I signaled, moving my free arm slowly back and forth.

Turning my attention to Ong I kept my voice confident. "Okay, we go *bac-si*. Go Stabo. Understand?"

"Okay, me understan."

I peered upward and yelled to let Flint know I was in

position. I instructed him to guide the chopper in as near perpendicular to me as possible when it came to hover overhead.

Looking back down I studied the ledge. There was enough space for me in the small area near his feet, but I'd have to straddle him while hooking the Stabo rope on his shoulder harness. I decided the safest thing to do was drop down and stay linked to my Swiss seat until I got Ong secured. I still wasn't sure the ledge would support the combined weight of both of us.

"Okay, Ong. I'm going to—"

Suddenly a burst of full-auto AK fire screamed through the wind, riveting the stone wall. Shattered rock spewed over me. Jerking my head back I glimpsed a muzzle flash as the rounds hammered again. Lead venom chewed a rock-splintering path along the outer side of the ledge.

Shots crackled in the distance. The sharpshooters had spied the muzzle flashes and were pouring it on the sniper.

Releasing my brake hand I dropped madly to the ledge, slamming my body face forward—hugging the cold stone wall. Hurriedly my fingers pulled a grenade from my pocket and jerked the pin free.

I grabbed my lifeline in one hand, leaned outward, and hurled the lethal steel ball in an arcing hook shot up and into the tunnel mouth.

The jarring grenade explosion belched a gray, fragmented cloud of debris out into the windy sky like a hot cannon blast.

Clinging to the rope my labored breath shouted, "Ong, Ong! You . . . still . . . with me, partner? You okay?"

"I'm tink maybe okay!" he shouted back.

I glanced at his wide eyes peering up at me. "Okay," he repeated while shifting his eyes down to my trembling legs.

Pressing my knees tightly together I tried to stop the quivering chill that rippled through my bones.

I took a deep breath and forced a frowning grin at him. "You don't tell anybody about this, all right?"

The little Montagnard smiled. "I'm tell nothing cep you being number focking one!"

Our Stabo exfil from LZ Cliff Hanger went smoothly and without further incident. Between the sharpshooters and my grenade tossing, Charlie lost interest in messing with us anymore.

After hooking Ong into the Stabo rope I tied a slack knot several feet above him and snapped in using my Swiss seat carabiner. As we lifted away I noticed frays on my rappel rope—it had been partially severed by the VC rounds.

The ride over to the camp dispensary was quick and as the chopper lowered us to the sandy earth of home a crowd of men cradled Ong in their arms.

Before being carried inside he smiled and gave me a Montagnard style double-eyed wink.

As I untied my seat and began rubbing some well-deserved circulation into my crotch Colonel Kahn shouted while trudging toward me. "Good show, Yancy! Out-fuckin'-standing!"

I accepted his firm handshake and grinned. "Looks like you'll have to name that bar stool after someone else, sir."

Smiling, he tapped me on the back and motioned toward the camp honky-tonk. "Come on, looks like you could use a cold beer."

Walking away he glanced over at me. "Don't worry about that bar stool, Yancy. You'll get another chance at it sooner than you think."

Chapter 2

The hot Asian sun glistened off the amber beach that spanned the eastern perimeter of CCN. Clad in cutoff fatigue shorts, I trudged barefoot through the warm loose sand toward the South China Sea. I clutched the strap of a small rucksack draped over my bare shoulder while keeping my gaze fixed on the blond-topped profile of a lone surfer.

Sergeant Swede Jensen maneuvered gracefully up and down a lofty green wave while stretching a leg forward toward the nose to the surfboard to hang five. A crisp offshore breeze scattered a jagged line of whitecaps along the crest of the gently rolling wave.

I stopped and watched him crouch beneath the windblown curl. He leveled his long red board, a human tracer cutting through the emerald tube. As the wall of water subsided Swede raised and skillfully turned back over the whitewash. He dropped into a prone position, digging his hands into the water, then paddled out to catch another wave.

If it weren't for the high rolls of concertina wire, machine-gun bunkers, guard towers, and mine fields girdling the vast perimeter of CCN, the camp could easily be mistaken for some low-rent vacation resort. I opened the gate

at the beach entrance and walked onto the hard-packed
sand. My nostrils filled with salt-scented ocean air.

Moving toward the water my eyes scanned the beach surface, looking for any mound or break in the smooth sand
that might indicate a recently planted VC booby trap. None.

During daylight hours the beach area was considered
secure and commonly used for team training and recreation. We'd recently nicknamed the area "Buffalo Beach."
The name was coined the day after my team had conducted night guard duty. That night, my new One-One,
Arnold Binkowski, mistook a water buffalo on the beach
for a king-size VC. Ski proceeded to empty a full automatic magazine of 5.56 into the hapless vagrant, blowing
buffalo hide, blood, and a large quantity of bullshit over
half the beach. The next morning the camp medic gave
Ski a handful of APCs and a thorough eye examination.

My attention turned back to the surfer. As he mounted
another swell I quickly pulled a fifth of Jim Beam from
the ruck. I yelled out to him while holding the bottle high
above my head. "Hey, Swede! How about a Beam break,
compadre?"

He darted a glance toward me, then jutted a thumbs-up
response. He cut an angular turn toward the shallow white
water tide pools separating us.

Jensen was from Santa Cruz, California. He was a wry
character. Although his laid-back style wouldn't allow him to
admit it, everyone knew he was the best One-Zero in camp.

He'd been in 'Nam twenty-six back-to-back months,
running over thirty missions across the fence into Chuck's
turf, the NVA stronghold—Laos. I'd been assigned as his
One-One, assistant team leader, when I first came to CCN
forty-nine weeks earlier. I'd learned "the ropes of Recon"
from the best teacher in town.

Over the past couple of years Swede had been awarded

a rucksack full of awards and decorations. Recently, he'd refused a DSC, Distinguished Service Cross. He'd told Colonel Kahn, "I can't accept an award for an operation that cost us three lives."

After two months and four missions with Swede's team, RT California, he recommended me for One-Zero status. Soon after that I was assigned my own team—Recon Team Texas.

Swede Jensen had taught me a lot with his personally honed tactics and techniques—things that weren't in the book. Since taking over RT Texas, those methods had saved us from the NVA meat grinder more than once.

I smiled, remembering some of his homespun recon philosophy: "Never take the same trail out that you took going in, and if you're on a fuckin' trail going in, you're wrong in the first fuckin' place."

But the most important lesson I'd learned from him was to trust the little people—the Montagnards. He told me, "Let the Yards be your nose and ears when you're in the bush. They know the sounds and smells that belong there and ones that don't. They can smell the difference between monkey shit and communist shit, and can tell a cockatoo chirp from a well-mimicked NVA whistle signal." His favorite phrase in referring to the NVA and the VC was "Those scum-suckin' communist globs of spit."

Sunlight sparkled off his wet body as he strode toward me. He lowered his board to the beach, glancing at the bottle of Beam in my hand. "What's the occasion, Brett?" he said with a lopsided grin. "Didn't we celebrate Ho Chi Minh's death last month, September? This is still the year of the chicken, isn't it?"

"Roger that," I replied, taking two canteen cups from the ruck and blowing the loose sand out of them.

He ran his fingers through the wet tangles of his hair.

"By the way, you did good on that rescue yesterday up on The Rock. Damn good."

He narrowed his eyes. "I'll bet I know what this is all about! You've decided to marry that good-looking journalist you met on R and R in Thailand? What's her name?"

"Tracy. Tracy Gibbs," I said, pouring a hearty dose of Beam into each cup. "No, Swede, marriage isn't the occasion. But it has kicked around inside me a couple of times."

He sat cross-legged facing the sea. "Well, let it kick around some more, buddy, before you bite the hook. No man coming out of this fuckin' war is ready for domestication. Besides, I haven't met a round-eyed woman yet who understands Special Forces types."

I handed Swede a quarter-full cup and sat near him. "Maybe so, partner, but she's the greatest thing since thirty-round magazines and napalm. You might meet a gal like her if you'd stop hanging around Tudo Street. There are some round-eyed women over here, you know. Nurses, journalists—"

He butted in with a wry tone. "Speaking of Tudo Street, did you hear they canceled the Virgins Day Parade?"

He continued without waiting for a reply. "Yeah, it seems one girl broke her foot, and the other girl didn't want to march alone."

Swede peered out at the waves as if talking to them. "I read somewhere that a Special Forces wife views her husband as a guy who passes through Fort Bragg once or twice a year with a rucksack full of dirty clothes, a hard-on, and an urge to get knee-walking drunk before heading back off to war."

He grinned, then glanced over to me before drinking. "But, shit, you didn't come down here to listen to my philosophy on marriage and women. What's on you mind?"

I tapped my cup to his and looked back at the white-capped waves. My jaw tightened remembering the names of a dozen friends who'd been kill during the past year.

Raising my cup I spoke slowly, "Here's to Wald, Brown, Dexter, Shoe, Villerosa, Davis . . ." I paused and peered down at the tide water rushing toward my feet. "And William Washington."

A frown crossed my face. I looked over at Swede. "And on, and on, et cetera, et cetera. Here's to camaraderie, and round-eyed women." I raised the cup to my lips and drank. The familiar sharp bite of sour mash whiskey tremored through me like the opening jerk of a parachute.

Jensen was silent. He drank slowly.

A strong breeze blew a puff of sand across my back. I sensed the damp smell of impeding rain laced through the warm air and turned to study the dark clouds hovering over the naval compound at Monkey Mountain a few miles north of us. A bright finger of lightning stabbed into the sea.

Strangely, the distant storm reminded me of some words spoken by William Washington. Will had been hit and killed, two months ago today, August twenty-ninth. It occurred during a body recovery mission we'd conducted in a southern Laos target area called Hotel-5.

A few months prior to the fatal firefight we'd been on a POW snatch mission in northern Laos. We'd just crept into a RON, remain-over-night position, when it started to rain heavily. Will looked over at me and whispered, "Boss, I'll take the first watch. I got a feelin' in my bones Charlie's gonna come 'round tonight. You know how those little bastards love to work in the rain. It's like they gettin' paid overtime or something."

Will's bone prophecy meter was right. We got hit hard around midnight. We managed to run, trip, and stumble our way out of the RON and get to a suitable defensive position. We set up a hasty claymore-mine ambush and when Chuck pursued and rushed us we blew his scum-suckin' ass all the way to the great rice paddy in the sky. I still remember the rank smell of exploded blood strewn through the wet shadows with the agonized screams of dying men.

I gulped down the last of my Beam, poured another, then turned to Jensen to refill his cup.

"Whoa!" he said, pushing the bottle upward with the lip of his canteen cup. "We got that 'Saydem' briefing with Colonel Kahn at 1500. I don't want to be carried into the War Room on a stretcher!"

I grinned and withdrew the bottle. Saydem was the popular pronunciation for the letters SADM. All One-Zeros and One-Ones had gotten the word to be in the command bunker War Room today for a briefing about it. But, at this point, nobody knew what it was. We didn't know if it was a new tactic, a new aircraft, or a new venereal disease. What we did know was that it was top secret.

I checked my watch: 1145 hours. After scooping out a shallow hole in the moist sand I set the half-full bottle into the depression and glanced over at Swede. "You're on your third extension tour here—all C and C time. Right or wrong?"

"Roger. That's right," he answered casually.

"How come you're staying here so long? You got a parking ticket back home you're trying to beat?"

He glanced at me with a quick smirk. Then a slow grin came over his face was if a light bulb had gone on in his head.

"Now I get it, Yancy! Now I know what this fucking impromptu drinking session is all about. You're short. And you're thinking about extending your tour, and you want me to give you some goddamn reasons to stay. . . . Well, no fucking way, amigo."

He lay back on the sand, propping his head on the edge

of his board, and rested the cup on his chest. "No fucking way," he repeated. "The decision to stay in 'Nam is about as personal as things get.

"In fact, it's kind of like surfing. Nobody can tell a man which wave to catch. You pick it yourself. That way, if you wipe out, there's nobody to blame but you!" He tilted his head forward and took a sip of Beam.

Jensen's perception wasn't exactly center target, but it was close. Although I'd already made up my mind to extend, I was curious to see if my motivation had any correlation with his. It was apparent he wasn't about to reveal anything more on the subject and I figured that was his prerogative.

Extension tours were six months in length. During the past year I'd lost a lot of friends and the best partner anyone could ask for—Will. I didn't need a pep talk, drum rolls, or flags waving to decide on staying. Simply put, I figured I owed another six months in the combat arena to some damn good men I'd had the privilege of serving with. Men who gave their lives to defend the freedom of a little country that most people couldn't find on a map with a magnifying glass.

I took the last gulp of Beam from my cup, then tucked it and the bottle into the pack. I stood, lifted the ruck, and looked down at Swede. "I gotta get back up to my team. It's almost chow time. You coming?"

Jensen opened one eye, glancing up at me. "I'll be along in a while. You know I've never liked long mess-hall lines."

I turned to walk away, then looked back at him. "I know why you stay here, Jensen. It's because you're the best surfer in camp."

Walking on, I said loudly, "Of course, you're the only surfer in camp! . . . See you at the Saydem briefing."

Chapter 3

Approaching our small, tin-roofed team hooch I saw Tuong clad only in tiger-striped fatigue pants emerge from the doorway. His eyes quickly found mine. He bounded toward me. His hurried pace indicated he had a problem that needed immediate attention.

Tuong, the team tail gunner, was the youngest of my four Montagnards—sixteen. Rham, Lok, and Phan were older, but even if you combined their ages you'd still get a figure less than seventy. They were all dead-serious warriors when we were in the bush, but somehow when we were on stand-down, in camp, they returned to the playful habits of youth.

Montagnards, the Dega mountain people, were the original inhabitants of South Vietnam. Just like our American Indian, they got prejudicially classified as primitives, savages in their own country, and were cast off into the Central Highlands and other remote sectors of Vietnam and Laos. For my money the Yards were the best and most loyal fighters we had. I made it a point to never ignore the little people, as we fondly called them.

The Dega Cowboys worked, fought, sweated, and died for us. Their allegiance was to Americans, not the South

Vietnamese. They had felt the hard sting of Vietnamese
discrimination for a long time. They knew damn well that
if this war ended tomorrow and we left, they'd be back
under the Vietnamese whip the next day. We owed them
our allegiance.

Officially I was their boss, but the close-knit relation-
ship was more like father and sons. If I had had a car,
they'd be trying to borrow it—since I didn't, they borrowed everything else including my razor; although none
of them had any beard to shave.

Tuong flashed a frowning smile as he trudged emphatically toward me. "Sar Brett, you pleasing tell Skee he
touchie piece he must move piece."

It was apparent there was a team chess match in progress back in the hooch, and next to a firefight, that was
about as competitive as things could get.

I slipped my arm over his bare shoulder as he turned to
walk beside me. "Well, babysan," I said, keeping my
gaze toward the hooch. "Ski really needs to win a game.
He's never won a game yet, has he?" Binkowski had been
on the team six weeks. He only had one mission under his
belt and I knew, for his own self-esteem he needed to win
a game of chess.

The standing rule was, if you touch a piece you had to
move it. But Binkowski was always changing his mind
about a move and it drove the Yards up a wall. When that
occurred I was the designated referee. Chess was more
like a group contact sport with the Yards. They'd playfully
punch each other and go through verbal jousting matches
as the game evolved. Although it was all in fun, there was
a certain honor in being team chess champion—even
though the title had a habit of changing hands every week
or so.

Tuong quickly answered my question. "That right. He never win game yet. But close sometime."

I glanced down at him and smiled. "Well, close only counts in horseshoes and hand grenades. It's not like winning. Maybe we need to let him win a game. You know, he's kind of apprehensive right now."

Tuong stopped in his tracks just as I'd expected. A gust of wind danced through his jet-black hair. "What do appy-hen-see mean, Sar Brett?"

My diversion had worked. I stopped and looked back at him. Tuong was always concerned with improving his English and wouldn't hesitate to ask a question anytime any-place. So, sometimes when I felt a need to divert from the subject at hand, I'd toss a new word into our conversation.

"*Apprehensive* means *beaucoup* careful, cautious. Ski is trying hard to win a game so you guys don't think he's dumb. You understand?" I wasn't giving him a full defi-nition because I didn't want to get it too complicated.

Tuong smiled. "I'm understan," he said, looking to-ward the beach at Jensen. "I'm see you bee talky wid Swee. What you talky bout?" He questioned with a slight tilt of his head.

"Women," I answered while turning to walk onward. "We talked about women."

He ran to catch me. Grabbing my hand he looked up at me with questioning eyes while walking backward in front of me. I knew what was really bothering him. For the past several days they'd all been wondering if I was going to extend my tour and stay with them.

I'd gone through the alpha and the omega of reasoning during the decision. A part of me that included thoughts of Tracy Gibbs said, "Get the hell out of this marathon war while I'm still in one piece." But the dominant side echoed with what boiled down to a one-word rebuttal to reasoning—camaraderie.

And there was something else that weaved into my decision. The Yards had loved William Washington as much as I had. They'd seen him fatally crushed into hot earth with a swarming maze of communist lead. Now, if I left them, it would be like walking away and giving the kids up for adoption—I couldn't do it.

I looked down at the imploring dark, faithful eyes standing silently in front of me. His voice was almost a whisper. "Sar Brett, you signee paper yet? You know, stay wid us?" He cast a glance over his shoulder toward the admin hut, then looked back at me.

I smiled and winked. "I signee paper after chow, babysan. Now let's get the team and go eat."

Releasing my hand he shouted "Number-focking-one!" He turned to run ahead of me, then halted and yelled back into the face of a cool wind. "I think maybe we nee let Skee win game, okay? He no be appy-hen-see then."

After chow I went to the S-1 shop to sign my extension papers. Tuong insisted on coming with me as if he planned on inspecting and notarizing the paper. He walked by my side with all the enthusiasm of a youngster on his way to buy his first bicycle.

While we were in the admin office our squatty camp sergeant major, Twitty, made it a point to tell me that I was suffering from some psychiatric disorder by extending my tour.

Twitty squalled, "You probably ain't aware of it but our mortality rate is over two hundred percent. You done been on borrowed time since you got here, Yancy. And now you're borrowin' some more!"

I ignored his statistical edification, signed, and left.

Twitty was more of a displaced bureaucrat than he was a soldier. He'd never seen any field in 'Nam, but he frequently boasted in the camp club over a table full of beer cans that he'd "kicked ass and took names in Korea." The absence of a CIB, Combat Infantryman's Badge, on his starched fatigues didn't do much to authenticate his slurred war stories.

He'd made no secret of his contempt for me ever since I'd kicked the living feces out of one of his teletype operators for calling Will a nigger. The incident occurred they day after Will had been killed. Even though Johnson, the kickee, was only in the hospital for a few days, Twitty was still steaming about it.

The good news about Twitty was, he rarely showed his face down in the recon barracks area. So, unless we accidentally encountered one of his filibuster war-story acts in the club, the only time we saw him was when we had to go to the S-1 for some admin requirement. When that occurred Twitty always treated recon personnel like we were some walking disease. Our scuffed, rough-cut appearance was in sharp contrast with the starched, spit-shined world of the sergeant major and his "Remington Raiders."

Once, when I was working as Jensen's One-One, Swede and I bumped into him near the isolation compound. Twitty immediately broke into a song-and-dance routine about how our boots needed a good shine. Jensen began to light one of his Eastwood-type cigars, talking while he puffed at the match. "Sergeant Major, as I understand it, it's your job to act as a primary support element for recon operations. That right or wrong?"

"That's right," Twitty replied with a controlled tremor in his voice. "That's right . . . but what the hell has that got to do with the goddamn price of tea in China or fuckin' boots?''

Jensen smirked. "Everything, Sergeant Major. Just send one of your support boys down to my hooch and I'll be glad to let him shine my boots.''

Twitty was about ready to blow a gasket when he saw Colonel Kahn approaching. The colonel's congratulatory words directed at Swede took about half the air out of Twitty's bagpipes. "Those were some good pictures you and Yancy got of that NVA bunker complex during that last mission. Good show.''

After returning our salutes he looked at Twitty. "I guess you've already told Sergeant Jensen and Yancy about the photos?''

Jensen butted in with a broad grin. "Yes, sir. The Sergeant Major never misses a chance to tell us what a good job we're doing.''

The befuddled expression on Twitty's face was priceless. It was all I could do to keep from bursting out laughing.

Chapter 4

A light rain began to fall as Arnold Binkowski and I approached the gray concrete bunker that was the Tactical Operations Center, TOC, commonly called "Big Bunk."

I glanced at my watch: 1430 hours. I'd deliberately arrived early for the briefing to try to gain some advanced intel on what SADM was all about.

After showing our passes and signing in, we entered the large bunker. The thick steel door closed behind us with an ominous echo as if we were locked in a tomb.

The TOC was perhaps the best built bunker in South Vietnam and for good reason—it housed the communications and command center for some of the most highly classified operations being conducted in the war. The structure was unusual for a bunker. The upper level extended eight feet above the ground. The lower level descended ten feet into the earth.

The high outer walls of the fortress were composed of steel-laced cement forty-eight inches thick. It was surrounded by an eight-foot-high chain-link fence. The fence was positioned not so much as a barrier to prevent intrusion, but as an outer buffer to detonate NVA rockets before

they hit the walls. A massive VC assault on the bunker
back in August didn't even dent Big Bunk.

Taking a left turn down a dim empty hallway, Ski and I
walked toward the east end of the complex. We stopped
at the door marked: WAR ROOM—Knock before breathing!

I glanced at Ski. This was his first trip inside the nu-
cleus of CCN. The wide-eyed look on his face as he studied the door made it seem as if he were taking the sign
instructions literally.

I slipped my CAR-15 carrying strap over my head and
placed the weapon in a long rifle rack beside the door.
"We check our guns here, partner." The empty rack told
me we were the first ones to arrive for the SADM briefing.

"Yes, sir . . . I mean roger, Brett."

I looked at him as he removed his rifle. His six-foot
four-inch mesomorphic frame put him about three inches
taller than me. Binkowski was a bonified Boston Yankee,
and up until six seeks ago he'd been assigned as one of
Twitty's "Remington Raiders." That tour in the haven of
bureaucracy was one reason Ski was still suffering from
the "yes-sir syndrome."

Right after I lost Will, Colonel Kahn had queried me
about assigning Binkowski as my One-One. It was Ivan
Kahn's habit to always check with his One-Zeros before
making final decisions about related personnel changes,
tactical SOPs, and mission directives.

I'd been hesitant about Binkowski at first even though
he'd volunteered for the combat slot. Colonel Kahn informed me that although Ski had made it through jump
school he'd been dropped from Special Forces Training
Group at Fort Bragg. He'd been terminated for fighting.
The colonel and I both agreed that it seemed paradoxical
that a soldier being conditioned for combat arms should
be terminated from that pursuit simply for fighting.

The team was initially resentful of Ski taking over Will's slot—but four weeks later, on his first mission, Arnold Binkowski earned his salt. We'd been in the tiger's mouth two days when we made heavy contact and I was hit. After my lights went out, Ski, while carrying me, led the team, broke contact, and got us all to an exfil LZ in one piece.

Now, even though the Yards still weren't too crazy about Binkowski's chess-playing habits, they did respect his combat intestinal fortitude. Binkowski still had some rough edges. In the six months ahead I planned on making him better. I knew that when it came time for me to leave, Ski would inherit my One-Zero slot. A big part of my job now was to make sure he was ready for it.

I nodded toward the door in front of us. "Go ahead, Ski. Knock."

He rapped lightly on the door.

"Louder, Arnold. You sound like a pawnbroker tapping on a watch crystal."

He frowned as if to emphasize his heavier knock, which was only about half a decibel louder.

I recognized the gruff voice of Master Sergeant Luther Hayes as he growled from behind the door. "Who's there? Sounds like fuckin' Bambi!"

"RT Texas. Yancy, Binkowski," I shouted.

The sharp metallic sound of a bolt echoed and the heavy steel door swung open revealing the short, stout appearance of the sergeant. He smirked as we walked in. "Damn, Brett, your knock sounds weak today. Maybe you need to start eating breakfast."

I ignored his attempted wit. "Loot, this is my One-One, Arnold Binkowski. Ski, this is Loot Hayes, the senior operations NCO. He claims his dick drags the ground. Some people say that's why he steps on it every now and then." I cracked a half grin.

Binkowski poked his hand out before Loot could respond. "Glad to meet you. Call me Ski."

Hayes frowned while his arm jolted from Ski's handshake. "Y'all are early," he said, yanking his hand away from Ski's grip. "Coffee's over there. I got work to do." He walked away, flexing his fingers as if to make sure they were still functioning. I glanced around the room. It was empty except for Loot, Ski, and me.

Walking to the small coffee table I noticed Ski's mouth gape when he looked up and saw the enlarged picture of a dead NVA above the table.

"Holy shit," he muttered, staring at the photograph.

The photo showed a contorted blood-soaked figure sprawled across a pile of bodies. Bullets had literally shredded his entire torso into a glob of what looked like decayed hamburger. Above the picture someone had written the words:

Right now there is a controversy in the Senate about the firepower credibility of the M16. Try and convince this communist bastard that the M16 can't do the fucking job!

Ski looked silently around the room at the ceiling-to-floor maps of Laos, Cambodia, and Vietnam that covered three walls. In one corner a teletype machine pecked relentlessly while scrolling out a long message. A massive desk occupied the center of the room.

"This place is something else." Ski muttered.

Ignoring his awed observation I poured a cup of coffee and walked toward the teletype. Ski quickly poured himself a cup and followed me. As I neared the machine I caught the faint aroma of what smelled like perfume.

I turned my head sniffing the air. The fragrance reminded me of Tracy. Stopping, I looked around the big room. "Ski, do you smell . . . Never mind."

Binkowski frowned, looking down at his shirt. "Do I smell? Did you ask if—"

"Skip it. I must be imagining things." I knew there were no women assigned to any administrative positions at CCN. The only women in camp were the cleaning and laundry girls and they weren't allowed anywhere near the TOC.

Loot noticed me staring at the teletype message and moved toward me just as my eyes caught a glimpse of a page heading: TOP SECRET LIMDIS NOFORN. I'd learned that "limdis noforn" stood for "limited distribution, no foreign distribution," which meant that the Vietnamese did not have access to any part of the message. I understood the necessity for security precautions in handling intel, but I'd always thought it strange that we were referring to the Vietnamese as "foreigners" in their own country.

Loot Hayes stepped between me and the teletype. "Sorry, Brett, this is hot stuff. Can't let you see this!"

As the message ended I said, "Loot, what is that cologne you're wearing? Smells like a French whorehouse in here."

He scowled up at me while removing the message from the machine. "Don't use no fucking cologne. It's probably—" He halted his words in mid-sentence.

"Probably what?"

"Nothing . . . nothing. Now, like I said, I got work to do. Why don't you and Squeeze, I mean Ski there, go on down to the briefin' room. Colonel'll be along in a minute."

Loud knocks pounded on the War Room door. Loot turned the message facedown on the desk and hurried toward the door.

"Brett, now that you mention it, I smell something too," Ski said, sniffing the air. "It reminds me of Chanel number five. I had a girlfriend back in Boston who used it." Ski smiled, staring at the ceiling as if looking back in time. "She'd rub some of it along the inside of her thighs. Then she'd say, 'Come closer and smell my Chanel, honey.' "

Arnold's dream dissertation was beginning to ignite memories of Tracy Gibbs in me. I cut in to his fantasy as two other team leaders entered the room. "Let's get down to the briefing room."

By 1455 hours a collective assemblage of twelve One-Zeros and One-Ones sat in the small, musty lower-level briefing room awaiting Colonel Khan's arrival. The gathering was unusually quiet. Commonly, there would be a lot of chatter, joking, and a general bullshit session in progress. I reasoned that the absence of conversation was due to the fact that no one knew what to expect in today's meeting.

A large 1:250,000 scale contour map of Southeast Asia dominated the entire wall behind a small mahogany lectern. The red-lettered words TOP SECRET were boldly printed at the top and bottom of the map.

Ski pulled a pack of cigarettes from his shirt pocket and started to light one.

"Hold off on that, partner. The ventilation down here is terrible unless they have the fans going."

"Roger, understand," he said, tucking the pack back into his pocket. "I really didn't need one anyhow. I can wait. I can wait." His voice trailed off in a melodic tone.

Suddenly the door swung open and Colonel Ivan Kahn strode briskly into the room. He was accompanied by the S-3 officer, Major Henry Jinx.

"A-ten-shun!" the major shouted.

"Don't get up, gents. Keep your seats," the colonel said while quickly unfolding a notebook on the lectern. He removed his beret, slid it under the left epaulet of his shirt, then looked out at us. He ran his fingers over his short-cropped silver hair and spoke in a personable tone. "Gents, this is one of the few occasions I've had to assemble all of you in one room in a long time. It's good to have you here.

"I say all of you, but actually we have three teams in the field right now, so it's not really the whole crew. But close enough for government work."

He glanced at Major Jinx. "Henry, how about turning the fans on in here."

Ivan Kahn pulled a panatela from his pocket and spoke around the match while lighting the cigar. "Smoke 'em if you got 'em."

After taking a puff he stepped forward. "I'll kick this off with some good news. I'm proud to say that every pendulating Richard in this room is doing a damn fine job." His eyes narrowed as he darted a smiling glance back to the map behind him, then gestured toward it with his cigar. "We, namely you, are now responsible for digging out over eighty percent of the reliable combat intel coming out of the Prairie Fire and Nickle Steel Area of Operations. The other twenty percent is coming from the CIA, CAS, and aerial photos.

"Our teams are hoeing some tough, fucking roads to get the job done, but in a word, gents, out-fucking-standing!

"Prairie Fire is as hot as its name," he said while walking toward the map and pointing to Laos. Moving his cigar upward toward North Vietnam he spoke as though talking to the map. "Now, Nickle Steel up here has a new game for us."

He paused, turned, and dropped his smile while looking over the entire group. "That new game is what this meeting is all about. Saydem!"

The colonel looked at Binkowski who was puffing on a Marlboro. "Ski, what is Saydem? Do you know?"

Arnold stuttered, trying to answer the unexpected question. "No . . . no, sir."

The colonel's eyes shifted to the back of the room. "Iron Oak. What is Saydem?"

I looked around toward James Iron Oak. Iron was a full-blooded Ute Indian from Durango, Colorado—Swede Jensen's One-One. He was usually a quiet-type person. He smiled a lot while nodding his head when anyone spoke to him. But when he did talk, it was either dead serious or hilarious—no in-between.

Iron Oak grinned back to the colonel and nodded a few times. Then, about the time everybody started to think that was all the reply he was going to emit, he said, "I'm not real sure, sir. But the word is that it's a great new flavored douche from Procter and Gamble."

A roar of laughter flooded the room. Everyone was laughing except Iron. He just grinned and nodded around to everybody as if saying thanks for the audience response.

As the noise faded Ivan Kahn wiped his eyes with a sweep of his hand, then crushed his cigar into a butt can. "I wish it were that funny, Iron. It's not. But I am glad to see that we've been able to keep a lid on this."

His voice straightened to serious. "Be advised, gents. From here on everything in this briefing is top secret.

"Saydem," he said emphatically, "stands for Special Atomic Demolition Munitions. Simply put, that anagram means man-carried nuclear bombs!"

Binkowski coughed loudly and dropped his cigarette.

The colonel continued as Arnold groped to find his cigarette and extinguish it.

Colonel Kahn explained that the Army had introduced SADMs into the covert military arsenal in 1966. I'd heard rumors about the high-level ordnance during my time at Fort Bragg, but this was the first valid report I'd received about them.

A few minutes later the colonel hit the high-spot technical aspects of the bomb. He told us they came in ten-, twenty-, and thirty-megaton capacities. All were similar in size, but each was proportionately heavier with the larger megaton load.

As he talked questions crept silently through me. Were we being prepared to implement nuclear demo into this marathon war in order to bring about an expeditious end—shades of, more like clouds of, Hiroshima? I checked myself realizing, if that were the case, surely aerial delivery would be the more likely method of deployment.

Ivan Kahn's next words snuffed the room full of silent conjectures. "Right now you're all probably leaning toward the thought that MACSOG may be considering deployment of Saydems in ground combat. Negative!

"MACSOG does maintain the devices in their arsenal at Ton Son Nhut Air Base, but it is only as a last-resort contingency. You have to keep in mind that the Soviets have their own version of Saydem. If push comes to kicking and gouging, it is fundamental that we are prepared to meet their firepower capability."

He turned and withdrew a piece of paper from his notebook. He grinned, looking down at the message, then glanced up before reading. "So that you can all have a greater appreciation for the MACSOG message mystique, I'll read this to you. It's dated 0715 yesterday. Priority, flash. 'Be advised of significant nuclear threat in the Prairie Fire and Nickle Steel Areas of Operations.''

He ran his fingers over his hair, then replaced the message into the folder and looked back at us. "Well, I'll skip describing the interim back flips we all went through in the S-3 shop after reading that! By late morning I'd managed to find out what 'significant nuclear threat' meant."

The colonel turned and began pacing as he talked. Every eye in the room followed him as he spoke. "Gents, right now, significant nuclear threat boils down to a gang of dope-head dissidents that have commandeered"—his hands jerked upward—"more like fucking hijacked, a Saydem device from the Ton Son Nhut arsenal. That event occurred eight days ago. Now, MACV has received a message from these peace-punks demanding an end to all allied combat operations in Southeast Asia or they will detonate the Saydem somewhere in North Vietnam!

"They've also thrown in a ransom demand of four million dollars. So, it's apparent these sons of bitches aren't without a little profit motive in their peace crusade.

"The larger headache in this scenario is what the potential Soviet reaction may be in the event of the detonation of an American nuclear bomb in Southeast Asia. That issue is currently being addressed by the Diplomatic Corps and God only knows if those bureaucrats can screw things up any worse, they will!"

He moved slowly to a position behind the lectern and leaned forward, placing his tanned forearms on the varnished wood. His eyes narrowed, looking at each man in the room, then stopped on mine. "You've already guessed where CCN fits into this nightmare. I'm directed to insert two teams into the Nickle Steel AO to locate and recover this loose nuclear cannon. RTs Texas and California will jointly conduct the mission.'' His eyes shifted to Bin-kowski, then back to Jensen and Iron Oak.

A moment later the colonel showed us an eight-by-ten black-and-white photograph of a Saydem. He stepped forward to let everyone get a good look at the photo. The ordnance, pictured horizontally beside an M16, looked like a huge M-79 round. It appeared that it could possibly be fitted into a large rucksack, but if so, it would be tight.

The colonel moved the photo slowly as he spoke. ''Primarily, Texas and California will be concerned with the details of the device. The reason I'm showing this to the rest of you is to let you know what Saydem looks like just in case you happen to inadvertently discover it in the conduct of your unrelated missions.''

The colonel went on to say that each team would now be required to carry two thermite grenades with them to use on the bomb if they discovered it. It was apparent in the colonel's tone that he did not consider ''inadvertent discovery'' likely, but, nonetheless, he was covering all the bases.

A few minutes later, after pointing out the correct placement area for the thermite grenade, he concluded the briefing and dismissed everyone except Texas and California.

As the room cleared Jensen and Iron moved forward and took seats in the front row with Binkowski and me. Swede gave me a quick roll of his eyes, indicating ''what the fuck are we into now.'' Iron just grinned at me and nodded.

Major Jinx exited after the last man and closed the door, leaving the four of us and Colonel Kahn in the room.

Colonel Kahn pulled a chair out of the row and sat facing us. ''Gents,'' he said softly, ''I don't have to tell you this mission isn't exactly up our alley, but then I don't know of anyone in the Army who's trained to go after nuclear bombs.'' He tried to smile while looking at me.

"Brett, Sergeant Major Twitty told me you signed your extension papers earlier. That's one reason I selected Texas as the sister team on this mission. However, you're due a thiry-day extension leave so if—''

I butted in. "Wouldn't miss it for all the flavored douche at Procter and Gamble, sir.''

"Good,'' he said with a smile. "Now, for the next two days the four of you will be receiving a crash course in everything we can put together related to this mission. Keep in mind, we haven't had much time to get ready for this so it's going to be shake and bake, catch as catch can, all the way. I don't like doing it that way but we don't have any choice.

"You'll get some technical training in Saydem, area study briefings, profile outlines on the three deserters . . . all that. And the CIA is sending in a rep with some special equipment for you. The agent will also brief you on the CAS linkup plan and some other related information. You'll launch at 2300 day after tomorrow so plan on putting in some long hours between now and then.''

He stood and glanced at his watch. "I know you've got a lot of questions, but hold off for now. Major Jinx has prepared a complete mission briefing for you. Also, Colonel Bendell has flown up here personally with a specialist on Saydem, so after the briefing, you get the fifty-cent spiel on that. We'll roll the ball on the briefing in about five minutes. Y'all take a break in place.''

He walked to the door, turned, and said, "By the way, this is all limdis noforn, gents. The Yards can't have a peep of intel about Saydem. As far as they're concerned you can tell them you're out to locate three deserters.'' He nodded and exited the room.

The low rumble of the exhaust fans dominated the silence. We'd just been dealt a mission like none other I'd ever heard of. It was 180 degrees opposite our normal mission spectrum. I felt like a quarterback who had just been handed a baseball mitt.

The fact that Colonel Bendell, SOG chief of operations, was on hand for the briefing told me things were red-hot. He'd never attended a CCN mission briefing to my knowledge. And this was the first time I'd been told not to disclose the complete mission to my Yards. I understood the directive was to prevent possible mission compromise. If we were captured and interrogated during the mission, there would be no chance of the Cowboys revealing sensitive information about Saydem.

But Montagnards never broke under interrogation. Recently I'd conducted a Brightlight, emergency team rescue attempt, on RT New York. We'd found the team Yards castrated and dead. The One-Zero and One-One, Morris and Wilder, were still MIA. One of the dead Montagnards had a bloody plug of some NVA's ear in his mouth—a dying testimony to a fierce sense of loyalty.

Chapter 5

Jensen struck a match and walked toward the wall map while lighting a small Eastwood-type cigar. "I wonder where these little pukes are right now?" he said, staring at the Nickle Steel zone.

Iron leaned back in the chair and crossed his legs. "That's probably anybody's guess. But one thing's for sure. Stealin' a friggin' nuke means they're either as dumb as corn bread or they got balls that drag the floor."

I walked over to Jensen. "Have you ever conducted a dual team mission?"

"Negative. But my guess is they have two possible areas of interest to cover. You'll get one, I'll get the other." He blew a puff of smoke over the map area of North Vietnam.

Looking back at me he smiled. "The way I see it it's a piece of cake. We simply cruise into North Vietnam and inform Chuck that we are there to recover a lost nuclear bomb. If they're smart they'll give us a hand. Right, Iron Oak?" We both glanced at the near-reclined figure of Iron.

Iron laced his fingers behind his head casually. "Right, Swede. And if that dream comes true, maybe they'll even tell Hollywood Jane to give us all some pussy while we're there."

41

Ski stood smirking at Iron. "I wouldn't fuck that commie bitch with Castro's dick!"

I'd noticed a recent increase of resentment in Ski about anything related to, or associated with, the hippie movement. It started several weeks ago when he got a "Dear John" from his girlfriend in Boston. She'd joined the antiwar fad. As a final twist of the knife she enclosed a bumper sticker in her letter that read: If there were no soldiers there would be no wars.

Binkowski made his own bumper sticker out of a C-ration box and sent it back to her. It read: If there were no soldiers you would be speaking a different national language, asshole!

Iron Oak ignored Ski's comment. He stood and walked toward Swede and me at the map. I studied the vast Nickle Steel AO.

North Vietnam was almost 63,000 square miles—about the size of Florida. Like Florida it had coastline, rivers, lakes, and swamps. But the similarity ended as you moved northwest into rugged mountains. Trying to locate a Saydem up there would be like trying to find a contact lens in a rice paddy full of leeches.

I hoped that Jensen's guess about two areas of interest was correct. But even if SOG intel had managed to narrow down the location of the deserters, we still had some taller hurdles to leap on this hide-and-seek mission. Covert operations into North Vietnam contrasted sharply with our target areas in Laos.

In Laos we had the availability of quick air support if we got into a flaky-feces situation. The reaction time of air support into North Vietnam was like cold molasses. One other good thing about Laos was that we could count on Laotian support in some areas if the going got tough. But in Nickle Steel every civilian was vigilant to intrusion.

Add to that the fact that President Nixon had just author-
ized the resumption of bombing in the North and you had
a situation like a big foot on an anthill—everybody was
stirred up.

Ski spoke, walking toward the map. "You know, it's
crazy that we have to go up there and risk our lives to find
three—"

Iron butted in sarcastically. "That's what it's all about,
Binkowski. Today's Army wants you to see the world; to
travel to exotic lands, meet new and interesting people,
and fuckin' kill them. Shit, nobody said it was gonna be
easy being a star!"

Ski smiled but his tone revealed irritation. "You know,
Iron, you have a way of inspiring people. Maybe you
should have been a missionary."

Iron's grin broadened. "You must be psychic, Binkowski. I signed up to be a missionary, but the fuckin'
clerk typist spelled it wrong and they made me a merce-
nary."

I knew how sensitive Ski was about clerk typist jokes.
I decided it was time to diffuse what was obviously about
to turn into a pissing contest. I took the Saydem photo
from the lectern and stepped between Ski and Iron.
"Wonder what this thing weighs? Man-carried leaves a lot
of room for speculation.

"For example, Ski here can do strict squats with five
hundred pounds, so he could probably carry several of
these. But on the other hand Don Knotts might have trouble rolling this thing across a parking lot." My comment
was geared to compliment Ski's physical development—
something Iron couldn't argue about.

Iron shrugged, then turned away to study the map with
Jensen.

Arnold Binkowski's camp weight-lifting records were

unchallenged. He could clean and jerk 350 pounds, flat back bench 450, and curl 225. The problem Ski had was that when it came down to a verbal jousting match he was unarmed. He'd rather end the contest by caving in the opponent's speaking orifice.

Ski didn't necessarily walk around playing barney-bad-ass, he just didn't have much patience with bullshit. In that respect Ski and I were a lot alike—the exception being his fuse was shorter than mine.

I placed the photo back on the lectern just as the door opened. "A-ten-shun!" Major Jinx shouted as he hurried into the room. He was followed by Colonel Bendell and Colonel Kahn.

"At ease!" Bendell barked while striding to our huddle near the map. He had an unlit cigar stub clenched in his teeth. He spoke without removing it like he was chewing his words. "Colonel Kahn says you're the best he's got. I've just apprised myself of your talent for recon by reading a dozen of your after-action reports. I think he's right."

Dark half-moon troughs craddled beneath his gray eyes. The strong voice seemed out of sync with his tired expression. Six months ago I'd seen him at a mission debriefing in Saigon; today he looked ten years older.

He removed his cigar and motioned toward the map with it. "I know you're not strangers to this AO. I also know you've performed outstandingly up there in that patch of real estate we call Nickle Steel." Light glistened off the bright silver eagle insignia on his starched collar.

"So," he said, taking a step back from the map. "I know we've got the right crew for this goddamn mission. I'm tasking you to kick a sixty-yard field goal into the wind and I want those points on the fucking scoreboard ASAP.

"If anybody can do it, you can." He looked at Ski who

was still standing at the position of attention. "I said, at ease, Sergeant."

"Roger . . . I mean, yes, yes, sir."

I caught a glimpse of Henry Jinx standing behind the lectern holding a pointer stick. Tapping his leg with the stick he said, "Sir, I'm prepared to deliver the briefing, if you're ready."

Colonel Bendell darted an irritated glance backward. "Hold your horses, Henry. Where's Lieutenant Blair?" His questioning gaze went to Colonel Kahn, but Jinx quickly answered.

"Blair will deliver the second portion related to Saydem, sir. There's really no need for—"

"Damn it, I want her in here. She needs to know the total picture. Don't you think so, Ivan?"

"Her?" I muttered to myself. Now I knew where the perfume smell came from.

Ivan Kahn replied to Colonel Bendell while nodding for Jinx to go and find Blair. "Roger, sir. She's the expert on Saydem. She might as well know what we're planning."

A moment later we were all seated and waiting when Major Jinx walked in with Miss Chanel number five. I had to consciously halt my urge to gape. She was a goddess— a tall bona fide brunet goddess. The fatigues she wore had been tailored to accent her bosom.

Colonel Kahn stood and introduced her. "Gents, this is Lieutenant Megan Blair. She is the SOG technical expert on atomic demolitions."

She returned eye-to-eye contact to each of us along with a smart nod as the colonel pointed us out by name.

Maybe it was my preoccupation with the fact that she was the resident Saydem expert, but one look into her almond-shaped blue eyes and I got the immediate impression that sex with her must be on a scale with nuclear explosions.

"And last but not least this is Sergeant Binkowski. He's Sergeant Yancy's assistant team leader."

Arnold stood abruptly like a spring had been triggered under his ass. "You can call me Ski."

Megan Blair smiled and nodded.

I tried to keep from laughing but it didn't work. Henry Jinx was clearly irritated. He slapped the side of his leg with the pointer and bobbed upward on his toes. "Sergeant Binkowski, if you and Lieutenant Blair will take your seats we'll get on with our intended purpose here."

After announcing that the security level was top-secret-crypto, he told us the briefing would be broken into three segments consisting of his initial briefing, Blair's portion on Saydem, and the final phase by Colonel Bendell.

I was surprised to hear that we were going to be briefed on information pertaining to crypto. We all had top-secret clearances but a crypto security clearance was one notch above top secret.

The major began in his usual dramatic baritone style. I'd listened to many of his briefings in the past. I liked Jinx, but I'd developed the impression that he was a frustrated thespian.

Jinx was a very competent S-3 officer. But at times he was so oriented to mission detail that he often lost sight of the human elements inherent to high-risk covert operations. Months ago, while going over our after-action report, he asked Will and me where our soil sample was. We knew soil samples were required on all missions into Laos, but due to the fact that we'd been hotly pursued and shot out of our AO just six hours after infil, we hadn't bothered to procure the sample.

I remarked to the major that we were up to our ass in

alligators and really didn't have time to make a wallet. As he chided us for our failure Will reached down and dug a crusted chunk of mud out of his boot cleat. He tossed it on the table saying, "There's your soil sample, sir. If you need a stool sample I think there's still some in my pants!" That was the first and only time I'd seen Major Henry Jinx laugh.

The major frowned while reading from his notes. "On October twenty-first at approximately 2330 a group of three Army personnel assigned to the nuclear containment facility at Ton Son Nhut Air Base commandeered a man-carried nuclear device. Dossiers on each of these individuals will be provided during your mission prep phase."

He paused, then continued: "Four days subsequent to the theft MACV headquarters received this surreptitiously delivered message: 'To MACV pig headquarters. The SADM device, serial number 47539501, is in our control. We demand cessation of all combat operations in Southeast Asia NLT November sixth. We demand withdrawal of all allied troops from South Vietnam to include Australian and Korean forces NLT November thirtieth. We demand that the sum of four million dollars be deposited in the Bank of Switzerland located in Lausanne, account number 3421009-473, NLT November thirtieth. You have trained us as technical instruments for your jingoistic rampage in Vietnam and we have learned well. Make no mistake, we are proficient in the arming and placement procedure of the SADM and we are in possession of the crypto cycling code Zula Tango 7551. Your failure to comply strictly with our demands will result in the detonation of this SADM somewhere north of the seventeenth parallel at an unannounced time. Upon compliance with all of our demands you will be notified of the location of the device for your retrieval. There is no margin for compromise.

There is no margin for debate. The die is cast. Signed: The Mariposa of Peace.' ''

As the major replaced the message back into a folder Ski leaned toward me whispering, ''What does jingoistic mean?''

''Later, Arnold.''

Major Jinx made a quick bouncing motion on his toes and frowned. ''There you have it. The message is clear. It is meticulous. It appears to have been authored by an individual with a sense of literary style. Of course, this was a copy of the original, however, MACV informs us that it was typed on a military typewriter. The paper they used was—''

Bendell growled impatiently. ''Damn it, Henry, skip the extraneous stuff and get on with the meat of the matter.''

The major nodded smartly. ''Yes, sir. Recent CAS intel reports the presence of a blond Caucasian female in the coastal town of Dong Yen located here approximately three hundred klicks north of the DMZ.'' He hastily turned and pointed to the map.

''While no photo is yet available the description matches that of Spec-four Eva Gordon, one of the Mariposa group. This reported presence indicates the group may have departed Saigon via boat or sanpan and moved down one of the two intercoastal canal arteries out of Saigon. Then they proceeded north along the coast to Dong Yen. It is inconceivable that Mariposa conducted this hijacking and movement without enemy assistance.

''At this time there is no authentication or other confirmation on this hypothesis from either the CID, MI, or the CIA, or any of their collective operatives. However, as of this morning another CAS source, located west of Dong Yen, reported sighting one black male and once Caucasian male moving along a trail with a small NVA unit. This sighting occurred near the town of Bai Duc, forty klicks west of Dong Yen. The two men were wearing civilian clothing, were unarmed, and appeared to be under no constraints or duress. Again, no photos. But based on the description, it appears they could be elements of the Mariposa group: Lieutenant Donald Defrisco and PFC Malcolm Abbey.''

The major went on to outline the joint team reconnaissance mission. We were directed to infiltrate via night parachute drop into North Vietnam, locate and gain control of one or more of the Mariposa, by whatever means ''tactically feasible,'' and then conduct interrogation related to the location of the Device. After that miracle was accomplished all we had to do was recover the Saydem and neutralize it using a thermite grenade. The major, in his own dramatic way, made it all sound simple. Listening to Jinx sum up a mission scenario was like watching the ending of a Roy Rogers movie. You got the impression that he wanted to sing ''Happy Trails'' as his closing statement.

I'd conducted two enemy snatch missions. Commonly, we exfiled the snatchee and left the interrogation to the Military Intelligence pros once we returned to base. But due to the criticality of recovering the Device conjunctive with the mission, we were being required to conduct the interrogation.

Again, the major made it all sound easy. He informed us that we would be using the drug Sodium Pentothal. I'd never used Sodium Pentothal and I wasn't a pharmatoxicologist, but from what I'd read about the drug it was effective only in gaining yes and no responses. I reasoned that trying to ''yes and no'' someone through 63,000 miles of map finger pointing saying, ''is it here, is it there,'' could turn into a career effort.

Chapter 6

Major Jinx closed his show with a final security reminder about the classification of the briefing. In the same breath he informed us that from here on the preferred term for SADM was "the Device."

As he gathered his papers I expected the usual end-of-briefing, one-word invitation: questions? I had about a dozen weaving through my mind. His next words stalled me from asking.

"I know you may have a question or two but due to time constraints I'll have to insist that you hold them until Sergeant Hayes and I get with you during your mission prep phase." He nodded smartly and turned to Megan Blair, indicating the stage was hers.

It was unusual for the major to postpone questions after his briefing. I guessed that the presence of Colonel Bendell had a lot to do with it. The major knew that if we asked a question he wasn't prepared for it would put him in a command embarrassing situation. He'd cleverly decided to avoid that potentiality.

Jensen wasn't stalled. "Sir, I can't even spell Sodium Pentothal. Never worked with it. Are we—"

Jinx glared at Swede. "Just state your question, Sergeant Jensen.'' It was obvious that Jinx didn't like being pinned down, but since Swede was being adamant he had to respond.

"My question is, are we going to get some training in working with this wonder drug truth serum?" Swede leaned forward in his chair and looked toward me. "You ever use it, Brett?"

"Negative," I said, noticing an amused grin on Blair.

I was glad Jensen had pushed the question on Jinx. Evidently Swede felt that if we didn't get some firm training commitment on the drug right now, it could easily turn into one of those things that get swept aside. I could picture the major tossing us a vial and a syringe saying, "just read the label," as we boarded the aircraft. A similar situation had occurred once when I was Swede's One-One. We'd been required to deploy a high-tech acoustic sensor monitoring module in northern Laos without being properly trained in how to activate it prior to mission launch.

Jinx answered while doing his quick toe-bouncing routine. "Yes . . . yes, I believe we can work in some training on that."

"Thorough training, Henry!" Bendell barked. "I don't want anything fallin' through the cracks here. This is too damn important to let Murphy's Law get into it."

"Wilco. Yes, sir," the major said while hurriedly jotting a note on his folder. He glanced at Colonel Kahn, then nodded again at Blair before sitting.

As Megan Blair rose and approached the lectern Colonel Kahn stood. He waited until she opened her note folder on the lectern and looked back at him.

"Gents, just a brief bio on Lieutenant Blair. She has a B.S. in nuclear physics from UCLA. She was commissioned last January and she has excelled in every phase of training the Army ordnance branch has thrown at her.

She's new in-country, but at this point in time and place she is the undisputed authority on the Device.''

Colonel Kahn's eyes moved over each of us as he spoke. I reasoned that he was giving us the build-up info to enhance Blair's technical credibility. He knew that SF NCOs viewed second lieutenants, and particularly female lieutenants, as military mutants.

Before taking his seat he added, ''Lieutenant Blair will also be assisting you during your mission prep. Go ahead, Lieutenant.''

She gave a perfunctory smile to Colonel Kahn, then turned her attention to us. ''Thank you, sir. My phase of the briefing is fashioned to acquaint you with some of the technical aspects of the Device, as well as its capabilities, its limitations, and its intended usage within the military ordnance battle spectrum.''

As she spoke Ski leaned forward, placing his elbows on his knees. Glancing at him it appeared he was mesmerized. I wasn't sure he was hearing a word she said.

Her voice was soft, clear, and concise. Although she'd obviously rehearsed her briefing there was a hint of caution in her expression. And her choice of words like ''fashioned'' wasn't exactly in sync with normal military jargon. But that was understandable considering she'd been in less than a year.

Her demeanor was poised and confident but it seemed like the facade a Miss America contestant presents walking across a stage in a bathing suit. She was well aware that she was under the microscope.

Looking up from her notes she said, ''Contrary to normal Army style there is no numerical nomenclature associated with the Saydem. For our purposes today we will call the Device, type-one. And in some instances I'll refer to it as, five-zero-one, which are the last three digits in the serial number of the Device that we are herein predisposed to relocate . . . neutralize, that is.

"There are several larger versions of which you don't have a need to know." Her slender eyebrows raised slightly implying she was privileged to a higher authority.

After withdrawing several eight-by-ten photos from her folder, she stepped forward and passed them out to each of us. "These photos are to be returned upon completion of this briefing. However, they will be available to you during your mission . . . mission—"

"Mission prep!" Jinx interjected.

She nodded modestly to Jinx. "Yes. Mission prep. Thank you, sir."

As she turned to walk back to the lectern I pried my eyes off her shapely buttocks and studied the photo. The Device was photographed in three different positions—top, side, and end view.

I looked up as she spoke. "During this briefing, and for that matter at all times during our association, you'll find that I will be vague in relating some of the aspects and characteristics inherent to the type-one. This is deliberate. I've learned during my brief time with the Army that it is the nature of military personnel to want more than they need; information, that is. So, please don't pursue or solicit additional information. I know what you need."

I smiled at her, taking her last sentence literally.

As she looked up she caught my expression and quickly darted her eyes back to the notes. "If you will give attention to the photograph you'll see that the type-one is approximately thirty inches in length and fifteen inches in diameter. At the opposite end of the rounded frontal nose portion is a flat area that is covered by a circular steel plate. Beneath this removable plate are the arming controls of the Device.''

I noticed what looked like a wall safe combination lock wheel in the center of the circular plate. Blair didn't comment about it.

"Type-one," she continued, "is simple in its complexity. It is comprised of a large volume of composition-four plastic-explosive material, several prepositioned detonators, an internal timer, an arming cube, and a pull-button activation switch.

"When firing occurs it delivers a precise electrical impulse simultaneously to seven detonation points positioned around the C-4 bringing about an implosion. This implosion is what triggers the nuclear reaction of the explosive material.''

I understood the physics of nuclear reaction. I was impressed that she had explained, in her "vague" way, the fundamental dynamics in the fewest words possible. I'd taken an engineering physics course in college and listened to a professor rave on for one hour about the basics of a nuclear bomb without ever clarifying what Megan had in just a few words.

Megan Blair had a distinct talent for brevity. She also had a knack for balancing military bearing with her sense of femininity. Most women I'd observed in the Army, enlisted and officers, always appeared to be searching for the military behavior mystique—some even walked like halfbacks. It was apparent that Megan was comfortable with being a woman, and that it didn't bother or impair her professionalism one bit.

After glancing down at her notes she said, "Unlike conventional point-detonation bombs, type-one nuclear demolition is much safer to work with. You can drop it out of an airplane without fear of explosion because it requires precise electronic stimuli to detonate. You can even place it in the center of your campfire and all it will do is burn and melt. No explosion.''

She paused and gave us a comforting look. I withheld an urge to tell her we never used campfires, or marshmallows.

"Wow, I'm starting to feel better about this," Ski blurted.

Megan ignored Ski's impetuous comment. Jinx didn't. "Sergeant Binkowski, we'd appreciate it if you'd try and restrain your elation."

"In order to effectively neutralize the Device," she continued, "all you have to do is place and activate a thermite grenade anywhere on the forward outer casing and insure that it burns sufficiently through the center. This will destroy one or more of the detonation points. As I've mentioned type-one requires precise impulse. The nullification or omission of even one detonator will cancel the circuitry, thereby preventing what we call SCT—simultaneous Circuit Transmission.

"I will stress that at no time should you place a thermite grenade on the rear section of the Device; nor should you shoot bullets into the rear area. Any intrusion into that area by anyone other than trained personnel could result in detonation.

"I hope my explanation will allay your fears when the time comes to neutralize five-zero-one."

At first I was bothered by her implication that we were somehow dominated or gripped by fear. But after I riggor-rolled my ego I remembered what a demolitions instructor at One-Zero school had told us: "When you're dealin' with explosives and you ain't just a little bit on the shallow side of fear, it's time to quit!''

But the shapely lieutenant's comment about fear overlooked the more significant element of danger on this mission. While finding five-zero-one was obviously the queen in this anthill scenario, managing to evade the pismire NVA was the larger problem. Considering the slow reaction time of air assets to the AO, I knew that if we got in trouble on this one we'd be like a whore in a men's locker room—there was no way out without getting screwed.

Blair concluded her briefing with a spiel about the limitations and intended usage of SADM. She told us the Device was designed for use on industrial targets: electrical complexes, dams, bridges, et cetera, when ballistic or aerial delivery wasn't politically feasible or militarily practical.

We were informed that the only significant limitation to the type-one was its non-adaptability to a submerged environment. At a depth of one atmosphere, thirty-three feet, the O-ring seal on the circular steel retainer is subject to leak, thereby rendering the timer mechanism unreliable. Type-one was considered water resistant, not waterproof.

Supposedly, the happy ending about the limitation was that it meant we didn't have to worry about it being concealed underwater. I wasn't sure how consoling that was, but at least it eliminated lakes, rivers, and the entire South China Sea as a hiding place.

I was surprised when she closed her notes, looked out at us, and said, "Questions, gentlemen?"

Raising my hand she quickly acknowledged me. "Go ahead, Sergeant Yancy."

Although it was proper to refer to a female officer as ma'am, somehow it just didn't seem to fit Megan Blair.

Keeping my tone casual I asked, "Do you know these individuals we're going after, Lieutenant? Defrisco, Abbey, Gordon?"

She blinked for a moment as if she wasn't ready for a

nontechnical question. I had a dozen other questions, but right now I wanted a chance to read her reaction to something unexpected.

She glanced down and looked back at me with a sad stare that seemed to be aimed just above my head, as if she could see them all standing in the back of the room. "Yes . . . I know them," she said slowly.

I'd found out what I wanted to know. Her look registered emotion. However subtle, the emotion was an undisguised tremor. I didn't know how deep it ran or where, but I did know that as of now Megan Blair was a primary source of intel on the nature of the beast we were going to hunt.

Major Jinx spoke up sharply. "Sergeant Yancy, I don't see what pertinent value personal questions have here. I'm—"

Colonel Kahn cut him off. "Henry, I can see what he's driving at. He's trying to determine if this Mariposa gang is in fact technically proficient in arming this goddamn thing. Is that right, Brett?"

"Roger, sir." I glanced back up to Blair and covered my tracks. "The demand note SOG received says they are capable of arming and emplacing five-zero-one. Since you know them, the next question is, are they proficient in arming the Device or is that so much bull . . . baloney."

Blair grinned. "No, Sergeant Yancy, it's not bull-baloney. I was assigned as Lieutenant Defrisco's executive officer at the NCF. He is fully knowledgeable and capable in every aspect of type-one. However, Gordon and Abbey are not. They were assigned as admin personnel so you need not be concerned about them."

I squinted hearing her naive words. I could have let it slide but I didn't want Ski taking her last sentence seriously. "Lieutenant, these deserters have had five-zero-one

for eight days. It seems to me it's very possible that Defrisco could have easily trained the other two in the arming
procedure by now. Am I right or wrong?''

She gripped the sides of the lectern before answering.
''I—I suppose that is possible. I see your point. In fact,
giving consideration to their blatant act of treason and the
motivation of it, I would say it is very likely. The procedure is relatively simple if you have the—'' She stopped
as if about to say too much.

Jensen spoke up immediately. ''If you were about to
say crypto cycling code, you hit my question dead center.
If not, I'll ask it anyhow. What is it?''

Blair turned to Colonel Bendell. ''Sir, I'm not sure there
is a need-to-know on this. Can you advise me?''

I grinned at her fancy verbal footwork. The LT obviously wasn't adverse to answering Swede's question, she
was simply covering her well-contoured gluteus.

Bendell rolled his fingers around his cigar and removed
it like he was pulling the plug out of a bathtub. ''Fire
away, Lieutenant. I'd like to know what it is myself.''

Blair quickly gave us an explanation of what she called
triple-c, crypto cycling code. She explained that prior to
shipment to Vietnam each SADM was preprogrammed
with twelve internal revolving code requirements—one for
each thirty-day readiness interval. In order to activate the
timer mechanism, which was fundamental for arming, the
prescribed numerical code for the readiness interval had
to be dialed into a separate four-digit window area located
to the left of the timer control hours and minutes window.
The current code for five-zero-one was comprised of the
four digits mentioned in the Mariposa demand message:
seven-five-five-one. The letter indicators, Zulu Tango, denoted only the readiness interval period.

Once the code was dialed in, the operator then had two

minutes to complete the timer setting, place the firing cube
into the arming well, and activate the Device. She explained that triple-c was designed as a fail-safe step to
prevent predeployment tampering by unauthorized personnel.

It took another question by Jensen and another nod by
Bendell to learn that type-ones were equipped with either
a twelve- or a twenty-four-hour timer. The arming operator could set the Device with no less than thirty minutes
or no more than twenty-four hours to fire time, depending
on the type timer inherent to the Device. The suggested
set time for teams deploying SADM was ten to nineteen
hours, dependent on the timer, in order to give them suf-
ficient escape time from the target placement site.

Iron drew a laugh from everyone when he interjected
that if he were deploying SADM, he'd want a forty-eight-
hour timer and he'd use every minute of it.

The laughter seemed to ease Blair's tense mood. She
was even prettier when she laughed.

A half-dozen questions later she collected the photos
and gathered her notes. It seemed that she'd made up her
mind that she liked us. To me, that was important. She'd
be spending part of the next two days going over additional
info and the deserter dossiers with us; now it would be a
lot easier working with her.

As she turned and walked back to her chair the venti-
lator breeze wafted a reminder of her fragrance over me.

Chapter 7

As Lieutenant Blair took a seat Colonel Caleb Bendell snuffed his cigar into a butt can, rose, and strode briskly toward the lectern. Moving across the room he exhaled a stream of gray smoke like an inbound freight train. No folder. No notes.

He avoided the lectern, choosing instead to stand in front of the big wall map. "Every morning at my staff briefing I have the S-2, Major Griswall, give us an updated report on how many American soldiers have died in this goddamn war.

"If it sounds like I've omitted concern about Australian, Korean, and Vietnamese casualties, it's not true. I am concerned about them. But I'm an American commander and my foremost thoughts are about my troops.

"I really don't give a damn about how many communists we've killed. I know we're killing them at about a hundred-to-one ratio. But if it were a thousand-to-one it wouldn't be enough."

He glanced down, then stepped forward and placed a hand on the corner of the lectern. A hard frown gripped his face as he spoke. "As of this morning the collective total of Americans KIA was thirty-six thousand three-hundred and forty-five!''

He paused and looked down again. I felt my fingers coil into fists as a scroll of names and faces I'd known spiraled slowly through my mind.

''I'm not going to preach about what fine patriots they were. Some of them wanted to be here, some didn't. But all of them were Americans and they all died fighting our enemy just like generations of American soldiers before them.

''Now,'' he said, raising his voice. ''We have three traitors who seem to think that we're going to forget about our KIA! Our MIA! Our POWs. They think we're going to just pull up stakes and go home because they have us over a barrel. Well, bullshit!'' he shouted while moving a slow concentrated stare to each of us.

''Two days from today you will infiltrate Drop Zone Ghost Rider by parachute. Your mission is to locate, capture, and interrogate the members of Mariposa until they have disclosed the location of five-zero-one.'' His eyes squinted, studying us as he continued.

''Once you have recovered and neutralized the Device you will then eliminate and dispose of the Mariposa personnel!''

I caught a glimpse of Megan Blair as she jerked forward in her chair. She drew a quick hand to her lips as if horrified by the colonel's directive. Slowly she leaned back and cradled her hands on her lap. Her eyes glistened with a hint of tears.

Part of me could understand her emotion. Caleb Bendell had just issued an assassination order on three people she'd known and worked with—her colleagues, possibly her friends. I was reasonably sure Megan didn't support what they had done, but she was obviously having difficulty accepting their fate.

If it weren't for the sad expression in her eyes I probably wouldn't have thought twice about the colonel's order. A twisting path of falling dominos clicked through my mind searching for reasoning to justify the assassination of three Americans.

My jaw tightened. The answer was clear. These were no longer Americans. They were traitors—they deserved to die. Their treasonous act had nullified any allegiance to my country. They were now clearly the enemy, and worse, they threatened to incite a nuclear exchange between the two world superpowers. They had to be eliminated.

Colonel Bendell's next words advanced my reasoning. He informed us that MACV did not want Mariposa returned for court-martial because of the likelihood of media fanfare. A trial would possibly turn the traitors into hippie heroes and fuel the already growing antiwar fire at home. Not to mention exposing our nuclear potential in Vietnam.

A quick glance at Blair revealed that the colonel's words had no effect on consoling her bewilderment. Her face registered alienation and anger.

If I'd had a choice about it I would have preferred that Megan Blair hadn't been exposed to anything about the assassination directive. Now, it appeared I had a serious emotional bridge to repair if I was going to keep her on our side. We needed inside information on the target personnel—idiosyncrasies, weaknesses, possible drug dependency, things I knew wouldn't be in the dossiers.

I reasoned that if it came down to some hard-knuckled interrogation about where 501 was cached it would help if I knew that Defrisco was spastic about snakes. I remembered something Tuong had told me about a Montagnard interrogator who taped the mouth of a deadly mangrove viper, then coiled the snake around an NVA prisoner's neck. After a moment the Montagnard looked closely at the snake, then casually mentioned that it appeared the tape was working loose. Suddenly the prisoner developed oral diarrhea—he started promising the interrogator everything but a blow job if he'd just get the snake off him.

A moment later Colonel Bendell completed his spiel and turned the floor over to Colonel Kahn.

Ivan Kahn stood and walked to the map. Placing his finger on the target area he glanced back at us. "After infiltration into the common drop zone California and Texas will split. Texas will link up with a CAS agent and proceed to a safe house near Dong Yen."

He glanced at Jensen. "Swede, you and Iron will move southeast toward the village of Vinh Son. We hope to have another CAS agent intercept you on infil but right now the CIA has lost contact with the agent. We'll firm that up prior to launch time. But be advised, you may be operating without CAS support."

CAS stood for Controlled American Source. Essentially, they were indigenous spies. They were well-trained, intelligent components of the CIA. They were also well paid.

Colonel Kahn turned away from the map and assumed a position behind the lectern. "During the mission both teams will carry standard fox-mike PRC-25 radios equipped with KY-38 secure voice mode. I recommend that you establish a daily contact between you and report your situation to each other.

"You're already aware that the NVA are using Soviet radio direction finding equipment so keep your transmissions short."

He looked at me. "Brett, you'll make the daily sit-rep to Moonbeam monitor aircraft and report mission status for both California and yourself. That will eliminate one more RDF window by keeping Swede off the air. Contact times and freqs will be in your SOI packet. I think you're scheduled for two contacts daily.''

He glanced at Major Jinx. "Is that right, Henry?"

Jinx appeared surprised. "I'm sorry, sir. What was the—"

"How many daily contacts do you have Texas scheduled for?"

"Two, sir. One at 0600, one at 2100."

Directing his attention back to me the colonel said, "If you miss three contacts and we haven't heard from you on the guard freq we are going to assume you've been compromised. At that time we will implement plan Bravo."

For obvious reasons Colonel Kahn didn't elaborate on what plan "B" was, but the mention of it told both Swede and me that they definitely had a contingency plan if we got nailed.

He went on to recommend that we develop a dead-letter drop somewhere between our separate AOs as a backup in case we lost commo. A DLD was simply a prearranged secret location to leave and pick up messages in case our primary method of commo became inoperative or infeasible.

Thinking ahead I studied the map. I figured if we found a good site for our DLD we could also incorporate it as a primary team rally point if we were compromised and had to beat feet—escape and evade.

The distance between Dong Yen and Vinh Son was about fifteen klicks, roughly nine miles. If the DLD was somewhere about midway, that meant four to five miles travel for each team. Looking closer at the map I realized I was probably being too optimistic. The coastal topography wouldn't offer much concealment for movement. We'd have to locate the DLD farther inland in dense vegetation.

Colonel Kahn spoke while leaning forward on the lectern. "Gents, I don't have to tell you this is the quickest mission we've ever had to glue together on short notice. Major Jinx and Sergeant Hayes as well as Lieutenant Blair and the entire SOG staff have done an outstanding job on this so far.

"The Agency has rolled everything over for us and they'll continue to provide all the intel they can for the next two days. You'll launch at 2300 hours on the thirty-first from Da Nang airfield. Drop time will be approximately 2355. You'll only get one pass on the DZ.

"Your gear will be transported separately to the airfield to avoid any civilian observation. Prerigged rucks et cetera must be loaded on the truck at S-4 by 1600 hours. The gear, including parachutes, will be stowed and waiting on the Blackbird when you arrive at the airfield at 2100. You'll be chuting-up immediately after boarding. Be sure and conduct your weapons test firing and radio checks early that afternoon in order to avoid having to hurry it.

"Your primary method of exfiltration will be conducted in an area south of Dong Yen assisted by Navy Seal team two. We will try and provide an alternate means of exfil but as of now—"

Suddenly the door opened. "Sorry to interrupt, sir," Luther Hayes said, leaning through the doorway. "Brightlight's bringing Arizona in. They're about ten minutes out."

Colonel Kahn gripped the lectern and glanced down. He looked up slowly; first at us, then over to Hayes. "Assemble all Americans on the chopper pad ASAP."

The code name Brightlight meant one thing—team in serious trouble. If an RT was in heavy contact and called for help, CCN would launch a kick-ass hatchet force post-haste to the AO. More often than not it was too late to save the team, but at least the hatchet force was usually able to beat Charlie back long enough to recover the bodies.

A cold chill cut through me like a razor blade as I studied the expression on Loot's face—Arizona was coming home for the last time.

I knew the One-Zero, Hank Wheeler. He'd just taken over the One-Zero slot shortly after the former team leader, Captain Bob Pugh, had been hit and killed. Now, it appeared RT Arizona was one more name on the long list of fatally retired jerseys at CCN.

Dark furrows of skin gathered between Ivan Kahn's eyes as he turned to Colonel Bendell. "Sir, I'd like to wrap this up now if you don't mind and get out to the chopper pad."

Bendell nodded grimly. "Understand, Ivan. I'll go with y'all."

It was Colonel Kahn's long-established SOP that we all gather on the chopper pad and help unload the bodies of our comrades. Afterward, we laid them out and filed past to pay our last respects. It was the most gut-quaking rite a man could experience, seeing the guys you'd been drinking with, laughing with a few nights before, suddenly laid out on cold cement, then stuffed into plastic bags.

As we filed out of the room Megan Blair stepped in front of Swede. "Where you going, Lieutenant?" Swede said in a cold tone.

Megan stopped, turned slowly to him, and said, "I'm going to the chopper pad. I happen to be an American too."

Chapter 8

The soft murmur of distant thunder rolled in off the sea as
we stepped out of the bunker and into a crisp afternoon
breeze. The damp smell of rain laced through a bleak
windy sky. I checked my watch: 1605 hours.

Swede, Iron, Ski, and I walked abreast toward the large
chopper pad on the west end of camp. A few meters in
front of us Megan Blair walked solo. She trailed several
feet behind the colonels and Major Jinx. The wind lifted
puffs of sand from beneath her boots as she trudged ahead.
She kept her head tilted downward—hands in her pockets.

No one talked. Only the low moan of wind whistling
through a nearby machine-gun bunker broke the silence.

I searched the cloud-patched sky looking for inbound
aircraft. I knew the Brightlight force would very probably
be comprised of two or three choppers.

In the distance I saw the specks of two CH-53s moving
beneath the cloud bases toward us. The Jolly Greens were
above the zone near Da Nang airfield, about four minutes
out.

Generally, RTs used UH-1Hs for operations but Bright-
lights needed the big Jolly Greens because of the larger

number of personnel that always comprised the hatchet force.

A small group of Americans was already standing near the edge of the pad as we approached. Half a dozen other men moved slowly up the gravel road on the north side of camp. A gusty swirl of sand bit at my neck as my eyes darted glances at the somber faces gathering around us.

Colonel Kahn peered skyward, then shouted across the windy LZ. "All right, gents, let's get formed up."

Twitty, standing off to one side of the pad, took a step forward and cocked both hands on his hips. "You heard the colonel. Get formed up. Move it!" he squealed.

Ordinarily, sergeant majors were key vertebrae in the backbone of the Army—somehow, Twitty was a slipped disk.

As everyone moved into ranks I could see the expressions of awe on their faces when they noticed Megan. She assumed a position adjacent to Colonel Bendell directly in front of us.

Within moments the growing shadow of the lead Jolly Green engulfed the pad chorused by the steady *whop-whop* of its rotor. A shroud of sand washed across the cement surface as the giant chopper landed.

Vietnamese, Americans, and Montagnards spilled quickly out of the tailgate and hurried through the sandy fog to the far side of the LZ. The huge, six-bladed chopper continued to idle as several Americans standing at the tailgate lip reached upward through the rotor downdraft to receive the first body.

I squinted, trying to see through the dirty cloud of movement to determine who it was. The smaller size of the first body told me it was one of Wheeler's Montagnards. Looking closer I could see it was Kosh. Kosh was from Tuong's village in the Central Highlands. They were best friends and anytime they had a rice-wine gathering both always playfully argued about the correct mixture of rice, leaves, and water.

The men quickly carried Kosh to the edge of the LZ and placed him faceup on the surface. A few moments later six bodies had been laid side by side.

The Jolly Green revved its howling turbine scattering another wave of sand out over the LZ. As it faded with the chopper's departure the hushed curtain of death rose over the grim carnage.

Now, a once bold and courageous fighting team lay silent just thirty feet in front of us. The gentle drift of wind lapped at their collars and caressed their tangled bloody hair giving a macabre animation to the still warriors. A chilling tremor narrowed my stunned eyes as I gazed at Wheeler's One-One, Curt Bolan—half of his skull had been ripped away from the left eye socket up.

Colonel Kahn removed his beret and walked slowly across the LZ. Hearing the approach of the number two chopper he halted, looked upward, and signaled it toward the alternate camp LZ near the beach area.

The hatchet force indigenous personnel stood gathered behind the bodies. The presence of only six dead indicated that the HF hadn't taken any KIA. It was common for the HF to lose several personnel on recovery operations. This time they'd been lucky.

Ivan Kahn nodded a silent thanks to the HF members, then knelt at the blood-soaked torso of Hank Wheeler. He gripped Hank's shoulder and whispered a short prayer as he always did, then drew his beret up to wipe the tears from his eyes.

A salty flavor on my lips hit me a second before I realized that it was my tears. I tightened my jaw and blinked, trying to restrain the flow. I didn't know if I was weeping for Hank Wheeler or Ivan Kahn. Perhaps, I thought, it was my own fear welling up inside me. It could easily be my team laid out there.

Many times I'd seen Colonel Kahn reverently kneeling before the lifeless bloodstained bodies of his soldiers—it never got any easier to witness my commander weeping.

Suddenly my eyes caught a glimpse of Megan Blair swaying. For a second I thought it might be the stout breeze moving her, then I saw her knees begin to buckle. I lunged forward to catch her as she wilted backward.

Bendell and Jinx quickly turned to me as I lifted her limp body and cradled her horizontally in my arms.

"What's . . . what's the problem?" Jinx muttered.

Colonel Bendell squinted and touched her pale face. "She's fainted. I had a feeling this might be too much for her. Brett, how 'bout taking her in, will you?"

"Roger, sir. I'll carry her into the admin office."

"Brett, you need some help?" Ski said, leaning toward me.

"Negative, partner."

As I turned and trudged toward the admin building I could hear Colonel Bendell telling Sergeant Major Twitty I didn't need any help. I was glad he'd stopped Twitty. I knew it wouldn't take much to revive her, and when she regained consciousness the fewer people around the better. Megan Blair was a proud woman. The last thing she needed now was a gang of men glaring down at her when she woke.

Upon entering the office the Vietnamese mail clerk jumped from behind his desk and hurried toward me. "Oh, oh! What wong? We hit? We hit? I'm no hear nothing. I—"

"No hit. Get *nuoc da*," I said while edging sideways down the narrow hallway toward Colonel Kahn's office.

I gently laid Megan on the couch, then took the seat cushion from the colonel's chair and placed it behind her head.

"Here *nuoc da*. What wong her? Her tired?" the clerk said while hurrying into the office with a canteen cup full of water.

"Roger. Her tired," I said, taking the water. Pulling the cravat from my neck I dipped a waded portion of it into the cup, then knelt and dabbed Megan's forehead lightly. I had several Amyl-nitrate capsules in my shirt pocket but decided not to use one because it had a way of waking someone with the chemical kick of a mule. I folded the cravat and placed it on her brow.

A few seconds later she groaned. I glanced up at the clerk standing beside me. "You *dee*."

As he left Megan began to blink slowly. She tried to pull her head forward.

"Just lay back and relax, Lieutenant. You're okay."

Hearing my voice she opened her eyes. A crack of thunder caused her to dart a glance toward the open window. "Is it . . . is it raining?" she murmured.

I stood, set the cup aside, then moved to the window and looked out at the darkening sky. "No, but it will be anytime time now, *Trung-'uy*." I closed the window and turned to see her trying to sit up. The wet cravat dropped off her brow and into her lap without her noticing it.

"What did you call me? Trung . . . trung something?"

"*Trung-'uy*, it's Vietnamese for lieutenant." I smiled at her and withheld the urge to tell her it was also the name of our team dog.

Looking down she noticed the cravat on her lap. "What's this?" she asked softly while picking it up.

I leaned against the desk. "It's my cravat. I used it to dab some water on you."

Leaning forward she placed her elbows on her knees. "Thank you. Was it you who brought me here?"

"Roger."

Her eyes avoided mine as she spoke. "Damn it, I'm sorry. I'm truly sorry. I just wasn't ready for that out there. I—I thought they'd be in body bags. I—I thought."

She jerked the cravat to her eyes. "I don't know what I thought. I feel so damn inadequate. So—"

"Hold it!" I said sternly. "Look at me."

Her tearstained face tilted upward sniffling. She drew her lower lip between her teeth as I stood.

"Don't start cornering yourself into some guilt trip. Pure and simple you walked into a situation you weren't expecting. There ain't a goddamn man out there on that LZ who doesn't tremble, shake, and cry when we go through this, and we've been through it a lot."

I softened my voice and looked directly into her eyes. "You are not inadequate. You're just human, that's all."

After seconds of silence I turned toward the door. "I gotta get back. The latrine is down the hall if you want to clean up."

She looked away clutching the cravat between her hands and spoke angrily. "Well—well why don't they put them in body bags? Isn't—isn't that what they are supposed to do? What the hell is wrong with—"

I turned, hurling bitter words. "They don't put them in body bags because that's the way Ivan Kahn wants it! That's why!

"Those men are our comrades. They fought, sweated, and died with honor for a noble fucking purpose and my commander doesn't want us saying good-bye to some bundled-up plastic bags. We say our good-byes face-to-face."

Lowering my tone I said, "It's the right thing to do."

I turned and left. As I exited the admin office I noticed a light rain had begun to fall. Through the gray mist I could see Binkowski lumbering toward me. Beyond him I could see the formation beginning to disperse.

Plodding toward the LZ I felt a gnawing anger with myself for letting my temper fire on Megan. She didn't need both barrels of my frustration unloaded on her, and more practically, I felt that it was now very possible that I'd completely alienated my number one source of target personnel information.

Approaching Ski I noticed his eyes were intense. He spoke loudly through the wind. "How's Megan . . . the lieutenant, I mean?"

"She's okay."

"I was just coming to tell you that Major Jinx wants us in the TOC at 0800 tomorrow."

I was glad to hear they hadn't decided to schedule any mission-related requirements for tonight. "That's good news," I said, stopping in front of him. I glanced back at the office, then faced Ski. "How about picking up our weapons at the TOC and meet me in the club. I've got something to do. I'll be down there shortly.

"And if you see Tuong, don't tell him about Kosh. It's better that I break it to him."

"Roger, Brett," he said, looking down. He looked up, avoiding my eyes, and spoke quietly, "Would it be all right if I skip that club ritual, Brett? I don't—"

I reached and gripped his shoulder. "Hang in there, partner. Arizona would be doing it for us. We need to be there. Copy?"

He looked up with a tight-lipped expression. "Roger, copy."

I understood Ski's reluctance to attend what was referred to as the "Blood Bash." I didn't like it any better than he did, but it was expected of us and the SOP had been in place ever since the conception of Command and Control.

When a man was assigned to a team as the One-Zero he was required to put one hundred dollars in an envelope along with his personal epitaph and give it to the club manager. If the team leader got zapped, the next step after the chopper pad ceremony was the "Blood Bash." All One-Zeros and One-Ones assembled in the club, listened to someone read the epitaph, then drank free until the one hundred dollars was expended—at fifty cents a drink that was a lot of booze divided among fifteen or twenty people.

Arnold Binkowski had only been with RT Texas a couple of months—not long enough to know that skipping a "Blood Bash" was not only a violation of recon protocol, it was also considered bad luck.

I turned away from Ski and headed back toward the admin building.

"Where you going?" he shouted through the thick drizzle.

"I'm going to get out of the rain. Didn't your mother ever teach you to come in out of the rain? See you in a few minutes."

I didn't have much time to intercept Megan before Twitty got to the office. I'd decided I wasn't going to let my ego ambush the opportunity to get some info from her. My mission right now was to try to set up something for later this evening with Megan Blair.

After entering the admin building I hurried past the clerk and down the hall. I found Megan standing at the window. She held an unlit cigarette in one hand and my cravat in the other.

I tapped on the door before entering. "Thought I'd check and see how you're doing."

She turned. "I'm okay," she said while taking a step forward. "Here's your scarf. Thank you."

I moved to take the cravat, keeping my eyes fixed on her. I started to tell her to keep it but quickly thought she might interpret the courtesy as an implication of some future emotional breakdown.

I stuffed the cravat into my pocket. "I was a little heated answering your question a while ago. I'm sorry if—"

"No apology needed, Sergeant Yancy. I wouldn't have understood it any other way. This is my first introduction to the raw side of war. Thank you for being straightforward with me."

"Well, I guess I should say 'you're welcome,' but it was purely accidental. I tend to be a hair trigger on the emotional side at times. I probably need to work on that some."

She smiled. "I don't agree. My father once told me that without passion there can be no compassion."

Her words floated over me like a net. I felt my eyes squint as I gazed into her placid face, and for a moment I lost my grip on my motive for being there.

I deliberately glanced away, then centered a smile back into her indigo-blue eyes. "How long has it been since you had a good American cheeseburger?"

She blinked, catching herself before she laughed. "What? I can't remem—"

"Well, that's too long. There's an R and R center called China Beach up the road a few miles near Da Nang. Best burgers this side of the International Date Line.

"I've just learned we're not kicking off the next skull session until tomorrow morning, so how about us forgetting the war for a while. I'll get a jeep and drive us up to China Beach for a burger and a beer." I looked at my watch. "Say . . . in about two hours: 1830?"

She took a step backward and studied me. "Okay, that sounds good. I'll have to check with Colonel Bendell and make sure—"

I grinned. "Don't worry. I'll get it cleared." I wasn't completely sure I could get his approval, but I did feel confident that if I could convince him it was in the best interest of the mission he'd give me an immediate nod.

Turning away I said, "I'll pick you up over at the officer billets. Bring your poncho."

"Wait, I don't have . . . I mean, I left it in Saigon."

It may have been completely unfair of me but I wasn't about to give her any excuses to back out or change her mind. I shouted while continuing down the hall, "Don't worry. I'll bring one for you!"

The light afternoon drizzle had evolved into a full-fledged pelting rain by the time I reached the club. The low drone of voices mixed with the loud rasping beat of the jukebox rushed over me like a smoky wave as I entered the small honky-tonk.

I removed my soaked bush hat, slapped it hard against my leg, and tucked it into my side pocket. I walked through the crowded room and found Ski leaning his big frame against the bar.

He saw me approaching. "I got you a drink already, Brett. Here," he said, sliding the Beam and Coke across the plywood bar to me.

I lifted the glass, tapped his, and spoke before drinking. "Here's to Arizona, partner."

"Arizona," he echoed, lifting his Budweiser and drinking.

I caught a glimpse of a stout figure nearing me. It was James Iron Oak.

He edged into the bar adjacent to me. "Did you get the

word about tomorrow? Zero eight hundred at the TOC?" he asked, glancing at me, then Ski

"Roger," I replied.

He took a sip of his beer. "How's the girl?"

I turned to him. "The lieutenant is fine."

Iron flashed his famous grin and nodded. "I'll say she's fine. Man, I'd eat a mile of telephone cable just to hear her fart over a Princess phone!"

Any other time I might have laughed but I just wasn't in the mood. Ski stayed silent too.

I took a long draw on my drink and turned to Iron. "Any word on what happened to Arizona?"

Iron nodded toward the far side of the room and told me Swede was over there talking to Colonel Kahn. He said all he'd been able to find out was that they got hit in their RON last night and had been running hard all morning trying to get to an LZ. When they got there they rolled straight into a point-blank ambush.

I turned to survey the smoky room. "Have you seen Colonel Bendell in here?"

"Negative," Iron answered.

"Ski, you seen him?" I asked.

"No. I don't think he's here. Why do you need him?"

"Nothing important," I said, finishing my drink. I set the empty glass on the bar. "Get me another will you, partner. I'll be right back."

I moved through the crowd and found Swede and Colonel Kahn sitting alone at the table by the jukebox. The jukebox table was Swede's favorite spot to sit when he didn't want anyone overhearing his conversation. Once, when I questioned him about it he said, "This is the most private spot in the joint. If anybody can eavesdrop over five hundred decibels of rock and roll, they deserve to hear what I'm sayin'!"

Swede noticed me approaching and slid a chair out for me.

"Mind if I join y'all for a minute?" I shouted while Chuck Berry wailed "Mabeline."

Jensen stood as I sat down. "I'm gettin' us another round. You ready for one, Brett?"

"Roger." When Swede left I leaned closer to Colonel Kahn. "Sir, do you know where Colonel Bendell is?"

"He's returning to Da Nang airfield to catch a flight back to Saigon. He left on the second Jolly Green about fifteen minutes ago. What do you need to see him for?" he shouted.

I breathed a little easier knowing that it was now Colonel Kahn who would make the decision about me taking Megan to China Beach.

I leaned closer to made sure he could hear me. "Sir, I was going to get his approval to take Lieutenant Blair up to China Beach. I've got a chance to drill her tonight and—"

"What?" he shouted, jerking back to look at me.

I realized immediately that I'd used the wrong choice of words. I reshuffled my deck and shouted again. "What I mean is, sir, I have a chance to get a little discreet intel on the Mariposa personnel from her. She's accepted my invitation and I figure if—"

"Say no more, Yancy," he said, breaking into a grin. "Take my jeep and drill away. The more we know about them the better! I want a full report in the morning."

Suddenly the music stopped. I hadn't noticed Jensen return with the drinks. He'd evidently set the drinks down and unplugged the jukebox.

"Listen up!" he shouted while holding a small piece of paper. "I'm now gonna read Hank's last transmission to us."

Everyone stood. A hush fell over the room.

Jensen waited for a second, then began reading. " 'Chances are if you're hearing this right now then I'm already zipped up inside cold plastic and canvas. I'm not much on long-winded spiels so I'll make this short and let y'all get back to drinking. A guy named Shakespeare once wrote, "To be or not to be, that is the question." Don't shed no tears in your beer for me, gents. Win, lose, or draw, I chose, "To be," and I had the privilege of working with the pros. Press on, Recon!' "

Chapter 9

The rain had let up some by the time Ski and I left the club and walked toward the team hooch. I glanced at my watch: 1715 hours.

"When we get to the hooch how about you taking the Cowboys on to chow, partner. I'm going to hang back with Tuong and break the news to him about Kosh. I'll be gone for a while this evening so remember what Colonel Kahn said. Don't say anything to them about Saydem."

"Where you going tonight?"

"I've got to go up to China Beach for a while."

"What's gong on up there?"

"Nothing, I just—"

Ski stopped in his tracks. "You've got a date with her, don't you? You have a date with Megan! Right or wrong?" His tone sounded dejected, like he had a flat tire just as he got to the starting line.

I stopped. "It's not a date damn it. It's—"

"I understand, Brett. I fully, I mean , no need to ex . . . Hey! How about if I tag along? It's been weeks since I've been up there."

Taking Ski with me was out of the question and I really

didn't like explaining my reasoning. I reminded myself that he was my partner—I'd always been straight with Will.

I glanced at the gray misty fog hovering over the beach area, then looked back at his forlorn face. "I say again, partner. This is not a date. But it is something I have to do alone. I'm going to drill . . . question her about the Mariposa personnel.

"She worked with them. There's no doubt in my mind that she knows more about them than anything we're going to find in those dossiers tomorrow. Right now we need to dig up anything we can."

I turned and walked on. "Now do you understand? This is important."

Ski hurried to catch up with me as I neared the steps of the hooch. "Sure, but what makes you think she's gonna open up to you?"

"You'd be surprised what cheeseburgers and beer can do to lower a lady's resistance to courteous interrogation."

"Yeah," he said in a pleading voice. "But if I went along we could 'Mutt and Jeff' her. How about that? It might work better."

Mutt and Jeff was a term common to military and police methods of interrogation. It pitted two people against one individual—after one fired a question the other would hurl another, eventually confusing the prisoner. Ski's concept was way out of sync with the method I planned on using, but it was apparent that he was intent on trying to wangle a way to come along.

I turned and stood face-to-face with him. Looking into his anxious eyes I felt like I was having to tell my little brother he couldn't go to the movies with me tonight. "Look, partner, thanks for your suggestions, but this is a solo mission."

Without waiting for an answer I turned and strode up

the wooden steps and opened the hooch door. Looking back I noticed him walking onward toward the latrine.

Upon seeing me Tuong jumped up from the big home-made picnic table in the center of the room and hurried toward me. "Sar Brett, what do *see so* mean?"

I slipped my weapon carrying strap over my head, walked to my bunk, and began wiping the water residue off my rifle with a towel. *"See-so?"* I said, giving Tuong a puzzled look. "Are you sure that's an English word?"

Lok sat up from his bed and quickly answered while pointing toward the radio. "Rogee, Sar Brett. We hear song call see-so on radio."

Tuong squatted by my bed. "Song say, 'rhy my see-so.' "

I hung the rifle on the nail above my bed, then sat on the bunk facing Tuong. "Rhy my see-so," I repeated while mentally flipping through the current top forty songs on the Armed Forces station.

A second later it came to me. "You're talking about that new Moody Blues tune. 'Ride My Seesaw.' That's it."

Tuong grinned. "That what I'm say, rhy my see-so. I'm know abou rhy horse like Clin Eezwoo. What mean, rhy see-so?"

Clint Eastwood and John Wayne were the unofficial heroes of the Montagnards. Whenever we showed a western at the outdoor theater every Montagnard in camp was always seated and waiting an hour before showtime.

I looked around the room while digging through my mind to find a quick explanation for *seesaw*. Up until now the toughest word I'd had to describe was snowball. I decided a picture was worth a thousand words.

Pulling a pen from my pocket I stood and gathered the Yards around the team table. I drew a seesaw on the table surface and sketched two stick figures on each end of it.

I'd learned from past experience to choose my words carefully when describing something. If a word was used they didn't understand it was like opening up a can of worms—questions would pop up from everyone.

Binkowski walked into the room as I began my explanation. He stood peering down over the huddled Yards at my sketch.

"See, gang, this end goes up and this end goes down. It's like a big toy for kids to play on." I held my hands out raising and lowering them to simulate the rise and fall of each end.

I knew the Yards didn't have a full concept of what domestic American toys were—they'd grown up with spears, crossbows, and guns as their toys. Nonetheless, they all seemed to accept my explanation.

Tuong leaned toward the etching and lowered his head for a closer look as if studying a map.

"There's a song out now called 'Ride My Seesaw,'" Ski exclaimed.

I scowled at him. "Yes, we know, Arnold. Why do you think I'm going through all this?"

"Oh," he said, shrugging and turning away toward his bunk.

Tuong stood. "Sar Brett, why song say, 'rhy see-so'? They want play?"

Binkowski cut me off before I could answer. "It's a metaphor, Tuong. A metaphor about the ups and downs of life you know, like a seesaw."

"Damn it, Arnold, they don't know what a metaphor is. How do you expect them—"

"I'm know! I'm know!" Lok shouted, jumping up from the table. Next to Tuong, Lok was second in command of English knowledge.

He hurried to a shelf near his bunk and grabbed a metal

mess-kit fork. He held it proudly in front of his face. "This is metal-for. Right, Sar Brett?"

The lid on the worm can was coming off quick. I decided it was time to ring the bell on today's class.

I smiled at Lok. "Roger, that's a metal fork." I quickly darted a stare at Ski to short-stop him from saying anything.

"Ski, how about you taking the gang on to chow. Tuong and I will be along in a minute."

As they all grabbed their hats and headed to the door, Binkowski looked back. "You never did tell me what jingoistic means. What is—"

"Later, Arnold."

After the others left I sat alone with Tuong at the table and told him about RT Arizona and Kosh. He quietly stood, lit a cigarette, and turned away toward the closed door. It was his way of concealing grief and I understood it was the way of the Dega people not to demonstrate their sorrow outside the family.

Only the soft murmur of monsoon wind touched the silence.

The religious belief of the Dega about death was that if a man's spirit was pure and he had been brave throughout his life, he would remain in the spiritual world in harmony and eventually return to life.

After a moment Tuong turned back to me and walked to the table where I was seated. He sat across from me and ran his finger in a circular motion around the sketch I'd drawn on the wooden surface.

Studying the careful movement of his finger he said softly, "I'm think maybe Kosh take rhy see-so." As he looked up a tear gathered in his eye. "Him brave Dega. Come back soon maybe."

I marveled at his tender search to find logic in the wake

of sorrow. I reached to touch the coarse texture of wood near his finger. "Kosh was brave Dega. I think you're right."

After chow I assembled the team in the hooch and gave them a brief warning order about the forthcoming mission. Although I couldn't disclose the place or purpose of the mission, it didn't seem to concern the Yards. To them a mission was a mission, and they were all aware that their primary role was to provide fire support if we made contact.

When I told them we would be making a parachute infil into the target they got ecstatic. Phan and Lok immediately hopped up onto their footlockers and performed a simulated parachute landing fall onto the floor.

It had been four months since I'd taken them through a one week jump school at the One-Zero training facility at Long Tan. They'd all done well during the training. We made five jumps—two from a UH-1H helicopter, and three from a C-130 Blackbird. But that had been four months ago and those jumps had been under optimum conditions. We'd only made one jump with equipment.

Our infil into Drop Zone Ghost Rider would be different. This one would be at night, and that, combined with the fact that this was a combat equipment jump, made things a lot more difficult. None of us, including myself, had ever conducted a combat parachute infiltration.

I'd learned during the briefing that this jump would be a "pop-up" infiltration. That meant the C-130 would contour fly at treetop level to avoid enemy radar, then "pop-up" to nine hundred feet to give us adequate jump altitude, then drop back down after we exited.

DZ Ghost Rider was estimated to be approximately three hundred meters in length. A quick mental calculation told me that at 125 knots jump speed we had less than six seconds to exit the plane when the green light said "go." I reasoned that two teams totaling twelve personnel would look like rice-wine diarrhea unassing the Blackbird.

The ability to maintain noise discipline and conduct a quick assembly once we hit the DZ were fundamental factors for the infiltration. But if the wind was anything more than twelve to fifteen knots, it was very likely one or more of the lightweight Montagnards could be blown and carried way from the DZ. If that happened, we'd have the additional problem of locating them before we could start the show, not to mention dealing with possible injuries if they had to make a tree landing.

The more I pondered the potential problems and complexity of this mission the clearer it became that there was a definite disproportion of nuts to bolts.

After telling the Yards that town was off limits until our return from mission, I went ahead and told them I had to conduct some intel gathering tonight and would be gone for a few hours. I didn't want them thinking I was deliberately violating our team SOP by going to town without them.

When I returned from the shower and began putting on fresh fatigues Tuong walked casually over to my bunk while wiping his rifle. He waited for a moment, then spoke while holding his CAR-15 out to me. "See, Sar Brett. Very clean."

I always stressed the importance of a clean weapon, however we generally cleaned weapons after range firing or upon return from a mission. There was no obvious need for Tuong to be asking me to inspect his rifle. I knew there was something else on his mind.

Accepting the weapon I glanced it over and handed it

back to him. "Number one," I replied, giving him an inquisitive look.

He took the rifle, then squatted holding it across his lap while watching me dab some cologne on my neck. "You go Da Nang tonight get boom-boom?"

Boom-boom was the Dega term for getting laid. "No boom-boom tonight," I said, replacing the cologne bottle into my wall locker. "I've got some intel gathering to do."

"What do intel gaddering mean?"

"It's like asking questions. You know like a certain Dega friend of mine does a lot of." I winked.

He grinned. "You smell good. Maybe I'm go wid you Da Nang. Watch for VC."

Tuong was aware that the road to Da Nang had been a VC ambush corridor in the past, but that was several months ago. Since the 3rd Amtrac Marines had initiated armored personnel patrols along the road there hadn't been a sighting of VC anywhere in the area.

I slipped my Beretta shoulder holster on and winked at him. "Thanks, babysan. I'll be okay. *Beaucoup* Marines kick Charlie's ass off Da Nang Road." I removed the pistol from the holster, pulled the sliding bolt back just enough to make sure a round was chambered, then flipped the safety on.

After putting my shirt on I donned a rain jacket and picked up a poncho for Megan. Lok, Phan, Rham, and Tuong all accompanied me to the door as if to tell me to be home early.

Ski had left moments before saying he was going to the dispensary to feed Trung-'uy. Our team dog was in observation quarantine since one of the Vietnamese in camp had contracted rabies from a rat bite.

As I walked out of the hooch and stepped into a light

drizzle, Tuong shouted from the huddled gathering at the door. "Sar Brett, you being careful gaddering. Okay?"

I smiled back to them. "Roger, gang. I'll be careful."

I'd timed my departure to allow me a few minutes to drop into Swede's hooch and let him know what I was doing tonight. As I entered his hooch a heavy veil of marijuana smoke floated over me. His team Montagnards were squatted in a circle passing a joint around.

"Mary-joe-wanna" was a way of life with some of the Yards, a kind of respiratory recreation. Will Washington and I had always discouraged use of it with our Cowboys, and strangely, ever since Will's death I hadn't seen one of them light up anything but regular cigarettes.

After letting Swede know about my plan for the evening, he stepped over to a footlocker and opened it. Pulling a new AK-47 out of the locker he grinned and tossed it to me. "This might help win her over a little, Brett. At any rate it'll be a nice souvenir for her to take back to Saigon and hang on her wall."

"How many do you have left? This isn't the last one, is it?" Swede and I had found eighteen of the new rifles still in Cosmoline in a village cache on my first mission with California. I knew he'd traded some of them to the staff director at China Beach for a surfboard. I didn't know how many.

"No sweat," he said, reaching into the locker again. He pulled out a full magazine for the AK and handed it to me. "I've still got three. Maybe you'd better give her some range time with it. Wouldn't want it on my conscience if she hurt herself!"

"Thanks, Swede."

As I turned to leave, Iron, who'd been reclined on his bunk, leaned upward and said, "Yeah, and I'll be glad to take her out to the range tomorrow. Man, I'd love to watch her firing that AK on full automatic. I'll bet the recoil would have those big bazoos of hers bouncin' like two cantaloupes on a trampoline!''

Trudging out through the marijuana fog I grinned at him. ''Sure thing, Iron. You can do it right after you get through eating that mile of telephone cable.''

Chapter 10

A young Vietnamese gate guard scurried through the heavy drizzle toward our jeep carrying his M16 in one hand and a clipboard in the other.

He smiled and handed the board to me. "*Chao-ong,* Sar."

"*Chao-ong,*" I repeated while brushing the drops of water off the paper and signing the sheet with name, time, and destination. Megan Blair leaned slowly forward, peering up through the rain-splotched windshield at the large sign above the gate.

I could hear the skulls that dangled beneath the sign clacking in the stout breeze like a satanic wind chime. The skulls had been brought back by the hatchet force Montagnards. They had boiled them, then hung them under the sign as a barrier against the intrusion of evil spirits.

As I handed the board back to the guard he glanced slyly at Megan, then to me. "You stay Da Nang tonie, Sar?"

"Negative," I said, holding up two fingers. "Be back in a couple hours."

He smiled and hurried toward the big chain-link gate. I

flipped the windshield wipers on and waited for him to unlock the gate, then swing it open.

I'd decided to hold off on giving Megan the AK right now. There was no need to tip my hand with a gift that might make her think I was trying to butter her up.

I pulled slowly out and turned north onto the main road. The old French-built highway was badly deteriorated. It looked like a practice corridor for B-52 bombing sorties.

"This gets a little rough in places," I warned, keeping my eyes concentrated on the puddles and potholes.

"Were those real skulls I saw hanging off that sign?" Megan asked, looking back over her shoulder.

I grinned while steering wide to avoid a pothole. "No. I made those in our Wednesday night ceramic class."

She started to turn toward me but instead she pretended to study the murky path of ditch water paralleling the road. I caught a glimpse of a smile in her reflection on the windshield.

After a short pause she reached under her poncho and withdrew a pack of cigarettes. "Very creative."

"What? My driving?"

"No. Your ceramic skulls."

I kept a stoic face. "Thanks. But that's nothing. You should see my skull canister set." I smiled and glanced over at her. "You need a light?"

"No," she replied, tucking the package back under her poncho.

"Oh."

"How long have you been in Vietnam?"

"Almost a year now," I answered.

"So, after this next job . . . mission, I mean, you'll be going home?"

"Not exactly. I've just extended my tour six months.

I'll probably take leave after the mission. How about you?''

"Where's home?" she asked, completely ignoring my question.

"Fort Worth. How about—"

"That's west of Dallas, isn't it?" she interjected.

"Roger. Fort Worth is where the West begins," I said, giving her a glancing smile. "Dallas is where the East peters out."

She nodded and cracked a half grin. "Do you have a wife? A girlfriend?"

I downshifted into second gear and slowed to ease through a large crater in the center of the road. "Negative, no wife. I guess you could say I'm sort of engaged to—"

"Sort of engaged!" she interrupted. "How can you be sort of engaged?"

"Well . . . it's like . . ." I stopped while pondering her barrage of questions. I was beginning to feel as though I'd lost a grip on who was in charge of this conversation.

I theorized that allowing her to feel a certain control would make her more comfortable and potentially receptive to my questions later.

"Did you hear me, Sergeant Yancy?"

"Roger, ma'am," I said, raising my voice. "I heard what—"

"Please don't call me that! I really don't care for that term. It sounds too matronly."

Her reaction had been exactly what I'd expected. I gave her a dramatic frown of agreement. "Roger. I never cared for it either. How about this? As long as we're not standing by the flagpole, why don't you call me Brett, and I'll call you Megan?"

She nodded. "Yes. It's a deal. You can—"

Suddenly I plowed head-on into a wide pool of water.

The jeep swerved, jolted, and bounced into the center of the dark pool and stopped abruptly.

"Are you okay?" I shouted.

She released her grip on the dashboard and pushed away, raising her feet. "Yes!" she cried, looking down at the water sloshing over into the floorboard. She grinned back at me sympathetically. "Are you sure this hamburger and beer excursion is worth going through this inclement weather obstacle course?"

I reached and shifted into four-wheel drive. "Absolutely!" I said, yanking the transmission lever into first gear and revving the engine. "Just think of it as part of the mystique. You know, like going to Germany for Wiener schnitzel."

An arc of muddy water sprayed up from the front and rear wheels as we spun, thrashed, and bounced, in place. She jerked toward me, grasping my shoulder to escape the deluge pouring in from her side.

The sweet scent of her perfume grabbed me as dominantly as her grip. "Would you like for me to do this?" she muttered.

I released the accelerator, flipped the gear lever to neutral, and turned nose to nose with her. Darting a smile from her indigo eyes to her scarlet lips and back again, I whispered. "Do what? What is it you'd like to do?"

Keeping her timorous eyes on mine she slowly released my shoulder and started to pull away. Raising my right arm I caressed her hair and pulled her closer to me, feeling the warm rapture of her cautious submission. I thought, Forgive me, Tracy, this is in the line of duty.

Monsoon winds blew ebony strands of hair across my face as she pressed her moist lips to mine in a full declaration of desire. Her firm breasts pushed against me. The soft pressure of our lips weakened as our breath labored with desire.

In the distance I could hear the irritating roar of an approaching truck above the idle purr of the jeep. I whispered through our kiss, "Darlin', I—I think we've got company coming down the road. Can you—can you discipline yourself long enough to let me get us out of this mud hole?"

Reluctantly she pulled back, scrutinizing my intoxicated smirk. "Maybe," she murmured. "I don't know. Depends on how long I have to discipline myself?"

I glanced at the black cloud of diesel smoke rising from the stacks of the truck into the gray drizzle. The big deuce and a half truck had stopped twenty meters ahead of us.

The driver leaned out the cab window and shouted, "Hey! Are you okay in there? You need some help?"

Megan pulled back to her seat and straightened her poncho.

"Hang on!" I shouted out into the heavy drizzle. I shoved the lever into second gear and rode the clutch while accelerating to gain traction. We moved steadily, fishtailing, through the water and up onto the solid ground adjacent to the truck.

I leaned outward from beneath the canvas roof of the jeep and looked up at the driver. "Thanks anyhow, partner. Looks like I got it handled. How's the road back north?"

"You green and good all the way to Dang-a-lang city, man," he yelled down while dipping his head and trying futilely to see below the roof line of my jeep. "You know, man, maybe it's the rain or my windshield needs a good cleaning; but it sure looked like someone was attackin' you when I was pullin' up here."

I knew he couldn't see into the passenger side of the

jeep. I frowned. "Roger. That's exactly right! I'm taking this NVA prisoner into Da Nang. He tried to jump me back there! Lucky you came along and distracted him!"

His eyebrows raised. "Well, shit! Don't fuck around with that prick. Gonna be dark soon. Why don't you just shoot the bastard and save yourself a trip, man."

Megan's fist jolted my shoulder.

"Can't shoot him. He's too important. See ya 'round partner," I said, releasing the clutch. Grinning, I quickly accelerated and sped onward down the wet, fog-patched highway.

Chapter 11

Megan Blair and I sat quietly by a rain-pelted window in the empty snack bar area finishing our meal.

"What do you plan on doing when you get out of the Army? Or perhaps you plan to stay in?" she asked gently, dabbing the corners of her mouth with a napkin.

I took the final bite of my second cheeseburger and chased it with the last swallow of Victoria Bitter. "I don't know. I never really saw myself as a career soldier, but I do like the people I'm working with. I guess it's a consideration. I still have two semesters of school I should complete. At any rate, I've got six more months in 'Nam to decide.

"You want another beer?"

She smiled and pushed her half-full bottle toward me. "No thanks. You can finish mine if you'd like. I don't care for this Australian beer."

I'd intentionally ordered the stouter Aussie beer hoping it would loosen her up some. Since our arrival at the R and R center she'd seemed withdrawn, indicating she had some inhibitions about our spontaneous heavy breathing exercise back on the highway.

I reached and picked up the beer, then pushed back

from the table and turned stretching my legs out beside her chair. I sipped the beer and watched her fondle the pack of cigarettes on the table. "Are you ever going to light one of those?" I asked through a grin.

Megan tucked the package back into her pocket. "No," she replied matter-of-factly while letting her eyes travel slowly up and down the length of my body. "I'm trying to quit smoking. I just carry them as a security blanket."

I glanced away from her eyes before mine admitted that I didn't understand carrying a knife if you were afraid of stabbing yourself.

Looking across the room I noticed a large wall clock: 1915 hours. I still had at least an hour before we needed to head back to CCN. Up until now I hadn't asked anything related to the Mariposa and Megan hadn't volunteered anything. For that matter, she hadn't even said a thing about the mission. My guess was that she was preoccupied about security precautions.

The only thing I'd learned was that she fostered a smoldering resentment for what she called "institutionalized male chauvinism." Upon her graduation from UCLA she applied for a position with a well-known nuclear medicine laboratory in Los Angeles. Although she was qualified for the position the male executive, who insisted on interviewing her over lunch, was more interested in her physical attributes than her academic standings.

When Megan didn't respond to his overtures he told her she was not what they were looking for. When she pressed him as to why, he remarked, "You have no grasp for the rudiments of analysis. You salted your food before tasting it!" The following week Megan joined the Army with the intention of gaining access to G.I. bill benefits in order to eventually return to school and get into a master's program.

She remarked that after six months in the Army she'd observed the military to be one of the few American institutions that allowed women to stand on the merits of their skill and determination to exceed.

Before speaking I looked around the room to make sure no one had entered. Two soldiers had come in but they were playing Ping-Pong on the far side of the room.

I took a sip of beer and kept my tone nonchalant. "What's this guy Defrisco like?"

She turned, avoiding my eyes, and looked out the window at the white line of waves rolling in out of the darkness. "You want to go for a walk on the beach? It's stopped raining."

I glanced out at the slow drops of rain falling off the window awning. "Let's wait a few minutes and see if it's a trap." I didn't like having my question ignored but decided not to get too adamant about it.

She leaned back and folded her arms. "You want to know about Don? He's a jerk. A well-disguised jerk. I'd prefer to avoid the subject if you don't mind."

I almost laughed at her casual assessment; it was like summing Hitler up as simply "a bad boy." But I sensed she was cloaking a deeper feeling of alienation. She'd used his first name and that told me there might be some cinders of endearment still warming inside of her. Megan was a passionate woman. It was possible that she had shared that passion with Defrisco.

After a short silence I probed again. "It's understandable that you may not like talking about him, but I need information on these people we're going to neutralize."

Her head turned quickly. "You mean kill, don't you? Isn't that the crux of this job . . . mission, I mean? To kill?" Her eyes narrowed into slits. Bendell's assassination order had resurfaced to haunt me.

I glanced out the window, then back to her. "Megan, I don't have to tell you what's at stake here. You know better than anyone what the magnitude of this threat is. Defrisco and his cronies have had one too many tilt-a-whirl rides. They're about to cause a damn—" I stopped myself before I said "nuclear war."

I leaned forward. "They've got to be nailed."

"You have a distinct dependency on euphemisms, don't you? You can't say the word *kill*. You have to use diluted words like *neutralize*, *nail*, and—"

"Look damn it! We are not here to analyze my vocabulary."

Her eyebrows raised melodramatically. "Oh . . . and when you get angry you degenerate from euphemisms to profanity. You're really not as cool a guy as I thought you were.

"So, tell me . . . what are we here for, Yancy?"

I took a deep breath, set the bottle on the table, and looked out the window. "Two months ago today a man named William Washington was killed while conducting a body recovery mission with me. He was my One-One and he's the best friend I ever had. I loved him.

"He came to this country like a lot of other Americans to help beat the communist thugs out of here to insure a chance of freedom for the South Vietnamese."

I turned back to Megan. "Now I'm not going to get maudlin with you, Lieutenant. I fully realize there is nothing in the book that says you have to tell me a damn thing about these traitors. But I'll tell you this. Will, and a lot of other good men, RT Arizona included, have died digging out a little foothold for freedom over here, and I'm not backing down to the threats of a gang of punks and forgetting about the sacrifices of my comrades.

"On Halloween night I'm exiting a Blackbird over North

Vietnam and I'm coming down on Defrisco's Mariposa with all fours with or without your help!''

I reached and lifted the bottle to my mouth and drank. Setting it back down I took a deep breath and looked over at Megan, ''But, understand this: I respect your right not to assist me in any way. Now, would you still like to go for a walk?''

Megan remained silent and still. Her gaze moved slowly from me to the window.

After a moment she spoke as though talking to the night. ''I understand your feelings, Brett. And I admire your sense of loyalty and dedication.'' Her soft eyes returned to mine. ''Don Defrisco is following his patriotic convictions too. Brett, he's doing what he thinks is right.

''Gordon, and Abbey . . . well, they're only confused dupes he enlisted to help him. In fact, he even duped me. But, in either case, do you think they deserve to be killed for trying to do something, however radical, to bring about peace?'' She reached and touched my arm.

I sensed that Megan was on the verge of helping me. Her tone indicated she was grappling for reasoning. There were two obvious rebuttals to her rationale. The most glaring was Defrisco's admitted malicious intent to ''detonate the SADM'' if his demands weren't met. The potential annihilation of innocent women and children wasn't exactly ringing the warden's phone off the hook with me. But the kicker was his demand for four million dollars.

Something told me that if I hammered too hard and completely renounced Megan's peace motivation theory I'd lose her. If I readily agreed with her she might think I was being conciliatory in order to pry information.

I decided to split the difference with a question. ''You heard Defrisco's demand note today. Do you think he's planning on writing a book about this? He could title it, 'Nuclear Extortion for Peace and Profit.' '' I grinned.

She didn't grin back.

"Is all this amusing to you?" she asked in a brittle tone.

"Ludicrous is a better word. Are you aware that the Army Officer Corps is strictly voluntary?"

"Yes. So?" She shrugged.

"So, if Defrisco didn't like being a part of this war he could have resigned his commission. They would have put him washing garbage cans for a while, then they would have discharged him, and he could have gone home and made himself a protest sign. He could write his congressman, demonstrate, all that.

"But no. He makes the decision to steal a nuclear bomb and turn it into a terrorist suppository so he can be an overnight millionaire . . . multimillionaire. You're right about one thing. He is a bona fide jerk. He simply decided to be a rich jerk."

I'd noticed Megan draw a pensive finger to her chin as I spoke. I knew some of what I was saying was getting through to her. I didn't like having to debate the issue, but it seemed there wasn't much choice about it.

I decided it was time to try another question. "You mentioned that Defrisco duped you as well as Gordon and Abbey. How did he do that?"

She glanced down at the floor before speaking. "I would enjoy that walk now if you're still game."

I smiled. "Roger that."

Twenty minutes and about a hundred slow strolling meters of beach later, Megan told me the basic story on the Earl of Extortion, Lieutenant Donald Defrisco. DD had befriended Megan upon her arrival and assignment to the Nuclear Containment Facility. He was a "personable and charismatic guy."

She accepted his friendship, believing he was just being professionally courteous to his new exec. He spent a lot of time with her both on and off the job. Megan didn't mention that she had been intimate with him, but it was apparent in her voice.

She eventually learned that in the weeks prior to her arrival Defrisco had been passed over for promotion to captain. When the disenchanted DD started smoking opium Megan backed away from spending time with him. The fact that she hadn't mentioned anything about the opium use to the CID or her superiors meant that I could not realistically tell Colonel Kahn of Defrisco's drug habit without implicating Megan in a negative way. The first thing Colonel Kahn would want to know is how I learned of Defrisco's opium habit.

Megan told me that on the night of the theft Defrisco came to her quarters and asked her to come with him to the NCF vault. He explained that he needed to conduct the required evening inventory check that he'd neglected earlier. The huge vault had a six-digit combination. Security SOP dictated that he had knowledge of the first three digits and the XO the other three. The dual security procedure was designed to insure that two officers were always on hand anytime the vault was opened.

After opening the vault they both initialed the log sheet and he dismissed her. Megan returned to her quarters and never saw Defrisco again. Early the next morning she was intercepted by the CID. She was told that a guard had discovered a type-one abandoned near the Ton Son Nhut POL dump. With Defrisco, Abbey, and Gordon absent it didn't take long to figure out what had occurred.

As we approached a thatched roof cabana Megan pulled her cigarettes from her pocket.

"Let's sit here," I said, gesturing to a rattan lounge beneath the lighted shelter.

"They had evidently stolen two type-ones initially," she said, leaning back on the lounge. A crisp wind danced through her dark hair. "The CID surmised that they discarded the second device because of a problem with concealing it in the jeep they had."

I could understand the problem they encountered trying to get three personnel and two SADMs into a small jeep without raising the suspicions of the air base gate guards as they exited. What I didn't understand was why Defrisco failed to foresee the problem beforehand.

"I feel very used. Stupid!" Megan exclaimed, crushing her cigarette pack. She hurled it at a trash can like she was aiming at Defrisco's head.

"Is it the nature of men to use women?" she said, standing and looking down at me. "I mean, you're using me right now. Frankly I don't like—"

"Hold it!" I said, remaining seated. "You're forgetting that you and I are on the same team here. At least I like to think we are. If you really believe I'm using you, then try and see some merit in it, outside your injured ego.

"I'm sorry you got fucked over by Defrisco. But don't lock me in the same breech with that bastard. Now, sit down please. I still have another question. After that you can lick your wounds and call me what you want to."

Reluctantly, she slowly sat down on the edge of the lounge. "You realize of course that by telling you some of this I'm opening myself up to investigation. I'm trusting you, Brett."

I moved closer to her. "You know, Ivan Kahn has this bottom-line philosophy that he always whips on his team leaders before leaving camp for a target. He says, 'Keep your mind on the mission.' I'm doing that, and you're part of it. So you see, dropping you in the grease doesn't have a damn thing to do with this mission. What's said here stays between you and me.''

Megan touched my hand. ''One question, please. Was that kiss we shared real or was it just to get—?'' The muffled pop of an illumination flare interrupted her words. She turned to peer at the bright glow hovering above the naval compound north of us.

I squeezed her hand. ''That kiss was about as real as that two-hundred-thousand-candlepower flare.''

Chapter 12

"Hey! Anybody out here named Brett Yancy?"

I turned and saw the Neanderthal silhouette of Arnold Binkowski plodding across the beach toward us. The light from the lume flare stretched his long shadow out ahead of him.

I stood as he approached. He was grinning from ear to ear and smelled like he'd just crawled out of a vat of Aqua Velva.

"Hi. I just came up here to get me a cheeseburger and remembered that you said you might be here and thought—"

"How did you get here, Arnold?" I asked dryly.

"Oh . . . I caught a ride with one of the teams coming in to town to get . . ." He glanced at Megan. "To get some—some—"

"Recreation," Megan quipped.

"That's it!" Ski grinned. "Recreation."

It was common for RTs to load into a truck and go into town for "recreation." The road into Da Nang passed right by China Beach. But Binkowski had deliberately interrupted me.

In his haste he'd forgotten his weapon. I didn't want to

embarrass him in front of Megan, but he was well aware of the team SOP never to leave camp without a rifle or pistol.

I glanced at Megan. "Will you excuse us for a moment? I'll be right back," I said, gesturing for Binkowski to follow me.

"Good to see you again. They've got great cheeseburgers here. Did you try one yet?" Ski asked, talking over his shoulder while walking away with me.

"Yes, I did. Thank you," Megan replied.

Nearing the main building I looked over at him. "Where's your weapon?"

"There's no alert status tonight, Brett. I didn't think—"

"You know the team SOP about weapons."

"Hey, well where's your weapon?"

I halted and turned, stopping him abruptly in his tracks. "My pistol is hanging under a hot armpit, Sarge. Hear this. You have just violated team SOP and that don't cut it with me! You ignored my directive to stay in with the Yards tonight, and that don't get it either!

"And, you have butted in. Copy?"

"Darn, Brett. I—I didn't know you would get this mad. I was . . . I mean—"

"I am not mad, damn it! Mad is something that occurs in dogs. I am bothered. Bothered that I can't trust your sense of discipline or judgment!

"Now go get your damn hamburger and get back to camp," I said, stepping out of his path.

He glanced down shyly. "Well, okay, okay. Can I at least get a ride back with—"

"No!"

"Well, how am I going to get back without—"

"There's the ocean. You can swim back for all I care," I said, walking away.

I knew Ski had a 40mm case of the hots for Megan but it didn't justify his actions. I remembered that Ski had been "dear Johnned" by his girl recently. I knew he was probably suffering from a simple need to spend some time with an American woman.

Taking an exasperated breath I turned. "Wait for me at the jeep. You can ride back with us."

"Roger, Brett. Thanks," he shouted melodically.

The last flickering embers of the lume round died as I approached the cabana.

"I heard someone talk about swimming a while ago," Megan questioned as I approached. "Surely he isn't going for a swim."

"No, he changed his mind," I said, gently gripping her hand. "Can we sit down for a minute?"

I felt comfortable enough with Megan to know that we were on frequency with each other. There was no need to delve into more questions right now. That could wait until tomorrow.

The rattan softly creaked as we settled into the lounge. I remembered sitting in a similar lounge with Tracy Gibbs.

"I don't know if I have any silver bullets left, but if I do I'd like to ask you a favor?"

Megan's fragrance drifted through the breeze as she moved closer to me. She studied my face for a moment. "You've still got a couple. What's on your mind?"

I slipped my hand over her shoulder. "That big Yankee in there," I said, nodding toward the snack bar, "is enchanted with you and I can't blame him one bit. If you could spend a few minutes with him maybe sometime tomorrow, you know talk with him, it would sure help recharge his ego. He's a gentleman, I can promise you that."

She edged closer and laced her arms over my neck.

"Yes. I'll be glad to," she said, smiling. "Now, do I have any silver bullets left?"

I winked. "Full magazine."

Moving her lips to mine she whispered, "Then I would like another candle, candle, kiss please."

On the trip back to CCN I managed to avoid the mud hole that trapped us earlier. Ski sat in the rear seat. He was quiet initially, but after I encouraged him to talk he wouldn't shut up.

When we dropped Megan off at the officer transit barracks on the north side of camp I gave her the AK-47 and told her it was a gift from Swede. She was elated. After telling me that she'd never fired anything but an M16, I asked Ski if he'd mind giving her some firing lessons tomorrow. Ski answered with a full-auto string of words, "Roger, yes, certainly."

I knew Jensen and I would be hammering out a long day working on our operations plan, so breaking Ski loose for a while wouldn't be a problem—getting him back could be.

After turning the jeep in at the motor pool Ski and I walked eastward toward the team hooch. The night stilled with only the soft murmur of the ocean waves intruding on the darkness. No wind. No rain.

I glanced upward at a guard tower as we neared it, then checked my watch: 2105. The box-topped tower appeared empty. I slowed my pace and held a finger to my lips, signaling silence to Ski.

Colonel Kahn had mentioned recently that he'd found some Vietnamese asleep on guard duty. Normally the guards were supposed to be posted at 2000 hours and rotated ever four hours thereafter.

It seemed too early to feasibly think someone could already be asleep, but after a closer inspection I still couldn't see a man in the tower. I moved to the ladder and began climbing it quietly.

As my head moved above the open entrance at floor level I peered into the dark interior. I saw the motion of a hunkered figure in the corner.

"You sleep?" I said loudly.

He jumped to his feet. "No sleep! No sleep!" he muttered, holding his rice bag outward. "Me eat. See, eat?"

"Ten anh la qi?"

"Nam, Nam Le," he answered quickly.

I descended the ladder without replying. He knew he was supposed to be standing at all times during duty. I figured the fact that I'd gotten his name and caught him off watch was enough stimulus to keep him vertical and vigilant for the remainder of his guard cycle.

The VN never seemed to take guard duty seriously. Weeks back I'd actually seen one of them mounting the tower with only a rice pot and a blanket. He'd either forgotten his rifle or didn't consider it important. It was like we were being guarded by hooded hawks.

"Was he asleep?" Ski asked as we walked onward.

"No. He was worshiping his rice bag."

"Oh, I see. Hey, you know that Megan she's something else, isn't she? I mean she's a fox. Did you smell her? Wow!"

"Roger all the above," I replied, feeling the warm memory of her kiss nudge me.

"Do you think she likes me? I think she does. I could kind of tell it during the briefing today. You know what I mean? By the way, thanks for setting up that date, I mean firing lesson tomorrow with her.

"Oh, I forgot to tell you; I won a game of chess today. I wonder if Megan plays chess?"

Ski's voice had graduated to almost musical and my response to his questions didn't seem important to him. He was clearly in another world. I was glad his spirits had improved because in the days ahead I needed my partner playing with a full deck. I just hoped he didn't turn into a lovesick puppy in the meantime.

As we entered the hooch Tuong immediately hit me with an interrogation about how my "intel gaddering" had gone. I told him it went well, then fired a quick question back to him. "What's the first jump command?"

He blinked. "Fur jum comman?" he repeated, scratching his head. "I'm tink, maybe, maybe—"

"Huk up!" Phan blurted with a smile.

"Negative," I said, darting a look to Rham and Lok. They shrugged.

I knew the question had caught them off guard. It had been months since we'd gone through the condensed version of parachute training down at Long Tan. Expecting the Yards to remember the nine fixed wing jump commands was a little farfetched. I knew I'd be lucky if they remembered half of them. My intention was simply to get their minds geared toward the mission, so they would gradually start thinking Airborne again.

"Ski, what is it?" I said, turning to him.

He grinned like he was answering a quiz show question. "The first jump command is 'get ready.' "

"Roger," I said, turning back to the Cowboys. "Phan, what's number two?"

"Huk up."

"Wrong. How are you going to hook up when you haven't even stood up yet?"

"Oh, I'm know. Stan up," he chimed.

I nodded. "That's right."

In actuality, the second jump command was "outboard

personnel stand up," and the third, "inboard personnel stand up." But, for practical purposes, we'd be using the shortened version due to the fact that we'd only have two outboard sticks of six men each during the infiltration.

A few questions later I had everyone pull their footlockers into the center of the room to form a mock-up outboard troop seating configuration.

I assumed the jumpmaster position at the rear of the imagined aircraft and talked the team through a simulated jump procedure. Their expressions were serious. With a little coaching they performed everything well except the "tight body position" upon exit.

TBP required a jumper to keep his chin tucked down, his feet and knees together, and his hands gripping his reserve parachute as he leapt from the aircraft. TBP was important—it put the jumper in a position to prevent the aircraft prop blast from spinning him like a top during exit. If spinning occurred it could cause a parachute malfunction, and at the very least, the jumper would have a twist in his chute risers and suspension lines all the way to the skirt of the canopy.

At an altitude of 1200–1500 feet a jumper had some time to perform a bicycling motion with his legs to produce counter-rotation and untwist—at 900 feet, combat jump altitude, there was no time. If the jumper had to expend precious moments untwisting, he lost that critical interval for canopy control that allowed him to steer to a safe landing on the drop zone.

After talking the team through another exit I noticed that Binkowski was the only one doing it correctly. Tuong performed the exit like he was spiking a volleyball, Rham and Lok appeared to be springing off a diving board, and Phan looked as if he was making a Hollywood free-fall exit.

I decided to focus our impromptu training on the proper body position during exit. I called Ski forward as my demonstrator. The Cowboys lit cigarettes and sat on the footlockers watching.

I knew the Yards considered Ski a little awkward at times. Using Ski as the example would make them try harder so as to avoid being criticized.

As he moved forward to my position near the picnic table Ski said, "It seems like we should tailgate rather than door jump. Wouldn't that be easier?"

Binkowski was essentially correct. Tailgating was simple. You just strolled to the back of the aircraft and hopped off—you seldom had to worry about spinning. I explained the difference, telling him that with combat jumping the concept was to get out of the airplane and on the DZ as fast as possible thereby minimizing your exposure to enemy detection and ground fire during descent. The point was, tailgating took longer to get a full canopy.

By exiting a troop door the jumper hurled immediately into a 125-knot prop blast giving him a quick canopy. It was like dropping through a hurricane.

It was Binkowski's nature at times to look for the easier way of doing things. But I was glad he'd asked. It gave me an opportunity to stress the importance of TBP to the little people.

At 2215 I dismissed class. Everyone knew the jump commands by heart and had improved the door exit procedure considerably. I made a mental note to ask Swede if his team was proficient in exit procedure. I also planned to let him know what I'd found out about Defrisco's opium habit.

I took off my shirt and shoulder holster and glanced at Lok. "Lok, *sau* Beam-Coke, please."

Our self-appointed team bartender hurried to the bar,

which was nothing more than a small triangular piece of plywood nailed in the corner of the room. We all sat around the team table as Lok blew sand out of cups and went about his careful mixing ritual.

Sitting across from Ski I could still smell the heavy scent of his cologne. As Lok passed out our drinks everyone lit cigarettes but me.

"Ski," I said, watching Phan pass a match to Rham. "Before we launch on this mission you need to take a couple of showers to get that Aqua Velva off."

"It's not Aqua Velva, Brett. It's English Leather."

"Smell like buf-lo ledder," Tuong said, laughing.

Ski grinned and nodded. "Okay, buffalo leather. If you so smart, do you think you can handle me in a game of chess?"

I butted in. "Let's hold off on the chess tournament tonight, gang," I said, taking my drink from Lok. "It's getting late and we've got early PT and a long day ahead of us tomorrow."

I held my cup toward the center of the table. "Here's to RT Texas and Airborne!"

Five cups touched mine as everyone chorused: "All the way!" A clatter of monsoon thunder resounded as if to applaud Texas team spirit.

Chapter 13

A booming concussion rattled the hooch, jarring me from a sound sleep. I jerked upward. A muddled chorus of voices penetrated the darkness. My team.

I leapt from the bed, groping blindly at the wall to find my rifle.

Ski yelled, "What the hell is—"

Another explosion thundered—more distant this time. I chambered a round and hurried to the door. My groggy mind tried to identify the blast sounds. It didn't sound like incoming and it wasn't claymores.

A flashlight beam streaked across the room. "Douse that light!"

"Okay, okay. But what's hap—"

"Sappers!" I whispered, partially opening the door to peer out into the foggy night.

A crouched figure darted out from between the hooches carrying two small packs.

Kicking the door wide open I leveled my CAR-15 and triggered a riveting stream of fire into the black-clad sapper. Expended brass clattered to the floor—as the VC jerked and twisted from the hot wads of lead pelting his body.

My adrenaline surged. "It's street-fightin' time!"

"I ready," Tuong cried, dropping to a kneeling firing position at the door.

I ran back to my bunk and yanked the web gear from a hook on the wall. Binkowski was hopping around trying to get a leg into his pants. "Forget the pants! Get your rifle!" I barked while slinging my gear on and heading for the door. I ejected my magazine and reached for another.

"But, but, Brett . . . I can't go outside like this."

"Damn it, I say you can. Let's move, Arnold!" I shouted back into the darkness while jamming a fresh magazine into my weapon and hitting the bolt release.

"Okay, okay, fuck it!" Ski muttered.

"Let's move, partner." I hurtled out the door and leapt off the steps. Wet sand crawled between my toes. The night drizzle poured a cool shroud over my bare shoulders as I stood peering over the knee-deep fog. Muffled pops of M16 fire echoed from the west end of camp.

Binkowski jumped to the ground beside me. "I'm here, partner. I'm here," he whispered.

Turning, I saw a face looking up at me. "Get back in the hooch and lock the door, Tuong. You know the SOP," I said, moving on into the night.

Months back Colonel Kahn had established a "sapper SOP" that directed that the little people stay in fixed positions while the Americans moved through the camp to hunt out and kill the sapper teams. The SOP was implemented to prevent Americans from mistaking the Yards and ARVNs as enemy.

Sappers could slip through concertina wire with the limber stealth of a snake. They usually carried two or three small satchels each, which were rigged with an explosive charge designed to detonate on impact when thrown.

If a mass attack occurred it was everybody on line, but

the absence of AK fire indicated sappers. Now, any small, skinny figure moving through the night was an immediate target.

Successive parachute flares popped high overhead, flooding the camp with swaying yellow light. Sporadic M16 fire cracked in the distance.

I knelt and pulled a satchel away from the bloody hands of the VC I'd killed.

"What are you, what are you doing with that?"

"I'm making sure his cronies don't stroll through here and decide to use this on us," I answered, moving to a sandbagged wall near a hooch. Using my rifle stock I quickly dug a shallow hole in the loose sand, placed the satchel into the hole, and covered it.

"Who's there?" a voice shouted as another lume round ignited.

I recognized the voice as Loot. "Yancy," I responded while standing. I scanned the area searching for Hayes. My eyes stopped when I noticed Binkowski. Except for the web gear hanging off his massive shoulders he was buck naked.

"Arnold, where the hell is your underwear?"

"I—I don't sleep with any. And, you—you told me to—"

"Well, shit!" I said, tilting my head up into the drizzle. "Go get your damn pants. Make sure Tuong knows it's you coming in or—"

"We nailed three of 'em up near the TOC," Hayes said, hurrying around the corner of a hooch. "Jinx sent me down here to check . . . Shit, looks like you chewed one up too!" he exclaimed, stepping back and gazing down at the sprawled VC.

His eyes caught a glimpse of Binkowski. "What the tarnation is he on? A nudist camp nature walk!"

Ski's fist coiled. I stepped forward. "Go get your pants, partner. I'm going up to the officer billets to check on Megan. You can meet—"

A blunt explosion resounded from the north side.

"That sounds like a hit on the officers' hooch!" Hayes yelled.

"Megan! Megan's in there!" Ski shouted, bolting northward.

I hurtled forward trying to catch him. "Hold up. You—"

"Yancy. Give me a hand over here!" Iron Oak yelled from somewhere. The lume round died, dropping a curtain of darkness over us.

I whirled back to Loot. "We'll cover this! Help Iron!"

M-60 fire hammered from the west end as I sprinted, following the naked glow of Binkowski's butt into the darkness.

In the distance flames sprouted from the far end of the officer barracks. I drew my CAR-15 into hip firing position to cover Ski. He hurled full speed into the open hallway on the near side of the billets.

A sudden burst of automatic M16 fire spewed wet sand over my legs. Hugging the rifle into my chest I dropped and rolled, trying to find the muzzle flash. The vicious fire howled again, ripping through my magazine pouches. Jagged metal from the shattered magazines cut into my side as I rolled wildly trying to escape the viperous path of lead. Finally, it halted.

The pop of another lume round flooded the perimeter in jaundiced light. A dull thump noise told me someone, somewhere, had fired an M-79 round. A second later high explosive raped the silence, raining splintered wood and shredded sandbags over me.

Turning over on my back I quickly brushed sand from

my face and saw two small figures running toward me. I
jutted my rifle at them.

"Sar Brett, no shoot!"

I raised forward as Rham and Tuong scurried to my
side. "What the hell are y'all doing out here?"

"You okay, Sar Brett?" Rham asked, quickly reloading
his M-79.

Tuong pointed at the northern guard tower. "Look. VC
do."

He smiled and reached to help me up. I stood and gazed
through the yellow drizzle at the tower. Rham's HE round
had blown away two sides of the tower box. A limp, black-
clad body hung over the edge.

Rham reached to brush the sand off the laceration on
my side. I ignored the sting and turned my attention back
to the barracks. "Follow me and stay close. I don't want
anyone mistaking y'all as VC," I said, quickly raising my
rifle and blowing the grit away from the bolt window.

We moved toward the flaming officer barracks. Approaching, I saw Binkowski edging sideways down the
smoky center hallway that spanned the length of the long
hooch. He carried someone in his arms.

I jerked my rifle sling over my neck and handed the
weapon to Rham. "Stay here. Cover!" I rushed inside the
smoky corridor.

Inside, I could see it was Colonel Kahn Ski was carrying. Megan followed Ski cupping a hand to her mouth.

"Is he hit?" I shouted grabbing the colonel's upper arms
and edging backward.

Ski coughed. "No. Don't think so. Smoke inhalation!"

Outside we laid the colonel on the ground. I knelt, feeling for a pulse. "He's alive." My fingers scanned his body
for wounds. None.

"Jeep coming!" Ski shouted, waving his arms. "Hey! Over here."

A thunderous cloudburst ripped the sky apart, unloading a stinging downpour over us.

As the jeep pulled up I saw it was Frank Romero driving. I reached into the vehicle and grabbed a small tarpaulin off the back seat. "Take the colonel to the dispensary. He needs oxygen."

"Roger. Get 'im in here. Be advised; I just made a quick loop around the perimeter. All clear near as I can tell. We killed two on the south side."

Ski and I wrapped Colonel Kahn in the tarp and lifted him into the right side of the jeep.

Turning to Megan I asked, "You okay?"

She coughed and nodded without speaking.

"You go with Frank to the dispensary."

Megan tightened the cloth belt on her robe. Ski took her arm, helping her into the back of the jeep.

"Go."

Romero revved the engine and drove away.

I turned to Ski. The rain melted gray streaks of soot down his face and chest.

"Damn, she's wonderful," he mumbled with a vacant stare watching the jeep disappear. "She could have run but she helped me find the colonel in there and even helped me drag him—"

"Binkowski!" Twitty's squeal penetrated the yellow rain. "You are outta uniform!" he shouted, trudging toward us through the downpour. He had a .45-caliber pistol in one hand and an unopened umbrella in the other. "Shit! You don't even have a fuckin' uniform on!"

I couldn't believe my ears. Twitty completely ignored everything and went right to the top of the page of his demented priorities. Somehow, he'd managed to get dressed during the attack.

"And you, Yancy," he squealed, jabbing his umbrella at me. "Look at you. What kind of example—"

I stepped square into his wet, ugly face. "That soldier just saved the colonel's life, Sarge. I don't think Ivan Kahn gives a damn what he is, or isn't, wearing!"

I turned to Ski, standing between Rham and Tuong. "Partner, no matter what this asshole says, I'm proud of you!

"Y'all get on back to the hooch. I'll be along in a while."

Tuong moved closer and handed me my rifle. "Sar Brett, you blee. Maybe nee go pin-ser-ree."

Glancing down I noticed the watery trail of blood oozing from my side. "I'll be okay, Tuong. I go later."

As they walked away Twitty fumbled to open his black parasol. He looked up at me from beneath it and tried to grin. "Well, guess I was a little tough on Binkowski there. Shit, maybe we need to put him in for a medal or something. Where's the colonel at now?"

After telling him I'd sent Colonel Khan to the dispensary, Twitty turned and waddled away clutching his umbrella.

Looking down at the butt of the pistol he held at his side, I noticed the magazine well was empty.

I glanced back at the barracks. The heavy rain was beginning to extinguish the fire on the other end of the building.

The poncho-draped figure of Henry Jinx hurried around the side of the barracks. "Yancy! Murphy said he thought he saw Binkowski carrying the colonel out of here. Is that right?"

I gave Jinx a quick summary of events and told him that

Romero had taken the colonel and Megan on to the dispensary.

"Are you sure it was Binkowski who pulled the Old Man out?" he said, yanking the poncho hood over his head.

I frowned, feeling a ripple of anguish run down my back with the cold stream of rain. The major didn't repeat the question. Instead, he remarked about the shattered ammo pouches on my web gear.

Looking closer he saw the gash on my side. "Have you been hit?"

"Negative."

"Well, you'd better get to the dispensary anyhow. That doesn't look like a sand flea bite!" he said, turning to survey the dying fire.

Gazing back across the camp he did a quick toe bounce and snapped his rifle to port arms. "Everything appears quiet. Looks like we whipped Charlie's ass again."

The mingled stink of cordite, sulfur, and smoldering wood cut through the rain. I saluted and turned to walk away.

"Hold up. I'll walk along with you, Sergeant Yancy. you know, that Binkowski is surprising. He may just turn out to be all right."

"Yes, sir, he's good," I said, sliding my rifle carrying strap over my neck. "He's even better when he's got his clothes on."

"What?"

Chapter 14

During the short walk to the dispensary I updated Major Jinx on the total number of known enemy KIA; based on what Romero and Hayes had said as well as my kill and the one Rham had blown away on the guard tower, the figure amounted to six.

After entering the busy medical facility Hayes told us the enemy score—four indigene KIA, two indigene WIA, two Americans WIA. RT California had taken the brunt. Swede and Iron were both wounded, two of the Cowboys were killed, two wounded. They had also found two Vietnamese guards with their throats cut.

I was standing near a sink washing the blood off my side when James Iron Oak hobbled in from another room with a crutch under his arm.

"Thanks for the fuckin' help, Yancy!" Bitterness laced his words. Crusted blood splotched his arms and hands. Gauze bandages girdled his upper thigh and forehead.

Moving near him I spoke softly, "I'm real sorry, Iron. Ski and I were—"

He flared. "Sorry don't get it, fella! They blew the holy shit outta us and you couldn't fucking—"

"At ease, Sergeant!" Jinx shouted, striding toward us.

"Get a grip! I understand how you feel, soldier. But Binkowski and Yancy had their hands full getting the colonel out of a fire."

"Hold it, sir," I said, glancing down. "What you're saying is only half true. We heard Jim's shout but . . . I figured Hayes could handle it. Didn't know how bad it was."

I thought back to the moment when Iron yelled. Somehow I'd misinterpreted his voice tone. Somehow I didn't decipher the urgency—the critical need. And I'd failed to correlate that the initial explosion proximity indicated it was a recon hooch that took the hit. Now, I knew that the sapper I'd killed was the same one that hit RT California.

"I was wrong, Jim," I said, looking into his grim eyes.

"Wasn't much he coulda done anyhow, Iron," Hayes said, stepping forward. "We had a lot of help within seconds."

Iron Oak had just lost two of his comrades and come close to death himself. I'd felt that knotted turmoil. He needed someone to strike. When I lost Will it ripped a piece of my heart out that could never be replaced.

But there was a difference in this—facing an enemy you could see and fight gave a man "recoil recourse." Facing the nightmare of a satchel charge ripping your teammates apart was a helpless feeling beyond comparison.

I leveled my eyes on his. "I nailed the VC who hit y'all."

He squinted. "How do you know that?"

I explained that at the time I cut down the sapper there had been only one localized explosion in the recon barracks area. The fact that the sapper only had one remaining satchel charge meant the other had just been thrown.

"How's Swede doing?" I asked.

Iron's chest heaved with a burdened breath. "Doc says

he's gonna make it. Khoi and Din, they're fucked up bad. Jard, Rhad, they're—they're . . . dead," he whispered.

The thudding noise of an approaching chopper mingled with the sounds of rain.

"Medevac coming," Loot muttered, walking toward the door.

I reached and raised Iron's arm, slipping it over my shoulder. "Come on, Jim. I'll help you out to the chopper."

Limping to the door he looked back. "Swede, where's Swede?"

"They'll bring him out on the litter," Jinx answered.

Cold heavy drops of monsoon rain splattered on my soaked head as I eased Iron forward and lifted him onto the floor of the chopper. The black corpsman inside took Iron's crutch, then pulled him carefully back into the cabin.

Glancing across to the other side of the interior I could see two men lifting Swede's poncho-covered litter into the cabin. Iron reached and pulled the cover away from Swede's face. He was pale, unconscious.

A moment later two more litters had been loaded into the cabin. As the chopper revved the corpsman yelled out to me, "Tell whoever's in charge there's a delay on the second dust-off. It'll be about one-five minutes! Clear the LZ!"

As the corpsman grabbed the door to slide it closed Iron yelled out into the rainy night, "Yancy! Glad you greased that bastard, buddy! Thanks!"

I bounced a quick salute off my eyebrow and hurried across the windy pad.

When I returned to the dispensary Binkowski was dressed and standing near a smiling Major Jinx. "Brett, I brought a set of my fatigues for Megan," he said, poking

them toward me. "I knew my boots might be a little big
for her so I borrowed these from Lok. Hope they fit."

I could see Lok cheerfully volunteering his boots to Ski.
Lok hated to wear boots. Once, he'd actually boarded a
chopper for mission launch barefooted.

I told the major about the second chopper delay, then
turned to Ski who was still holding the uniform. "Megan's
back in one of the rooms here somewhere. Why don't you
give those to her," I said, glancing at my watch: 0247
hours. "I'm going to take a hot shower and hit the rack.
Recommend you get some sleep too. We got a long day
tomorrow."

"Today," Ski quipped. "You mean, long day today.
You see tomorrow is already to—"

"I got it, Arnold!" I said, stepping to the door. Then,
Jinx proceeded to astound me with his perception.

"You realize that RT California is now out of the picture, Sergeant Yancy. There may be some changes in the
mission."

I nodded, saluted, and stepped outside before saying,
"No shit."

At 0740 hours RT Texas sat in the mess hall eating
scrambled eggs and rice. Although the rain had stopped
I'd called morning PT off to give the team some extra
sleep.

"You want my rice?" Ski said, glancing at Phan.

"Rogee," Phan answered, moving his tray across the
table.

"Why you no like rice?" Tuong asked.

Ski answered while raking rice onto the tray. "It's okay,
I guess. But I've got my standards. I mean, I like baked
beans but I don't eat 'em with my eggs."

The U.S. Government was doing everything it could to

boost South Vietnam's economy. That meant buying huge quantities of rice from them and distributing it to all the allied mess halls. At times I got a little burnt out on rice too, but I understood the dilemma for mess sergeants. Inundated with massive quantities of rice they had to dream up every conceivable way to serve it. In WWII the slogan was "buy war bonds." In Vietnam it was "eat more rice."

Ski pushed his tray aside and reached for a cigarette. "I gave that uniform to Megan. The boots even fit."

Looking at the ceiling his voice lowered to a near whisper. "She smiled and said, 'Thank you, Ski.' Oh, but the way she said thank you; it was more than that," he said, returning his eyes to mine. "You know how you can read between the lines."

I nodded and placed my fork on the tray, then glanced at the Yards. Looking back at Ski I said, "Yeah, I guess. Did you see California's hooch this morning?"

"Roger.

"It's a shambles," he said, flipping his Zippo open and returning to reality. "I don't see how anyone could have lived through that."

"Two of his Cowboys didn't," I reminded him. In the same breath I gave the team a warning reminder about locking our hooch door at night. Although October was on the tail end of monsoon season we still had rain and fog and that made it ideal sapper weather.

I wasn't sure if the door had been left unlocked on Swede's hooch but it seemed likely. I wasn't taking any chances on leaving a welcome mat out for Charlie the next time he came calling.

"With California out, do you think they'll scrub the mission?" Ski asked, taking a draw on his cigarette.

"No way, partner," I answered, glancing at the clock on the far end of the mess hall. "I'm heading up to the

TOC now. How about you taking the team over to California's hooch and going through the rubble to try and find any personal items for them.

"Any weapons you find, turn them in at S-4," I said, standing.

"What are we suposed to put the stuff in?"

"Get some empty sandbags. Use them," I said, looking down at Lok's bare feet. "Babysan, you come with me."

"Where we go?" Lok said, jumping up with a smile.

"We go supply. Get you some boots."

His smile drooped.

When we left the mess hall I routed by the hooch where I'd buried the VC satchel charge. I carefully removed it and took it with me.

As we walked toward the supply building near the center of camp a stout morning breeze pressed at our backs. Lok's expression looked like that of a youngster on his way to the dentist.

Peering through the morning haze I saw Twitty approaching in the distance.

"Hold up, Yancy! Where you goin'?" he shouted.

We stopped and turned. "Supply. How's Colonel Kahn?"

"Marvelous." He grunted. "And before you start askin' I'll tell you that the girl, the lieutenant, is okay too.

"Now, the Old Man told me to check with you . . . I mean, that is question you, about what award we need to put Binkowski in for."

"Bronze Star."

"That's about what I figured too. You want that with a 'V' or without a 'V'?" he said, pulling a small notepad from his pocket. He looked like a carhop taking an order.

"With 'V,' " I answered.

" 'V' for Valor. That's what I figured too," he said,

touching the pen to his tongue and talking to the pad as he wrote. "Course he was completely outta uniform; neck-id as a fuckin' jaybird he was.

"This'll probably be the first damn time in the history of the U.S. Army that a soldier's been decorated with Valor for running around with his damn dick flapping in the wind! Glad I'm getting ready for retirement."

I turned to walk on.

"Wait a minute," Twitty squealed while tucking the pad back into this pocket. He stepped forward, studying the dark canvas bag in my hand. "What's that thing?"

I cracked a half grin. "Oh, I almost forgot. It's a present for you. Ski wanted you to have this," I said, handing it to Twitty.

"Thanks. But what the fuck is it?" he said, shifting it around in his hands.

"A satchel charge," I said casually. "We pulled it off a dead VC last night."

Twitty froze. His lip quivered trying to speak. "Yan, Yancy, you take—take this fuckin' thing back," he stuttered, holding it palms up like it was a folded flag presentation.

My grin widened. "Now, Sergeant Major, why disappoint Ski?"

"Please—please take this thing and get it the fuck away from me. I—I got two months left in this—this hellhole and I ain't takin' no chances. No chances! You hear me?" His squealing voice pleaded.

I waited for a second, then took the satchel and turned away. "Okay, Sergeant Major, but Ski is sure going to be—"

"I don't give a flyin' fuck!"

Moments later I'd signed off on a new pair of boots for Lok and sent him back to the team.

Outside the TOC I noticed a portion of the wooden plank walkway riddled with bullet holes. When I entered the War Room Colonel Kahn looked up from a seated position at a desk. "Get yourself a cup of coffee, Brett."

I walked to the desk. "I'll skip the coffee for now, sir," I replied, shaking his hand and looking around the room. "Where is everybody this morning?"

He informed me that Jinx and Hayes had gone over to Da Nang airfield to pick up a CIA agent who had flown here to assist in mission preparation.

"Before I forget it, I want to say thanks for helping yank me out of that fire last night. Did the sergeant major see you about Binkowski's award?"

"Roger, sir. According to Ski, Lieutenant Blair helped find you and drag you out of the room."

The colonel grinned thoughtfully while lifting the cup to his mouth. I hoped the look on his face implied that he planned to include Megan in the award consideration.

He set the cup down, wrote something on a pad, and turned to me. "Have a seat, Brett."

After I sat down he lit a cigar and blew a long drag toward the ceiling. "It's a hard lick, about California last night. Aside from how I feel about the tragic losses, it puts us in a tough spot. I'd like to get your idea on some things before the room fills up with people.

"The only team I can use to fill in the gap right now is RT Missouri. They're without one Montagnard, but I can cover that. What do you think?"

I glanced away for a second in thought. I knew the recent history of RT Missouri; they had run some tough missions during the last months and they were a good team. I also knew that Tony Lions, the One-Zero, was short. He was looking forward to going home. He'd talked a lot lately about being back with his wife and kids. I had faith in Tony, but I didn't want to take my team into a hot area with a man who had going home on his mind.

"I'll take that cup of coffee now, sir," I said, standing and striding to the table.

Returning, I sipped my coffee and looked over into the silent face of my commander. "You know, sir, that's sparse coastal terrain up there where we're going," I said, looking toward the large wall map.

Following my eyes to the map he agreed, then looked back at me. Silent.

I chose my words carefully. "The fewer people we have stirring dust up there the better. If Texas were to go in there solo it would be easier getting in. I could eventually split the team and let Binkowski handle the southern area of interest." I shut up and sipped my coffee.

He drummed his fingers on the desk for a quick second, then rose and walked to the map. I followed.

Pointing to the highlighted area marking Drop Zone Ghost Rider, he said, "With only one team parachuting in, there would be fifty percent less canopies for someone to spot.

"Maybe you're right. Truth is, the thought of making this a one-team mission had crossed my mind. Do you think Binkowski can handle working a leadership position?"

I grinned. "He pulled you out of a fire last night knee-deep in sappers."

He grinned. "Okay. We'll try it. But the minute you determine that you need another team I don't want any hesitation about it, you get on the horn. Understand?"

I raised my coffee cup. "Roger, sir."

A strong voice broke in. "Morning, Colonel."

We turned, seeing a slender, mustached man carrying a briefcase walk into the room. He was wearing civilian clothes and had a black, tooled leather quick-draw rig circling his narrow waist. A chrome .357 Magnum was plugged into the holster. His ensemble was topped off with a large gold neck chain, a gold Rolex, and shiny black Roper-style boots.

I remembered the man immediately—Nakhon Phanom, Thailand.

"Good morning, Calvin," Colonel Kahn replied. "Where did you lose Major Jinx?"

"He'll be along. He and Sergeant Hayes told me to come on in here."

"Brett, this is Agency rep, Calvin Stapleton," the colonel announced, using the brevity term for CIA.

"I remember you, Calvin," I said, accepting his handshake.

He frowned. "Can't say as I—"

"NKP, a couple of months back."

He smiled. "Yeah, yeah, I remember now. You were on that Blackbird flight when we got the sky knocked out from under us over Laos. Didn't think we were gonna make it out of that one.

"Whatever happened to that foxy blonde who was on board? Journalist, I think she was," he said, stroking his mustache.

"She's back Stateside," I answered, turning to Colonel Kahn.

He gestured to the coffeepot. "Well, it's good you know each other. Calvin has a couple of pistols for you and he'll be helping you with CAS linkup information, codes, all that; and he's got a profile update on the Mariposa personnel."

I was surprised to hear about the pistols. I hoped they weren't the chrome style.

Calvin immediately informed us that the personnel profile update was courtesy of Military Intelligence and that it had nothing to do with CIA operations. "I want to give credit where credit is due. MI handles that ball of wax," he said, accepting a cup of coffee.

It seemed as though Stapleton was being honest, but it crossed my mind that he might be establishing a disclaimer in case the information turned out to be unreliable.

Some past experience with the Company boys had taught me that they prided themselves on autonomy. I knew they didn't like having to work directly with or be dependent on other government agencies.

When Major Jinx and Loot entered the War Room the major paced directly to Stapleton. He nodded to Colonel Kahn, then turned to Stapleton and said, "We have secured the Baby."

Calvin smiled. No one bothered to tell me who, or what, Baby was. I didn't ask.

Chapter 15

"Boldness has genius, power, and magic," Calvin Stapleton remarked while neatly stacking our code paperwork to one end of the conference-room table. He stood, took two pistols from his briefcase, and placed them on the table. He then removed four magazines, two silencers, and a box of .38-caliber ammo marked Super-val. He arranged it all with the care of a salesman displaying his product in a showcase.

"If there is any merit to that philosophy, then your key target leader has applied it directly to the scenario in which we are mutually concerned here," Calvin said while taking two nylon shoulder holsters and placing them to one side of his display. "I'm not saying there is necessarily genius inherent to this guy Defrisco, but he is definitely bold."

I was mildly irritated, but nonetheless awed with Stapleton's ability to talk about the mission and yet never say or divulge anything that could be construed as exposing it. For the past two hours I'd been his student while he gave me a technical class in the primary wheel codes, the contingency code, and code names I would be using during the mission. He hadn't mentioned anything about the

AO, the Device, or Mariposa, and only vaguely referred to the mission.

When I suggested that we pull Ski into the class he recommended otherwise, saying that I could perform a class for Ski later. I got the impression that Calvin preferred the one-on-one teaching method because it eliminated any potential student collaboration or questions about details and technical authenticity.

The other thing that rubbed me the wrong way was his insistence that none of the material covered be communicated to the Yards. That meant if Ski and I were zapped they would be up the proverbial tributary without any means of movement—no commo.

"Now for this! These little jewels are a gift from the Agency," he announced, proudly taking a pistol off the table. He yanked the slide to the rear and let it click forward.

"This is a refitted Smith & Wesson Model thirty-nine, nine millimeter. In this modified configuration it is called a Model zero Hush Puppy. It was developed primarily for Navy Seals and it just happens to be the perfect weapon for your intended purpose."

He quickly screwed a black, smooth-surfaced silencer onto the threaded end of the barrel. "Included in each box of ammo is a replacement sleeve insert for the silencer. It must be replaced every thirty rounds or so in order to maintain the proper silence level. Each pistol is issued with two nine-round magazines.

"It also has special plugs that can make it waterproof, however you will not be concerned with that need. What will excite you is that it is a very quiet way of doing business," he whispered the last words and arched his eyebrows like he was revealing a new secret way of entering the playground tree house.

I knew Calvin's reference to "doing business" meant this was the intended instrument for eliminating the Mariposa. I remained seated and listened while he droned on about the engineering merits of the pistol. A few sentences later I had to admit the weapon was unique.

The Super-val cartridge was designed to reduce muzzle velocity to 274 mps by using a 10.2-gram green-tipped parabellum projectile. The new subsonic bullet configuration eliminated the usual in-flight supersonic *crack*. The noise level could be further reduced by locking the sliding bolt closed for single-shot manual cartridge extraction use. The lower velocity round, locked chamber firing, and the silencer combined to make the Hush Puppy an impressive weapon for covert close-range kills.

Calvin handed the weapon to me and finished his spiel by telling me it was designed for killing enemy guard dogs. He assumed a hands on hips stance as if waiting for applause.

I glanced the pistol over, then placed it back on the table. I loosened the top button on my fatigue shirt, reached inside, and removed my Beretta.

"Three-eighty Beretta. Where'd you get that?"

"A gift," I answered, sliding the Hush Puppy carefully into my shoulder holster to determine if it would fit. The long silencer passed through the open end of the holster. The cold steel nose nuzzled against my skin. It was a tight fit.

"Two recommendations!" he said, making a peace sign. "Use the holster provided, and don't carry the weapon with the silencer attached."

I understood his rationale. But he'd forgotten that the CIA worked under different circumstances than recon personnel. While using the issue holster was probably best, keeping the silencer detached was not. In no-light, ultimate noise discipline environments that recon commonly performed in, it did not make sense to risk any telltale metallic sounds while fumbling around trying to attach the silencer. More importantly, if a target of opportunity suddenly revealed itself, the assembly time expenditure was prohibitive.

I removed the Hush Puppy, replaced my Beretta, and kept my opinion to myself.

"The next topic of extreme importance is your CAS counterpart. I will not provide you with any written material or photographs and you will not be permitted to take notes; so you'll have to listen close." He turned, glancing around the room curiously.

"We might as well take a walk during this. I like to walk some each day. As long as we are alone we shan't be breeching any security restrictions." He winked. "I will tell you this now, Yancy. She is a living doll; recruited and trained her myself." His dark eyes showed a flash of lascivious reminiscence.

I was surprised that our CAS agent was a woman. When I admitted to it, Calvin grinned and said, "Never sell them short. They can get into places men can't, providing they don't mind putting out.

"And believe me, Bacsin, that's her Vietnamese name, enjoys what we in the Company call 'undercover work.' " He bounced his eyebrows several times. "She also enjoys large men, if you know what I mean," he said, stroking an end of his mustache proudly. "Like I said, trained her myself."

As we exited the TOC into a crisp midmorning breeze I convinced Calvin that Ski should be included in our briefing stroll.

During the walk toward the recon barracks area I learned that Bacsin was the illegitimate daughter of a French bot-

anist who had cultivated a prosperous coffee bean planta-
tion in the Khe Sanh valley near route nine. Monsieur
Pollas was well liked and somewhat of a local deity in the
area. Although he was married and had five children, he
continued to provide for Bacsin and her mother until
the mother decided to move herself and her daughter to
Savannakhet, Laos, in early 1962.

Bacsin had grown to love her father during his occasional visits to her mother's house in the village. When a
Special Forces A-detachment arrived in Khe Sanh in November 1962 to establish a small outpost, Monsieur Pollas
was very helpful to them. Because of his long-term association with SF he was murdered by the VC less than two
years later.

The ever-vigilant eyes of CIA recruiters found Bacsin
and her mother three months later in Savannakhet and
"thoughtfully" informed them of the brutal murder complete with photographs. Bacsin was subsequently enlisted
as an agent-in-training, to "help defeat the enemies of her
father."

With her mother's endorsement Bacsin accepted the CIA
completely. Stapleton provided initial indoctrination and
training for her, then gave her the assignment cover that
would take her to the coastal town of Dong Yen on the
pretense that she sought to escape the encroachment of
Yankee capitalism and their bogus war.

She was provided with money to open a small restaurant
and bar in the town that had become a popular R and R
spot for NVA officers. To further strengthen the viability
of her cover story she said it was SF who killed her father.

Since her "positioning" and subsequent "activation"
in Dong Yen, Bacsin had performed well. She was a glow-
ing success story for the Agency. She gained access to
vital military information through both her casual and in-

timate contact with NVA officers. She relayed the intel via
a CAS network of fishermen along the coast.

The beautiful agent had also been instrumental in encouraging and arranging the defection of two junior-grade
NVA officers.

"She's a woman with a smoldering inner motivation for
revenge rooted to love, Yancy," Calvin said, talking into
the wind as we walked. "And I'm here to tell you that
there is nothing more fundamentally motivating than love.

"If you rolled the combined motivational merits of
greed, sex, and status into a ball it would look like a damn
BB beside a cannonball of revengeful love!"

Slowly I began to identify with Bacsin—I'd known that
"smoldering inner motivation" when Will was killed by
a communist sniper.

Bacsin had been "positioned" in 1965 and "activated"
in '66. That meant she'd been operational for over three
years. I wondered how three years of "undercover work"
had affected a young woman who was now twenty-four
years old. I knew it was doubtful that she still had that
same bright-eyed innocence of youth, but my concern now
was learning her current level of allegiance.

When I queried Calvin about it, it was obvious he didn't
like the question.

He stopped and gave me a look like I'd just farted in
his elevator. "Current level of allegiance? Damn it, the
communists killed her father, Yancy! It's like malaria. It
doesn't go away. Trust me!"

I slid my bush hat back off my brow. "There's a difference between allegiance and motivation, Calvin. Some
people will stand up and say the pledge to the flag, then
sit down and cheat on their income tax.

"Besides, people change. What I'm asking is, do you
know her level of allegiance as of now? What's the relia-

bility of intel coming out of her cell right now. When was the last True-blue test on this agent?''

True-blue was the code word for a method the Agency used to determine CAS agent reliability. The CIA would seed the CAS agent with false critical information from a ''plant'' and wait to see if the intel was passed on in a timely and unaltered way.

Calvin glanced away, then returned a hard frown back at me as if he was irritated with my knowledge of True-blue. ''That is information outside the bounds of my privilege and intent to divulge! You do not have a need to know!'' He dropped his hand to rest on the butt of his chrome pistol.

In the distance I caught a glimpse of Ski and the Yards approaching. I decided now was not the time to get in to a full-fledged pissing contest with Calvin. Still, without any answers to my questions, I'd found out two things. Calvin wasn't aware of the difference between motivation and allegiance, and he didn't like being questioned about his star.

Binkowski stopped at yelling distance. He had a full sandbag in each hand. The Yards held several large chunks of Swede's surfboard and some rifles.

''Where do you want us to take this, Brett?'' he shouted.

I instructed the Yards to take Ski's load and the rest of the items on to the supply sergeant, then told Ski to join Calvin and me.

''Ski, this is Calvin Stapleton. He's our Agency rep for the mission. Calvin, this is my One-One, Arnold Binkowski.''

''Glad to meet you, sir,'' Binkowski said, giving Calvin his infamous jolting handshake. ''Call me Ski.''

Stapleton jerked his hand away. ''Careful, son, that's

my trigger finger you're trying to crush!'' he said, stepping back and slowly viewing Ski with a detached awed look.

"Sorry, sir. Didn't mean to hurt you.''

Calvin laughed. "Hurt me? Shit, you must be kidding, son. Come on, let's keep walking. I like to walk. Let's move on down toward the beach. That beach is secure, isn't it?''

"Roger.''

Forty-five windy, strolling minutes later Calvin had told us about Bacsin's fluency in French and Laotian. He said her English was poor but quickly added that her current role didn't provide much opportunity to practice. He also told us her code name, the challenge and reply to be used on the drop zone to determine validity of the intercepting agent, and the Agency recommended escape and evasion route.

He walked and talked while looking down at his shiny boots. He kept one hand cocked on his pistol and the other on his hip. We flanked him on each side. Occasionally he'd look up and dart a glance to each of us to emphasize a point. He even answered some of my questions. He quoted everything including several eight-digit grid coordinates pertinent to the DZ and the E and E plan, without referring to anything but a white-capped wave now and then.

If I assumed that all of what he said was correct, then I had to silently admit that Calvin Stapleton was a marvel of photographic memory.

He refused my request to note several grid coordinates saying that he would give them to me again later this evening when he conducted a thorough map briefing with us.

As we approached the beach gate to reenter camp Calvin stopped us abruptly. He took a step forward, turned, and faced us.

His voice flowed with a distinct absence of dramatics. "I need to tell you that every man in the Agency, in this corner of the world anyhow, is aware of the job Command and Control is doing for our commitment here in Southeast Asia.

"We know, perhaps better than most, what it's like out there in the tiger's anal canal." He gave a quick northwest nod of his head. "And we're aware of the sacrifices and cost in terms of human lives, your buddies, your teammates."

He glanced down, then brought his head upward and removed his sunglasses. "Understand that this is not some loose-jointed pep talk, gentlemen. I guess what I'm trying to say is, thanks for the professional job you're doing."

A maverick ray of light sparkled off the corner of his sunglasses as he replaced them over his eyes.

I was speechless. Ski wasn't. "Thank you, sir," Ski responded, jabbing his open hand outward to him.

Calvin avoided the invitation to shake hands. He raised his Rolex to check the time. "It is now 1118 hours. I'm sure you have some things you need to take care of with your team, so why don't we break until after chow. I'll meet you in the briefing room at 1300.

"Also, sometime this afternoon I'd like for you both to try out those Hush Puppies." He turned emphatically. "Let's walk."

"Hush Puppies," Ski leaned over, whispering to me, "sounds like some new kind of CIA stealth shoes. Boots maybe. Yeah, probably boots."

Chapter 16

"I'm see you talk wid that Hollywoo man," Tuong said as we approached the hooch door. "What you talk abou?"

"Hush Puppies, Tuong. Hush Puppies," Binkowski confidently answered, following me inside.

"We talked about the mission, Tuong," I rebutted. "Did y'all get that gear turned in?"

"Rogee," Tuong replied, turning to Ski. "What mean hus puppy?"

"It's a new kind of boots, Tuong."

I scowled at him. "Arnold, they're not boots. They're—"

"New boots! I'm already have focking new boots! You see?" Lok exclaimed, pointing under his bunk where he'd thrown them.

"Hold it, gang," I said, raising my hands. "First off, we're not getting new boots. Hush Puppies are pistols and I'll explain that later. Second, you need to stop taking your conjectures for reality, Arnold. Third, I want you to go to supply and draw six H-harnesses with drop lines and twelve quick releases. While you're there ask Sergeant Beck if we can use the building tonight to conduct a class in there; around 2000.

"Tell him we'll need six parachutes, T-10s with reserves."

"Okay, roger."

"Rham, you go with Ski. Hurry it up. We'll wait for chow till y'all get back."

Binkowski started to move away, then turned around to me and pulled a note from his pocket. "I wrote this early this morning for Megan. I think it's pretty good. I'm going to give it to Megan later. Would you look it over for me? You do remember I've got to see her later and give her that firing lesson on the AK?"

I accepted the note and nodded. "Go." I knew it was doubtful that Megan's AK had survived last night's fire but decided not to rain on Ski's aspirations at the moment.

I sat on my footlocker and opened the note while Tuong mounted my bunk and peered over my shoulder.

"Sar Brett, you wan Beam-Co?" Lok asked.

I glanced up at him. "No, partner. That can wait until later tonight."

"What say, Sar Brett?" Tuong whispered, looking down at the paper in my hand.

I glanced around at him. "It says you need to get your shirt on and get ready for chow, amigo."

Tuong relented as I looked back at Ski's note-poem. It was titled: "Ode to the Flaming Monsoon Night." I controlled an urge to cringe while reading it silently.

Through the dark of the monsoon night
The booming sound traveled.
I thought of you and my heart came unraveled.
I turned and ran with all my speed
To get to you and meet your need.
I found you there within a smoky room
And I held you close to take you from the gloom.

Unselfishly, you thought of the colonel
And we searched for him through the smoke and flames.
We found the colonel and got him outside,
You had smut on your face but my heart swelled with pride.
Now all has quieted as the morning sun dawns.
I continue to compose and withhold my yawns.
I smile and think of you now as a kind of hero.
With a little recon training you'd make a swell One-Zero.
Love, Ski

I folded the poem, tucked it into my pocket, and peered across the room. "Lok, I'll take that Beam and Coke now, please," I muttered.

The H-harnesses I'd sent Ski and Rham after were a nylon rigging system used to secure a rucksack for jumping. It was rigged by strapping it around the rucksack and securing it with two prepositioned steel buckles. Two release straps were then threaded through additional mating buckles with the lead end pushed back through the opening to allow it to be "quick-released" at about fifty feet above ground level. This prevented the jumper from having to land with the additional weight of the rucksack. An 18.5-foot drop line was tied firmly to the H-harness. The line was rigged in a zigzag fashion across the back of the ruck, then secured with rubber bands on each end. The lead end of the drop line attached to the main lift web of the parachute harness, thereby preventing loss of the ruck after release.

When Ski and Rham returned with the gear I instructed the Yards to practice rigging their rucks after chow.

I told them Ski and I would be busy at the TOC so they'd be doing it without our assistance.

I didn't expect the results to be perfect. They'd only

made one equipment jump and they'd only had a brief class in equipment rigging prior to that. Again, my intention was simply to keep their minds geared toward jumping.

In less than thirty-six hours we'd be hurling our camouflaged bodies into the black skies over North Vietnam—it was time to keep our minds on the mission.

During chow I told the team about my request to conduct the mission solo. The Yards took it in stride, implying they preferred the solo concept. I looked at Ski, expecting a reaction from him.

He nodded without much surprise, then tilted his head to the side and asked, "By the way, what does conjecture mean?"

Seeing Tuong's antennas go up I kept my explanation short. "It means, guessing at something."

After chow Ski and I trudged toward the TOC. The windy sky massed with dark billowy clouds threatening more rain. I reached into my pocket, removed Ski's poem, and handed it to him without comment.

A few steps later he finally spoke. "Well—well what did you think of it?" Anticipation lilted his words.

Keeping my gaze straight ahead I answered casually, "I think it's a masterpiece, partner."

"Oh, come on, it's not that great! Is it?"

"No, no, I think you may have perhaps written the perfect love poem, but . . ."

"But what?" he asked quickly.

"Well, there's that middle part where you found the colonel. It didn't rhyme and—"

"Okay, okay. I know that. But you just try and find a word that rhymes with colonel. I racked my brain for—for . . . well, I couldn't think of one. Besides I've seen poems that do that; you know, don't rhyme in some places."

"Roger. Whatever you say."

"Well, what else? You started to say something else about it."

"Nothing. It's not important," I said, glancing at my watch.

"Darn it, Brett. Yes, it is important. I want it to be perfect."

"Okay. I think the title could be better."

He stopped. "Brett, if there's only one thing perfect about the poem it's the title! I mean, 'Ode to the Flaming Monsoon Night'; it's—it's . . . wait up."

He ran to catch me. "Okay, tell me. What's wrong with it? Tell me."

"I think it could be more descriptive. You know, after all you were naked during all that time. How about, 'Ode to the Naked Monsoon Night'?" I tried to hold my grin to a minimum.

"But—but that leaves out the most important word. Flaming! I mean, there were big flames. Didn't you see the flames? Surely you saw—"

"Yes, Arnold. I saw the damn flames."

"I got it!" he announced loudly as we approached the TOC. " 'Ode to the Flaming Naked Monsoon Night'! How's that?"

"That's it. Great," I answered, stopping several meters from the guard entrance. He stopped and faced me with a beaming smile, like he'd just applied the last brushstrokes to the *Mona Lisa*.

I kept my voice courteous but skipped the smile. "Now that we've got that handled I want you to do me a favor."

"Sure, Brett. Anything," he replied seriously.

"I know you're crazy about Megan and I think that's great. She's a beautiful woman.

"This afternoon, and tonight, we're going to have a

supersonic skull session that includes Stapleton, Jinx, Colonel Kahn, and Megan. Tomorrow night we launch and it's going to be too late to start asking questions about what we need to absorb today. I want you to keep your mind on the mission during this." I cracked a half grin. "Roger that?"

His head moved with slow, thoughtful nods. "Roger, partner," he answered in a serious tone.

I turned to walk on. His words halted me. "Brett, does this mean I can't take Megan down to the beach today for a firing lesson?"

"That's what it means," I answered, looking at the dark sky. "Besides, it looks like it's going to rain hard pretty quick. I'll promise you this. When we get back from the field I'll make sure you get a three-day pass. Maybe you could fly down to Saigon and visit Megan then."

"Wow! That's a great idea. Thanks, Brett. You don't mind if I give her the poem, do you? I mean, now that we've got it perfect it would be a—"

"Partner, it would be a tragedy if she doesn't get that poem," I said, smiling. "I mean, 'Ode to a Flaming Naked Monsoon Night' is going to make her day."

As I signed in at the guard booth I noticed Megan's name on the list above Stapleton's. I wasn't exactly sure how she would take Ski's poem, but considering what she'd been through during her last twenty-four hours at CCN I figured she might welcome the opportunity to smile and enjoy some home-grown poetry.

When Ski and I entered the War Room we were immediately intercepted by Major Jinx. We accompanied him to his desk where he began looking through a message file. While we waited I noticed a small WAR IS HELL! sign on the wall behind the desk. Below it someone had scribbled in the words: Actual combat is a son of a bitch!

"The message I wanted to bring to your attention seems to be missing," Jinx said, looking back at us with an irritated expression. "Perhaps Colonel Kahn has it. Anyhow, the crux of the—"

"Good afternoon, Sergeant Yancy, Sergeant Binkowski," Colonel Kahn said, approaching the major's desk.

We turned and snapped a salute to him. The colonel extended his hand to me, then to Ski. "Thanks for your assist during that hit last night," he said, smiling. "It was a tough night."

Ski tossed a grin to me, then back to the colonel. "Roger, sir. To put it more poetically, I guess you could say it was a 'flaming monsoon night.' "

"Sir," the major interrupted. "Do you happen to have that MACSOG flash—"

"Got it right here, Henry. Brett, Calvin has some time scheduled with you in a few minutes, but first I'd like to get with you and Ski about this message. We've got a new wrinkle in this mission."

We followed Ivan Kahn to an adjacent room where he handed the message to me as we all sat down. The colonel and Ski shared conversation about the sapper attack as I read.

The message had a DTG of 300115Z; priority, FLASH. It informed us that MACSOG headquarters had received a "brief phone call" telling them that Mariposa was aware of a planned mission to recover the SADM and that if such an effort were to occur it would result in the "inadvertent detonation" of 501.

The switchboard operator who received the message said the call had originated from a military phone in Saigon and that the caller sounded like a female American. Intel analysts at SOG surmised that the call was a "preplanned stratagem to deter what Mariposa perceives as a likely course of retaliatory action by SOG."

It also informed us of what appeared to be obvious; Mariposa had at least one additional operative in the Saigon area, if not more. The last paragraph instructed Colonel Kahn to initiate any precautionary measures he felt were necessary and to proceed with the scheduled launch time. It ended with "Bendell sends."

I handed the message over to Ski and looked at Colonel Kahn.

Ivan Kahn took a draw on his cigarette. "I'm inclined to agree with Bendell about this being a bluff. It just doesn't stack up that Mariposa could have an inside agent at SOG.

"At any rate, we've got to press on as planned."

I agreed with Colonel Kahn's assessment that we had to press on in spite of any threats—real or fabricated. However, I wasn't as confident about his "no inside agent" theory. I'd been at SOG headquarters twice during the last eight months. Some of the support personnel I'd seen there looked like candidates for the Charles Manson school for urban terrorism.

Although everyone at any level with SOG operations required a top-secret security clearance, that was no absolute insurance against potential treason; after all, Defrisco and his puppets all had TS's too.

What bothered me most was the quote "inadvertent detonation."

I glanced at the paper in Ski's hand before speaking. "That part about 'inadvertent detonation' seems out of sync, sir. It's my understanding that detonation of the Device is controlled strictly by timer preset."

He frowned. "Roger, I noticed that too. Perhaps they're just exaggerating the threat a little in order to emphasize the deterrent issue."

"I don't think so, sir. Major Jinx brought out in his briefing that the initial Mariposa demand note was written by a very articulate individual. I agree with the major. I think they chose their words carefully."

"That part bugged me too," Ski added while passing the message back to the colonel. "Could mean they've booby-trapped it somehow. Of course, I never take my conjectures for reality." He shrugged and grinned at me.

I darted a look at Colonel Kahn. His face registered the same astonishment I felt.

The colonel quickly stood. "Conjectures or not, you may have something there!" he said, jotting a note down. "I'll check with Blair and find out if it is in fact possible to booby-trap a Saydem. By the way, were you able to get any info from her last night?"

"Not much, sir. She did say that Defrisco was passed over for promotion to captain recently and he'd seemed withdrawn at times.

"She admits it's a guess, but she felt he could be using some type of drugs." Being vague about Defrisco's opium habit was the best way I knew to keep Megan out of the grease.

"Well, I wouldn't be surprised about the drug use," the colonel replied. "It tends to be a part of the hippie subculture. Not that I'm throwing Defrisco in the same tub with hippies, but according to the MI dossier, he'd been noted to occasionally patronize a bar in Saigon called the Mellow Yellow. It's a hippie kind of hangout.

"MI called it a 'head joint.' I always thought that was where a man went to get a . . . well, never mind," he said, checking his watch. "I think Blair is down in the conference room with Calvin. When you get down there send her up here.''

We heard Megan's voice as we neared the open door of the conference room. ''Remember, you only have two opportunities to use the scale,'' she chided.

Entering the room I smelled the soft fragrance of her perfume. Calvin was sitting across the table from her.

''Hi,'' she said, looking around at us. ''We've been waiting to see who gets first turn with you this afternoon.''

''Sorry you had to wait,'' Ski replied. ''We were conferring with the colonel. You know, RHIP.''

Calvin's head stayed tilted down concentrating on the table surface as if we hadn't entered. A step closer I noticed eight paper clips neatly arranged in front of him.

''What's this?'' I asked, moving to Stapleton's side.

''It's a damn brain teaser. I'll tell you that!'' Calvin mumbled without looking up.

''It's the light coin puzzle,'' Megan answered.

''I don't see any coins,'' Ski said, looking closer at the table.

Megan smiled. ''The paper clips simply represent coins.''

''Oh, I see. You have to use your imagination, huh?'' Ski nodded with a grin.

I winked at Megan. ''You look like you recovered well from the fire last night.''

''Yes, thanks to you and Ski.''

''The show was over when I got there. I'd say it was more like you and Ski handling things.''

I pointed to the table. ''Tell me about this puzzle. Looks interesting.''

As Calvin continued his silent contemplation of the clips Megan explained that the objective of the puzzle was to determine which of the eight similar-sized clips, coins, was the "light coin" by weighing them on an imaginary balance scale.

The complicating factor was, you could only use the scale twice. Although you could weigh any combination of coins during the two weighs, the conditional use of the scale significantly restricted any process of elimination.

"I got it!" Calvin announced while dividing the clips into two equal portions. "On the first weighing I weigh four on each end of the scale. The end that falls would obviously contain the light coin.

"Now, hypothetically, I have narrowed it down to one of the remaining four coins. I place two on each end of the scale and the end that drops would naturally contain the light coin." He pushed two more paper clips into the elimination pile, then looked up and smiled as though he'd just won a game of Clue.

I glanced at Megan. She stared at Calvin in disbelief, as if she was inhibited about telling him he had not rung the bell.

Ski wasn't inhibited about it. "Sir, it appears to me you still don't know which one of the two is the light one and you've used up all your weighs. Am I right or wrong?"

Megan smiled. "He's right. Looks like it's back to square one, Calvin."

"Yeah, yeah," he said, pushing them all aside. "I can tell you this . . . we got better things to do than be screwing around with puzzles.

"We need to get started here," he said, standing. "I need these gents for about two hours, Lieutenant. After that you can pitch your ball game and your puzzle too for all I care." Calvin's tone was condescending.

Megan stood and checked her watch. "Okay, gentlemen, it appears I've been preempted. I'll return at 1530 if that's satisfactory," she said, glancing at me.

I winked. "Roger, that'll work fine. Also, Colonel Kahn asked if you would meet him in the War Room. He mentioned he had some questions he wanted to run by you."

She returned my wink, then looked at Ski. "I'm afraid my new gun was sacrificed to the fire, Ski. Guess I won't need a range lesson today."

Binkowski grinned and glanced at me before replying. "That's all right. It looks like a storm is moving in anyhow. Maybe, well . . . I'll see you later when you're back here.

"I have something I want to give you," he said, tapping a chest pocket on his shirt.

As Megan turned to walk to the door I looked back at her. "That light coin puzzle, where'd you learn that?"

She cast a half smile. "Lieutenant Defrisco showed it to me. He collects puzzles."

Chapter 17

"So, Defrisco likes puzzles," Calvin said as I took a seat at the table by Ski. "It's really too bad he doesn't have much longer to live. Perhaps he could have eventuated into a good officer. He's obviously a thinker," Stapleton continued while giving the pile of paper clips a pensive look.

I felt a restless amusement with Calvin's hint of confidence in my team's ability to accomplish the mission. Listening to him you'd think we'd already neutralized 501, put the Mariposa's lights out, and were marching home at shoulder arms with a big smile.

But Stapleton was right about two things—Defrisco was a thinker and he was bold. The more I learned about him the more I came to respect his displaced intellect. His interest in puzzles was gnawing a hole in my acceptance of the popular theory that "inadvertent detonation" was a bluff.

Calvin opened a small black case and removed a camera—about the size of a can of C rations.

"This is another gift from the Agency," he announced, opening the back of the camera.

"What was the other gift?" Ski questioned.

"The Hush Puppies, partner."

"Oh, I see. But really I haven't seen—"

"I have them in my briefcase. I'll go over that later with you," the agent interrupted, raising his eyebrows.

"But first this. This is a Pen Double-E thirty-five millimeter half-frame camera. I will now load it with this roll of black-and-white four hundred ASA film," he said, tearing open a foil wrapper.

After loading the roll he closed the back and began advancing the film with the manual lever. "The film has thirty-six exposures, however since this is a half-frame camera you'll have double that amount, seventy-two. That's really somewhat extraneous because you'll only be required to use twenty-four frames."

Although I hadn't yet trained Ski in using the Pen-EE, I was very familiar with it. It was the principal camera issued by SOG for general purpose field recon photography and particularly for bomb damage assessment missions.

Months ago, during an area recon of an NVA battalion staging base, Will and I had snapped sixty photographs of enemy personnel so close we could have spit on them. The Pen-EE was a rugged camera with a no-glare flat-black housing. The feature I liked most about it was the soft, almost inaudible shutter click. Will had once commented that the click was so quiet that he had to look at the frame indicator to make sure it hadn't malfunctioned.

Calvin's next statement answered my unasked question about why we were being given another "gift" from the Agency.

He passed the camera to Ski. "Look it over, but do not, I repeat, do not snap a picture. You are accountable for every frame on that roll of film. Incidentally, the camera's to be stored in the waterproof bag when not in use.

"The purpose of this instrument is to procure photographic documentation of twelve subjects. You will take two photographs of each subject, totaling twenty-four, and you will take each picture consecutively.'' Calvin's voice had evolved to dramatic emphasis mode again. "I will add that should you encounter a subject of potential tactical value you have the latitude to photograph it. However, remember that you must take two shots of any subject.''

Ski passed the camera to me and I returned it to Calvin.

He picked it up, then stood holding it as if prepared to take a picture of us. "Please turn your hands over flat on the table, palms up, and hold them very still. You first, Sergeant Yancy. Move them closer together.''

I felt my eyes narrow, reacting to Stapleton's order. I complied while he leaned forward focusing the camera downward and about eighteen inches directly above my hands. He then snapped a picture of them. "Don't move. I'll take another now.''

After repeating the process with Ski he remarked that the first four of the essential twenty-four photos were now placed.

He then removed two small metal plates from his pocket, separated a cover shield from them, and carefully took our fingerprints. I was surprised that no ink was involved with the process. After replacing the shields back over the fingerprint plates he told us that upon return of the film, a CIA photo analyst would use the first four pictures he had just taken for fingerprint authentication to determine the photographic validity of the remaining twenty pictures.

The reason he avoided taking a facial photo of us was a security measure to prevent our pictures from being revealed to the enemy if the camera were stolen or lost during the mission. After hearing the explanation Binkowski commented, "That seems like a good idea.''

Calvin smiled. "I'm glad you can appreciate our keen attention to detail."

I wasn't nearly as impressed with the extravagant security of the procedure. In my estimation, if the camera fell into enemy hands it wouldn't matter if the film revealed our pictorial history from birth. In Indian country white boys stuck out like nipples in a wet T-shirt contest—Chuck didn't need our mug shot on the post office bulletin board.

Again, I withheld my opinion, reminding myself that the CIA operated under different tactical circumstances than recon. It was becoming apparent that Stapleton couldn't distinguish the difference.

As Calvin replaced the camera in the case I saw his eyes drift to the paper clips that still lay on the table.

"You mentioned we have a total of twelve subjects you need photos of, two pictures per subject," I said, interrupting Calvin's retro-puzzle study. "With four of the photographs now 'placed,' as you call it, what are the other subjects?"

"Yes," he said, returning attention to me. "You will photograph the Device before and after destruction, two photos each. Then you're required to photograph each of the three personnel to be terminated, before and after you kill them."

My mind tallied the total while Ski withdrew a small notebook and pen from his pocket.

"No notes, Sergeant!"

Ski quietly tucked his pad back into the pocket.

"That totals ten subjects equaling twenty pictures, including your shots of our hands. How about the other four pictures?"

He lowered himself to a seated position and placed his forearms on the table. "The other subject is simply a photo update on Bacsin for our file. Take two facial profile shots of her and two facial front shots.''

''What if she doesn't want her picture taken?'' I asked, leveling my eyes on his.

Calvin looked down and laced his fingers together. He raised his head slowly. ''That . . . is entirely possible. CAS agents do have a—shall we say—aversion to being photographed.'' He grinned. ''Good question.''

I grinned back. ''How about a good answer.''

Arnold's voice chimed in. ''We could always say please. Most girls I've met really appreciate manners.''

Calvin fell back in his chair, frowning at Binkowski in amazement. He appeared stunned. His lips began to move without speaking. Finally he muttered, ''Please? Did you say, please?''

Ski smiled. ''Yes, sir.''

''How long you been in Southeast Asia, son?''

''Four and a half months, sir.''

Stapleton turned to me with a wide-eyed stare. ''That's it, Brett. Just say fucking please.''

I didn't know if Calvin was being evasive or if he was trying to be witty. Either was unacceptable.

''We both know this isn't a campus photo tour, Calvin. When was the last picture of her taken?''

''I don't want to sound like a broken record, Yancy, but you don't have a need to know. How about this . . . I'm sending four hundred dollars' worth of sterile gold with you to pay Bacsin. Don't give it to her immediately. Tell her you need to take her picture. If she resists, simply say, 'no picture, no pay.' ''

I didn't like the idea of bartering with the woman who would essentially be controlling our local destiny in the AO. I decided the best thing to do right now was drop the subject and cross that rice paddy when I came to it. I reasoned that if Bacsin didn't want to cooperate with the photo session I was not going to let it get in the way of keeping rapport with her. RT Texas had enough hurdles already without creating another one.

"That'll probably do it, Calvin," I said reassuringly. "And like Ski says, if all else fails we can always say please."

I remembered that Colonel Kahn had mentioned during the mission alert briefing that they hoped to have another CAS agent working the Vinh Son area but that the CIA had temporarily lost contact with the agent. I knew if I had to split the team and send Ski and three Yards with him to Vinh Son it would help if he had a prepositioned contact. Now seemed like a good time to ask about the possibility of another agent in the southern target area.

When I tossed the question to Stapleton he informed us that the other agent had been "deactivated." In the same breath he gave me his well-used broken record recital.

Since we had no way of establishing the validity of Bacsin, other than the challenge and reply to be used upon contact with her on the drop zone, I asked the good agent to go over it again for Ski's benefit.

"Yes," he answered. He moved his chair slightly to a position directly across from Ski. "If it is you who makes first contact with Mighty-Tight, you will—"

"Mighty-Tight!" Ski exclaimed.

"Yes, that is the code name I assigned her. And if you ever bed her you'll know why.

"As I was saying, when and if you make contact with Mighty-Tight the first man, individual, initiating the challenge will say 'I need some water.' You must speak this phrase in Vietnamese. Now, repeat after me: *Ho bat coc toi.*"

Ski blinked. *"Ho but coc—"*

"Not but, *bat* . . . like in Batman."

"*Ho bat coc toi. Ho bat coc toi,*" Ski repeated.

"Very good. Now the reply must be, 'It will rain soon,' followed by raising your right arm and pointing skyward. Repeat after me: '*Troi sap mua.*' "

"*Troi sup mua. Troi sup mua.*"

"Not sup, *sap*, like sapper."

"*Troi sap mua. Troi sap mua.*"

"Okay. What else?" Calvin asked, leaning forward.

"I—I don't—"

"You forgot to point skyward!"

"Oh, oh . . . okay. *Troi sap mua,*" Ski said, jabbing his big right arm straight up.

I conducted a brief rehearsal with Ski, then looked at Calvin. "Since we don't have a photograph of Mighty-Tight, can you tell us any distinguishing characteristics about her? Does she have a scar, a mole, tattoo . . . anything that could help us in identifying her?"

Calvin brought a hand to his mustache, stroking one end of it slowly while casting a contemplative stare at me. I could tell he was thinking about giving me his standard put-off.

His eyes glanced upward, then down to the paper clips, then back to me. "No, no marks. Nothing like that. She has high cheekbones, dark eyes, straight black hair, maybe a little taller than average. . . . She's beautiful, like I said, but she doesn't have much of a French look about her.

"Her breasts! That's it!" he said, snapping his fingers. "She has gorgeous breasts. And you know how Vietnamese women have big, dark, protruding nipples?"

I nodded.

"Well, Bacsin's nipples are a splendid tone of pink and they're inverted. She has inverted nipples!"

He continued his excited revelation while I looked over

at Ski. Ski's eyes were gleaming. Calvin told us that with prolonged oral stimulation her nipples would swell out like miniature condoms blown up with compressed air. "Well, there you have it. That's the—"

"Have what?" I butted in dryly.

"Damn it, what you're asking for . . . a way to identify her!"

I stood, feeling a frustrated sense of heat. "That's great, Calvin," I said, walking toward the wall map. "What do I do? Shake hands with her on the drop zone and ask her to open her shirt so I can suck her tits!"

"I'll do it," Ski blurted.

I turned and studied Arnold's face. He glowed with a proud smile like he'd just volunteered for the first moon shot. It crossed my mind that he'd make a great sidekick for Calvin Stapleton.

I turned, walking to the door. "I need a fucking cup of coffee."

Chapter 18

Entering the War Room I noticed Luther Hayes placing a long canvas-cased piece of gear on a table. The object it contained appeared to be long and tubular.

His words caught my attention. "Here's Baby, sir. You want me to take her out of the case?"

I turned slowly, raising the coffee cup to my lips.

"No. I'm going to let Agent Stapleton handle this. The less we have to do with this thing the better," Major Jinx answered, laying his hand gently on the tubular-shaped object.

I walked toward the table. "What's this? Looks like it could be an old LAW."

Hayes glanced at Jinx. The major withdrew his hand from the object. "No, Sergeant Yancy, it's not a LAW. It's . . . well, I'll let the CIA fill you in. This is their baby. As a matter of fact that's what they call it: Baby."

Seeing me take an interest in the olive-drab–covered article, Jinx instructed Loot to deliver it on to Calvin in the conference room.

As Loot picked Baby up and cradled it horizontally in his arms I noticed the unusual absence of any identifying nomenclature on the case.

"Did you get finished up with Agent Stapleton?" Jinx asked.

"Negative, sir. We've still got about an hour with him. We'll go through a map and aerial photo session after chow."

Jinx did a quick toe bounce. "He's quite a guy, isn't he? I mean, those Company men are sharp. Wouldn't you agree?"

"Yes, sir," I answered, sipping my coffee. "They definitely seem to stay *abreast* of things."

Turning to walk away Colonel Kahn appeared in the doorway of the office and asked me to come in. Upon entering I saw Megan seated near the desk.

"Brett, I've just gone over this 'inadvertent detonation' booby-trap thing with Lieutenant Blair. She can't see any potential in it."

"That's right, Brett . . . Sergeant Yancy . . . with a type-one it is either armed with the timers running or it isn't. There really isn't any neutral status with it.

"You'll have a better understanding of what I'm talking about when I give you and Ski, I mean Sergeant Binkowski, my class."

Megan's stoic expression indicated she'd given the booby-trap scenario a lot of serious thought. I decided to hold off on declaring my interrelated puzzle theory until after I'd heard Megan's class. Once I knew the mechanics of a type-one I figured it would either blow my theory loose or at least give me a better perspective on what tricks DD could have up his sleeve. Inwardly, I hoped Megan's expertise would short-stop my suspicions. But I'd made it a habit never to ignore my sixth sense, and right now it was flashing *tilt*.

When I returned to the conference room Calvin and Ski

were finishing up with the Hush Puppies. The canvas-cloaked Baby lay near the end of the table.

Seeing me enter Calvin remarked, "By the way, Brett, I failed to mention earlier that these little jewels are not serial numbered, but you will be required to sign for them; and of course return them upon mission completion.

"We have strict control procedures just like the Army . . . camera too—nonexpendable items."

"How about Baby over there?"

"Yes, of course, that too! And since you mentioned it we might as well get to that right now."

Stapleton gently laid the Hush Puppy aside, then smiled while opening the end of the canvas case. Reaching inside the mouth of the case he carefully withdrew a long cylindrical camouflage-coated tube approximately four feet in length and six or seven inches in diameter. When he took out an antenna and began screwing in into the conical nose I knew exactly what it was—a sensor.

Peering down at his assembled display Calvin placed his hands together as if he were preparing to pray. He smiled. "This is an electronic marvel. It complements man and nature. It is the most ingenious creation that has ever been produced by our communications and electronics laboratory.

"I should add that it is not fully perfected yet."

"Wow. Looks like it could be a motorized mortar round," Ski interjected.

Listening to Calvin's excited preamble was like hearing a game-show host introduce a *National Geographic* documentary.

Months ago I'd conducted two sensor plant missions along the Ho Chi Minh Trail—one acoustic, one seismic. In recent months they, MACV, had begun seeding some sensors by aerial delivery.

Seismic sensors were designed to distinguish ground rumbling from communist supply trucks. The more sophisticated acoustic-type sensors were supposed to detect human voices. Commonly the internal transmitters had a battery life of thirty to forty-five days. Data was transmitted to a reception station located in Calvin's home away from home—NKP, Thailand.

From what I'd learned both types of sensors had adjustment flaws that resulted in unreliable data interpretation at the receiver facility. The acoustic version, called Acoubuoy, could not distinguish tiger and monkey sounds from humans; and the common seismic type, ADSID, had a problem differentiating elephants from trucks.

As far as I was concerned sensors were still in the experimental stage. But the question that nudged me now was: What could a sensor have to do with this mission?

As Calvin carefully snapped two large plastic camouflage leaves into position his eyes radiated with the excitement of a youngster assembling a new toy. "There!" he said, holding Baby upright. "Isn't she beautiful?" he continued while stroking it.

Ski reached to touch it. "I could set that in my living room for plant decoration. If I had a living room, of course."

Calvin smirked while lifting it higher to reveal four prong-type fold-out legs. "These small feet are used to stabilize Baby in an upright position once you have selected a well-concealed placement site," he said as if he were showing off his first-born child, standing it on the table.

"You mentioned something about it combining man and nature. Is—"

"Hold it!" he said, raising an index finger. "I know

what you're thinking, but the fact that it looks like a jungle plant has nothing to do with my allusion to nature.

"My choice of the word *nature* has to do with the best export to come out of Mexico since tequila. Bedbugs!"

Ski jerked back in his chair. "What? You mean like good night, good night, don't let the bedbugs—"

"That's exactly what I mean. In layman terms, this sensor employs the use of a Mexican bedbug glued to a phonograph needle. The . . ." Calvin suddenly went mute, drawing a thumb to his lips.

It seemed he'd realized that he was about to step beyond the need-to-know boundaries. Seeing the excited gleam in Calvin's eyes told me he couldn't resist the temptation to tell more.

His hands went to the praying position, touching his nose, then quickly down to his chin. "You fully understand this is all top secret?"

I grinned and nodded.

"Yes, sir, how does it work?" Ski added.

Calvin lightly petted a plastic leaf as he continued his spiel. He told us the basic problem with past sensors had been their inability to differentiate noises. Through "tireless research" the CIA had learned that Mexican bedbugs could sense human beings at a range of 150 yards regardless of weather conditions. When the vermin sensed humans they became irritated.

The bedbug, which was glued to a phonograph needle, was placed in a high-resonance small chamber within the sensor canister. A tiny wire attached to the phonograph needle activated a vibrating crystal within a transmitter. When humans came into the sensor radius the hapless import started playing his irritated version of that great all-time hit "La Cucaracha."

"There you have it . . . or should I say, *olé*?" Calvin

smiled. "The only potential limitation is that we don't know what the life span of a bedbug is. Some of them die unexpectedly and for no apparent reason," he said dolefully.

Arnold nodded sympathetically. "Maybe they're lonely. You know, Mexican Chihuahuas are that way . . . hyper, I mean, when they're lonely. I'll bet a Chihuahua would work in there and I know the life span of—"

Calvin frowned. "Hold it, Sergeant. Do you have any frigging idea the size of the canister we'd have to . . . besides, they bark. They shit. They . . . well there is just no damn way!"

I'd heard about all I needed. I took the last gulp of cold coffee. "I really don't give a damn what the life span of a bedbug is. How about telling me what this roach canister has got to do with my mission, and how it's going to help find three deserters and a nuclear bomb."

"Like I said, Sergeant . . . if you'd listen closer, I told you it is not perfected. We simply need to test it and—"

"North Vietnam is not Aberdeen proving ground, Calvin! I'll tell you straight out that unless you can show me that this Star Trek gadget has some benefit to my mission I'm opting not to take it."

He stepped back like I'd slapped him. "I'm—I'm not sure you have that option. Perhaps you haven't learned yet that the military service is not a democracy."

I stood and picked up my coffee cup. "I'll tell you what I have learned, mister. To keep my mind on the fucking mission."

"Sounds like somebody is quoting my favorite axiom," Colonel Kahn said, entering the room.

For some reason his strong voice indicated he'd heard more than just his "favorite axiom."

Chapter 19

"As you were, gents," the colonel barked, nodding a sharp frown at Calvin.

If he'd overheard the Stapleton versus Yancy low-level pissing contest, he'd apparently chosen to address the issue later.

He handed me a message. "Hot off the press, Brett. Looks like the State Department has decided to get into the act after all. Read this."

I read the short message and passed it to Ski.

The message directed us to not only neutralize 501 but to "recover and return all portions of the SADM not destroyed by thermite, including any particles larger than a thumbtack."

When Ski returned the message Colonel Kahn told us that as far as he was concerned we didn't have to recover anything less than the size of a brick.

As we talked I could see the silent profile of Stapleton out of the corner of my eye.

Stepping forward he assumed his Streets of Laredo stance. "Ivan," he said with one hand resting on the butt of his shiny pistol. "It seems we have a failure to communicate here, me and Sergeant Yancy, that is!"

168

His tone indicated he was prepared for a showdown, to pitch his bitch about my sensor rejection. My intuition was center target.

Colonel Kahn folded his arms and listened patiently as Quick-draw Magraw went through an elaborate lecture about the electronic wonderment and tactical importance of Baby Bedbug.

Within another minute I'd have the opportunity to state my point. I felt confident that my commander was strongly oriented to mission essentials and would understand my position. But even if he sided with me I knew it was possible that Stapleton could take his case to a higher court. If Calvin did that, Colonel Kahn was going to need more than just a recital about mission essentials to get Calvin overruled.

Watching the agent stroke his favorite plastic leaf as he talked, it dawned on me that Calvin truly cared for this electronic infant; he'd fondled, caressed, and stroked it during his briefing like a mother preparing a child for a trip to the zoo.

When Calvin shut up the colonel spoke. "Brett, it looks like this gadget is the latest technology," he said, stepping between Baby and Calvin. He turned his back to the agent and rolled his eyes upward to indicate he was about to snap the ball to me. "You've conducted sensor missions before; what's your objection to taking this in?"

I reached over the table and thumped a leaf with my finger, then grabbed it as if checking for a pulse. I smiled. "Nothing really, sir. In fact I have to admit I may have been a little overreactive initially," I said, grabbing its throat and lifting it with one hand.

"Careful, Yancy! That's expensive gear, damn it!"

Stapleton's face contorted as I jabbed the sensor toward Ski. Binkowski grabbed it abruptly in both hands like he was frozen in the position of port arms.

I continued, "Actually, my concern was that Baby might be too fragile to be jumped into a rough terrain drop zone."

I turned, darting my eyes from Calvin to Ivan Kahn. "You know, we'll be going in with heavy rucks. Two radios, extra batteries, and rations, water, ammo.

"But now that I think about it," I said, slapping Baby on the side, "a parachute drop may be just the place to test this pretty little bitch." I gave Calvin a subtle smile. "It'll make it . . . or break it, as they say!"

"Sergeant Binkowski, will you kindly return that to the table!" Calvin ordered, reaching out to make sure Ski didn't drop it.

"That's right, Calvin," Colonel Kahn said, giving me a wink. "It looks like a rugged piece of gear but this jump will be a good acid test for it. I'm assuming the Agency has developed some type of padded container for parachute infiltration."

"You know, to absorb the ground shock," I interjected, looking at Calvin.

He squinted when I said "shock." "Well—well no . . . not as of—"

"Now that you mention it," Ski uttered, "I'm worried about that bug and the pornograph needle they have glued—"

"Not pornograph needle, you word rapist . . . phonograph!"

"Oh, sorry."

Calvin looked mournfully down at the flimsy canvas carrying case on the table, then at Colonel Kahn. "By any chance do you have a team inserting by helicopter sometime soon?"

"First thing next week; Prairie Fire Target."

Stapleton's hands slowly went to the praying position again. "Perhaps it would be more realistic to use a less—

a less jarring method of insertion since this is somewhat of a pilot run for Baby.

"After all, I'm the first to admit it's not totally perfected."

Ivan Kahn glanced at me. "Sounds reasonable . . . what do you think, Brett?" he asked through a frowning grin.

I kept a poker face. "Whatever's in the best interests of the Baby, sir.

"But personally I like the make-it-or-break-it idea."

Calvin began quickly unscrewing the antenna. "Your choice of words clearly indicates that you have an impaired sense of reality about testing sensitive equipment, Sergeant. You'd never make it in the Agency."

"I guess that's the breaks . . ." I said, smiling at Colonel Kahn. "Metaphorically speaking, of course."

Calvin went through the last phase of his briefing about as briefly as possible. He hurried us through a few glimpses of aerial photos of the drop zone, Dong Yen, and Vinh Son. He seemed to have lost some of his enthusiasm.

We were told there were no significant enemy concentrations in the area, with the exception of the K-9 center and the occasional entry and departure of NVA officers at Dong Yen.

The civilian populace in the area was some rice farmers in the outlying regions and the local types in the city. The rice cultivation area was located to the north near the K-9 training facility.

Calvin informed us that there was a fishing village between Dong Yen and Vinh Son that kept a watch on the coast. Our seaside exfiltration point was in an area four klicks south of Dong Yen in an isolated area that was out of the vigil range of the fishing village. Supposedly, the Navy was maintaining a discreet monitor on the exfil location. If somebody or something moved into the area, our Seal assets would wait until our time for exfil, then move in and eliminate any opposition prior to our arrival.

I was given two 1:250,000 grid maps of the area with the DZ, safe house, and exfil point marked in red grease pencil.

The aerial photos weren't high quality but they were good enough. More importantly they were recent. They'd been taken by an SR-71 reconnaissance aircraft at 80,000 feet flying three times the speed of sound. Better pictures could have been taken from a lower altitude but that would have risked alerting the enemy to our area of interest.

Using a magnifying glass I carefully studied one photo and noticed what looked like a 37-millimeter antiaircraft position a few klicks west of DZ Ghost Rider. Near the AA battery there were some railroad tracks.

When I questioned Calvin about it he told me it was an NVA standby battery and currently inactive. He informed us that all bombing in the Dong Yen area had been curtailed since the deployment of Mighty-Tight. The intel she was producing far outweighed any strategic benefits of bombing—they didn't want to risk a bomb killing one of their key agents.

The photo of the seaside town of Dong Yen revealed a small harbor with two ships at dock. CIA photo analysts were unable to determine the country of origin, but they were believed to be either Soviet or French. Surrounding area photos showed rice fields to the north near Hoang Du, several large huts, and sections of a coastal highway. The road was splotched with bomb craters that looked like hobo swimming pools.

Calvin mentioned that the bombing had ceased some time ago. I was curious as to why the NVA hadn't repaired the road.

He smirked. ''Elementary! They think if they repair the

road we will intercede with bombing again. They want us to believe that Highway One has no tactical value to them. But of course, we know better." He paused without answering the obvious question as if to make me ask it.

"Okay. What is the tactical value?"

"It's an incoming artery from Dong Yen to a small Soviet K-9 training center up here." He turned and walked to the wall map and placed his finger on an area about five miles north of Dong Yen.

"K-9! You mean like in dogs?" Ski questioned.

"Precisely. But these are not your little fucking Chihuahua variety, Sergeant. They're like hounds." He smiled. "They are training dogs to hunt your recon teams."

"Have trained," I said, correcting Calvin. "We were tracked by hounds on our last mission. So they are definitely in the active status, as you call it."

Stapleton frowned. "What area was that?"

"Prairie Fire. Hotel-5."

"Yeah, but Brett had a trick for them they weren't expecting. Right, partner?"

"What trick?" the agent asked, pulling a small spiral pad from his pocket.

As Calvin made notes I explained the merits of chemical sulfide. CS came in two varieties—gas and powder. When the NVA trackers put the dogs on us I sprinkled a good quantity of the CS powder along the trail behind me. Moments later, as their snouts hit the acrid powder, the dogs went insane. I smiled, remembering the distant wild yelps and growls followed by the cries of confused men when the dogs turned, attacking their handlers. Within seconds I'd heard shots ring through the jungle as the handlers killed the mad dogs.

"Why wasn't I told about this?" Calvin asked the ceiling, then looked back at me.

"Sorry, Calvin. Guess I should have called you, but I didn't have your number handy. My question is why weren't we told about dogs in this AO?"

"Well, according to our reports they're not used in your AO. The Soviets conduct a two-week shake-and-bake training course, primarily to get the dogs climatized, then transport them to Cambodia and Laos to be used by the bad guys. I wouldn't worry too much about dogs in the Dong Yen AO, Brett."

The agent's assessment was shallow. It was common practice for any military training facilities to conduct a field exercise as the final phase of classes—the Soviets were no exception. I didn't bother to explain it to Calvin. I made a mental note that it was very possible we could encounter dogs in the AO and decided to take along a plastic pouch of CS powder, just in case the Bolshevik versions of Rin Tin Tin got into the act.

Glancing at his watch Calvin said, "That chesty lieutenant will be here in fifteen minutes so I need to wrap things up. I have one last question, then we can step outside and fire the little jewels before I depart."

I told Calvin there was no need to fire the Hush Puppies; that we would conduct that in conjunction with our standard weapons' test firing prior to launch.

"Well, then," he chimed, slapping his hands together. "All I need to ask is, how do you want your drop zone: wet or dry?"

At first I thought Quick-draw was using his cryptic dialogue again. I was wrong. His explanation revealed a phase of the CIA private war that I'd never heard of— Covert Weather Modification Operations.

I learned that the CIA, using aerial-dropped silver and iodine cloud-seeding units, was making it rain wherever and whenever it suited their tactical best interests. When

Ski asked about the volume they could produce, Calvin answered that they could "make it rain like a herd of King Ranch cattle all pissing on the same flat rock!"

We learned that recent precipitation in the Dong Yen area had been unusually light and that the weather forecast for Halloween night was no rain.

I opted for rain. A night shower would help obscure our silhouettes during the slow-descent jump. Additionally, if any of the hounds of Bolshevik-ville were in the drop zone area, the rain would help cloak our scent. At the same time I told Calvin that we didn't need the King Ranch version of rain.

"I think what we need is rain kind of like a pack of Chihuahuas pissing on a sponge," Ski said, giving me a studious frown. "Am I right, Brett?"

"Roger, Arnold."

Calvin chuckled while making an entry on his notepad. "Okay, Chihuahua piss for Drop Zone Ghost Rider. Sounds like a title for a great movie, doesn't it?

"Now, I gotta go say adios to the colonel and get myself over to the airfield, gentlemen. Best of luck to you on this mission. And if I don't see you again . . . well . . . of course I'll see you again." He grinned. "I mean, I've got to pick up the camera, pistols." He tried to smile while shaking my hand.

He avoided Ski's hand, choosing instead to tap him on the shoulder and give him a dramatic look of confidence.

"One question before you mount up, Calvin."

"I'm easy. Fire away."

"It hasn't been mentioned, but we both know that the NVA would love to have the Saydem, for their own toy box. For that matter, so would the Soviets.

"So, it has occurred to me that it's possible they may

have gained control of it by now. Question is, do you know of any intel that could substantiate my conjecture?''

Calvin looked down, picked up his briefcase, and set it near Baby. ''I see what you mean; be kind of like going into a beehive with no honey inside.'' He grinned.

''That, or like pissing into the wind,'' I said, transmitting a don't-give-me-any-fucking-tap-dance look straight into his eyes.

His grin faded. ''I know exactly how you feel, Brett. Truth is, the same thought has crossed my mind. But I haven't even heard a rumor to that effect. Sorry, I can't help you on that.''

''Excuse me, gentlemen.'' Megan's soft voice floated in. ''It is 1530. If you need some more time I can—''

''No, no, Lieutenant. Come on in here. It's time for me to get out of Dodge.''

As Megan's fragrance drifted into the room Ski hurried to help her with the folders she was carrying.

Seeing the stars in his eyes I decided now would be as good a time as any to let him spend a couple of private moments with her. I knew he was anxious to give her his poem.

Turning to Stapleton I said, ''Come on, Calvin, I'll carry Baby upstairs for you. I need another cup of coffee anyhow.''

Jabbing his briefcase toward me he muttered, ''Here, you take this. I'll carry Baby!'' As we neared the door Calvin turned back to Megan. ''Good to have met you, Lieutenant,'' he said, glancing at the paper clips on the table. ''I don't suppose you'd like to tell me the solution to that light coin puzzle, would you?''

Megan's head tilted to the side as she smiled. ''Sure, I guess—''

''No, no. Forget it . . . don't tell me. I'll figure it out during my flight back to NKP; it's probably easy. Adios, amigos!''

Chapter 20

When we got up to the War Room Stapleton immediately told Colonel Kahn and Major Jinx that Air America would initiate weather modification in the vicinity of Ghost Rider to insure light precipitation during our airborne infiltration.

When I asked Calvin how long the homemade rain would last he couldn't give me a straight answer. He said the duration and volume was dependent on variable meteorologic conditions, as well as the ballistic bursting radius of the seeding unit, which was controlled significantly by the prevailing air density. After that he shifted into esoteric overdrive and it got complicated. After Calvin completed his science class I made sure that both Colonel Kahn and Major Jinx were aware of the K-9 Corps while Calvin was there to substantiate it. Stapleton did confirm it, but at the same time made light of the potential threat. I marveled at his ability to shrug and say, ''Dogs? No big deal!'' when it wasn't his ass on the line. I'd felt the tense anal constriction that occurs when you first hear that distant yelping chorus of hounds and you know it's your blood they're coming after. It's one of those special sounds you don't forget.

After receiving four hundred dollars in sterile gold, neatly packaged in a wood box, I signed Calvin's issue receipt for the Hush Puppies and the camera. I refilled my coffee cup and bid him adios.

When I returned to the conference room I found Ski and Megan sitting at the big table talking. They were both smoking. It was the first time I'd actually seen Megan smoke.

Entering, I noticed her tuck Ski's poem into her pocket.

"Guess what, Brett? Megan likes my poem!"

I sat down opposite Ski at the table. "Well, I'm not surprised at that. You may just turn out to be another Joyce Kilmer, partner."

"Who's she?"

"Not she, he," Megan said, reaching to touch Ski's arm. "He was an American soldier in World War One. He wrote the poem *Trees*."

"Oh, yeah. I heard that once. Do you really think I'm that good?" Ski asked, shifting an enthused smile to each of us.

Megan looked at me with a subtle grin that said, "You started this, Yancy."

Up until now it had felt good to enjoy a little low-key conversation in the wake of Calvin's guest appearance. But now, short of telling a bald-faced lie, it seemed I'd painted myself into a corner.

Taking a gulp of coffee, I looked across the table at Arnold Binkowski; the Poet Laureate of CCN. "Partner, I think, with hard work, you could be that good. Yes."

Megan leaned forward. "You know, looking at you both I must say you have changed my stereotypical opinion of what is special about Special Forces.

"I think it's your sense of dedication to your job and each other. As I watched you just now another poem came to mind. It was penned by Amelia Earhart. She called it *Courage*.

" 'Courage is the price that life exacts for granting peace. The soul that knows it not; knows no release from little things. Knows not the livid loneliness of fear, nor mountain heights where bitter joy can hear the sound of wings.' "

Megan's clean, thoughtful words were complimented by her uninhibitedly glistening eyes.

"That . . . that is beautiful," Ski said softly.

"I agree."

She gave each of us a quick smile, then turned her attention to the small pile of folders in front of her. "Well," she said, taking a deep breath and straightening her posture as she reached forward. "As Major Jinx would say, 'we need to get on with our intended purpose' here."

She handed Ski and me a folder marked Top Secret. "The heart of type-one is located beneath the circular tungsten steel cover at the base of the Device.

"If you will open your folders you will find four one-quarter scale diagrams of a Saydem."

Glancing through the diagrams I noticed there was a side, top, and two end views of the SADM. One end view depicted the Device with the combination locking cover on and one view revealed the inner face of the "heart."

"Of the five diagrams, the two we'll be concerned with are the rear section views showing the locking cover in place and then removed, revealing the arming controls.

"The main reason I am elaborating on the control area is to make sure you can determine if the Device is armed when you locate it."

Studying the locking plate diagram she called our attention to two see-through glass areas. One small circular porthole allowed viewing of the pull-button arming switch.

The other elongated window exposed the four crypto cycling code digits to the left of the four separate hours and minutes numbers.

The CCC indicator showed the numbers one, two, three, four. The timer was also set on one-two-three-four. "Now can either of you remember what the CCC is for five-zero-one?"

"Zulu Tango seven-five-five-one," I answered.

"Very good, Brett," she responded. "This is pertinent to the Device you seek because if those digits in that precise order are not showing in the CCC window, then the Saydem has not and cannot be activated."

Ski repeated the numbers softly. "Seven-five-five-one."

Megan smiled and reached to point at the timer digits on Ski's diagram. "Now, Ski, can you tell me what timer rundown interval these numbers indicate?"

"Sure," he said, looking closer. "Twelve hours thirty-four minutes."

"Right. Now can you discern anything about the characteristics of this hypothetical Device based on the timer setting? I mean, other than the obvious fact that it will detonate twelve hours and thirty-four minutes subsequent to activation."

Ski was silent. While searching my mind for the answer it occurred to me that Megan's question was oriented to make us think and reason.

Ski looked up and blinked. "I . . . I'm not sure what you mean."

Megan turned to me. "Brett, can you tell anything about it based on the timer setting?"

I remembered that during her initial briefing she'd mentioned that type-ones had either a twelve- or twenty-four-hour timer. "I'd guess this particular Device must have a twenty-four-hour timer because the numbers indicate a time more than twelve hours.''

''Exactly. The reason I wanted to illustrate this is to let you know that if five-zero-one has a combined total of hours and minutes exceeding twelve, then it has been unwittingly disarmed.''

''That's good to know,'' Ski muttered.

I asked Megan if there was any other way to determine which kind of timer a particular type-one had. She informed us that if the serial number, which was engraved in the area directly below the timer windows, ended in an odd number it was equipped with a twelve-hour timer. An even number denoted the twenty-four-hour model.

Megan then outlined the six-step arming sequence necessary to activate the Device—remove the locking plate, implement the CCC, set the timers, remove the arming cube from the storage well and place it into the arming well, pull the activation button, and replace the cover rotating the combination wheel at least three times counterclockwise.

Megan admitted that our knowledge of the arming sequence was ''superfluous'' but felt that by having some in-depth knowledge, it would enhance our feeling of confidence.

She told us that upon locating the Device the most immediate way to determine if it was armed was to cup a hand near the small porthole viewing area, at the activation switch, and look for a red glow.

Megan remarked, ''The popular saying is, 'If it's red you're dead.' I don't know what mental giant thought that up, but I guess it does get the idea across.''

Chapter 21

"A-ten-shun," Ski shouted, springing to the position. Megan and I stood as Colonel Kahn entered.

"Press on with what you're doing," Ivan Kahn said. "I just wanted to let you know I'm headed over to the ninety-fifth medevac hospital to visit Swede and Iron. You got any message for them I can deliver?"

"Roger, sir," I answered. "Let them know that Ski and the Yards went through their hooch and salvaged their personal gear. Sergeant Beck has it at S-1."

"Oh, yeah," Ski said. "Sir, tell Swede he's going to need a new surf . . . no, bad idea. Tell him I hope he gets better soon."

"Please convey the same from me, sir," Megan added.

When the colonel left we sat down and continued the SADM technical briefing.

Megan reiterated the caution directive she had mentioned during the initial briefing. She made it well understood that a thermite was not to be placed anywhere near the arming controls.

Looking closer at the rear-view diagrams I asked, "Does the locking cover have to be repositioned in order to complete the arming sequence?"

Megan squinted, leaning back in her chair. "No. But why do you ask?"

I stood and walked to the large wall map. "It seems obvious that in a common tactical situation the operator would want to replace the cover," I said, turning. "But my concern is with the uncommon situation—namely how Defrisco could booby-trap this."

She smiled. "Maybe an explanation will alleviate your concern, Brett. Let me show you this."

I walked back to the table and looked over her shoulder as Ski moved his chair closer. She removed a close-up diagram of the activation button. The diagram depicted the button in a frontal and side view. In the frontal view I could see the small bulb she'd mentioned earlier that would glow if the Device was activated. The two side views showed the button in the inward nonactivated position, and in the pulled-out, activated mode. A circular flange on the button appeared to allow easy finger grip when pulling. The words DANGER-ACTIVATOR were stenciled in red letters above the button.

Using a pencil Megan pointed to the area that showed the button in the activated out position. "As I've explained, step five of the arming sequence requires the operator to pull this out. When that occurs a steel pin, which is behind the face, drops into a slot preventing the button from being pushed back in. The instant that this is pulled the light goes red and the timer starts rundown." She laid the pencil on the diagram and looked up at me.

I took a seat and studied the diagram. "Is there any provision for disarming a type-one once it's activated; other than the thermite grenade method?"

"Yes, there is," she answered. "But it requires a series of—"

"I know!" Ski shouted. "Why not just take that little cube, the arming cube, out! Wouldn't that do it?"

"No, it also locks into position."

She continued, "As I was saying, the only method of disarming a type-one is to perform a series of movements with the timer controls; six movements to be exact. But it is very evident that the method of disarming that you are allowed is the safest and the quickest, because even if five-zero-one is activated when you find it, all you have to do is place it on its side, set a thermite on it, and pull the ring."

"Pin. It's, I mean, we call it a pin. Like grenade pin. Not a ring," Ski said politely.

"Thank you, Ski," Megan replied with an amused grin. "Do you see what I mean, Brett?" she said, tapping the pencil on the table. "My point is, there's really no way it could be booby-trapped.

"And remember, the shortest time span that can be set on the timers is thirty minutes. So, even if it is booby-trapped in some way when you discover it, you still have more than adequate time to neutralize it."

Megan's explanation had loosened my grip on the bobby-trap theory. Glancing across the table at Binkowski I could see the wheels of his mind turning.

He stood abruptly. "Think about this," he announced, holding his empty palms out to us. "Do you remember that Gene Autry movie where he gets tied up in the mine and Black Bart lights the fuse to the dynamite and—and . . . well, Gene gets away of course. But you—you know what I mean."

"Look, Gene," I said, noticing a slow reaction of awe on Megan's face. "If we're tied up in the mine, why doesn't Black Bart just shoot us and keep all the gold for himself?"

Megan leaned forward, trying to restrain her laughter. I didn't.

Seeing us laughing Arnold turned away quickly, then looked back at us with a lopsided grin. "I know—I know what you're thinking. You're thinking my imagination is getting carried away. Am I right or wrong?"

"Roger, partner. You're right, but mine's been running wild too. I think what we need is a break and some fresh air."

Glancing at my watch, then over to Megan I said, "If we can put this on hold for about fifteen minutes, we'll take you down to the hooch and introduce you to the Yards. I happen to know they're dying to meet you."

"What did you call them? Yards?"

"Roger. Montagnards. They're great," I answered, standing.

"I'd like that," Megan said, standing. "Maybe you can show me your ceramic skull canister set while I'm there?"

As we entered the team hooch we found a mass of tangled confusion. The rucksack rigging had turned into pandemonium. Drop lines were strewn over a floor clogged with rucks, clothes, ration packets, and H-harnesses. I felt like a parent who'd just returned to the kitchen after instructing the kids to cook spaghetti.

The Yards stood in the midst of the mess frozen with silent gaping amazement as they looked up at Megan.

"The hooch usually looks a little better than this," I said, wading into the olive-drab clutter.

Tuong started digging into the pile of gear. He found his shirt and hurriedly put it on as I spoke.

"Gang, this is *Trung-'uy* Megan Blair. Megan, these are the Cowboys: Lok, Rham, Phan, and that's Tuong over there getting dressed," I said, turning back to Megan and Ski.

Megan smiled. "It is good to meet you all."

"You want Beam-Co, Sar Brett?" Lok asked happily.

"No. How about y'all moving this shi . . . stuff so Megan can get through here," I answered, glancing at Phan. His wide eyes stared at Megan's breasts as if he'd just encountered the eighth wonder of the mammary world.

The Yards began raking the gear aside to clear an isle for Megan to walk through. As we moved nearer the table Tuong stepped forward, bowed, and spoke through a broad smile. "You fur woman here dis place. Where you come?"

"She came up here from Saigon, Tuong," Ski answered as if he were Megan's official spokesman.

Tuong frowned at Ski. "You pleasing let pretty lady talk," he continued while pointing down at the sketch I'd drawn on the table surface. "You know song call 'Rhy my see-so'?"

Megan drew a finger to her chin, glancing at me with a questioning look.

" 'Ride My Seesaw.' You know, the song," I answered.

She looked down at the drawing. "Oh, yes. Very good song. I like it too. You draw very well, Tuong."

"No. I no draw. Sar Brett, he draw."

"Oh, I see," she replied, giving me a subtle grin. "In that case, you draw very well, Sar Brett. Have you considered becoming an art major?"

Lok bounded toward the table, interrupting before I had to answer. "Look see," he said, holding his fork proudly up at Megan. "I'm having metal-for like see-so song!"

Megan responded with a polite but dubious nod, then gave me that what-the-fuck-is-he-talking-about look again.

"It's a long story," I mumbled, seeing her eyes peering beyond mine.

"What's this?" she asked, walking toward Ski's bunk.

I looked up at the small sign above the bunk and explained that my partner, William Washington, had written the song verse down and placed it there a week before he was killed in Laos.

"It's the last verse in the song 'The Boxer.' Will kind of identified with those words. You see, he fought Golden Gloves back in Tennessee. He was real good. He won several championships and . . ." I felt my voice start to crack. "He was an all-around champion."

"I think I've heard this song," Megan said, stepping closer to the wall. She began to read it aloud.

As Megan's words finished I felt a rebel tear gathering in my eye. Turning to the door I walked ahead. "Why don't you show the Yards your puzzle. I'll be back."

I walked through the loose sand toward a bunker near the beach. The memory of Will rolled through me like a wave from the sea. Now, I needed to be alone for a moment.

I wasn't ashamed of my tears—I just didn't want to share my memories with anyone right then. The memories were sacred.

Leaning against a sandbagged corner of the bunker, I peered out over the fog-shrouded sea feeling the tingle of mist on my face, breathing the salty stink of Asian rain.

Moments passed while the aching memory of Will's death numbed me. I remembered holding his limp blood-soaked body in my arms and feeling the last of his blood soak into my chest. I remembered the helpless agony that gripped me as I listened to his faint dying message to his wife, "Tell Chunky I'm goin' 'cross the river, man. I'll see her and the kids over there. Might even see you there someday . . ."

"Brett, Brett, are you okay?" A voice wafted through the wind.

I glanced over my shoulder to see the intruder. Megan Blair moved with wayward steps toward me.

I looked back out to sea, took a deep breath, and tucked my memories away.

"I really like your Montagnard teammates," the voice said, coming closer. "I showed them the coin puzzle. They're working on it now. I think—"

"Good. Thank you," I said, turning to her.

She stopped. "Brett, I'm sorry . . . I feel like perhaps, well . . . like I should have known better than to read Will's verse. I didn't think about what—"

"Hold it," I said, taking a step closer to her. "You have nothing to apologize for. Your words complimented him and I'll bet he would have loved hearing it himself."

I smiled into her shy face. "I wish Will could have been there when you recited *Courage*. He would have liked that."

As we walked back toward the hooch a crack of thunder echoed in the distance. "You know," I said, looking over at Megan. "Somebody once wrote, 'When you part from your friend, grieve not, for that which you love most in him may be clearer in his absence, as the mountain to the climber is clearer from the plain.' "

"That's splendid. Who wrote that?"

I smiled. "A friend of Will's and mine named Kahlil Gibran."

Chapter 22

The next morning I woke at 0540 hours. I walked to the hooch door and peered out into a light rain as first light crept through the dim, cloudy sky. The restless sea was ebbing, leaving a wide span of hard-packed sand along the beach.

I rousted the team and by 0615 RT Texas was moving in a column, northward along the rainy beach with full web gear, rucks, and weapons.

I could have called PT off, but we'd missed it the previous morning and we'd be missing it for the next several days—in less than eighteen hours four skinny Yards and two roundeyes would be hanging beneath dark silk descending into the mouth of DZ Ghost Rider.

After a quarter mile of fast-paced walking I shouted forward to the point man: "Okay, Rham! *Mot* mile, double time!"

Jogging down the hard-packed beach I felt the rhythm of the heavy rucksack bouncing quietly on my back. I listened for sounds that would indicate someone hadn't packed their ruck to prevent noise. All quiet. Only the occasional splatter of boots hitting puddles along our amber pathway broke the silence.

I could have kept the pace limited to a fast walk, but experience had taught me that when you're dealing with Chuck it can save your ass at times if you are the undisputed district track champs.

Our column of tactical movement put Rham in the point position followed by me, Phan, and Binkowski. Tuong occupied the tail-gunner slot.

I shouted to the team as we ran. "Listen up! *Ho-bat-coc-toi! Ho-bat-coc-toi!*"

"You nee *nuoc*, Sar Brett?" Phan yelled from behind me.

"Negative. Everybody say, *ho-bat-coc-toi!*"

A muddled chorus jabbered the words through labored breaths.

"Now, *troi-sap-mua. Troi-sap-mua*," I shouted, raising my right arm.

The chorus responded while I glanced around insuring that each man raised his right arm.

After several repetitions the team knew the challenge and reply well. I'd wait and explain the significance of it to them when we returned to the hooch.

Although I was violating Calvin's directive not to share classified info with the Yards, my primary concern was for their survival. If in the event Ski and I got nailed somehow, prior to linkup with Mighty-Tight, I didn't want the Yards out on a limb with no way to identify themselves to Bacsin.

When we returned to the hooch we showered, dressed, and went to breakfast. I'd planned to cram all final mission prep: rigging, weapons' test firing, et cetera, into the morning hours in order to give the team some additional rack time prior to mission launch. I knew we'd be up most of the night and there'd be no time for sleep during the short flight to the drop zone.

After explaining the challenge and reply to the Cowboys as well as giving them a description of Bacsin, Ski interjected: "You know, if Calvin's Chihuahua piss show materializes, we'll be answering the challenge and pointing up into the downpour while saying, 'It will rain soon!' Won't that seem weird?"

When we completed chow I took the team to the range area at the base of Marble Mountain to test-fire our CAR-15s and the Hush Puppies. Upon completion of firing we taped our rifle muzzles with black electrical tape to prevent debris entry.

I left the Yards at S-4 to begin final rucksack rigging while Ski and I went on to the TOC for our Sodium Pentothal class.

Sergeant Dick Rector, a seasoned Special Forces medic, gave us the brief class. We learned that SP should be administered in a 150 mg. dosage. We learned that any amount higher than that could be fatal if the individual receiving the Pentothal had high blood pressure.

Looking at Dick I asked, "What's the reliability of this drug?"

"Well," he answered while packing the syringe and vial into a small padded box, "in my estimation it's about as effective as mud on a snake bite.

"No pun intended, but the truth is, truth serum is only successful in lowering the patient's, the victim's, inhibition level during questioning. If the recipient isn't guilt ridden about whatever it is you hope to find out, then chances are he's not going to tell you a damn thing."

As we left the TOC and walked to the S-1 it occurred to me that when I got face-to-face with DD, Sodium Pentothal was going to take a back seat to the Montagnard snake method of interrogation.

The S-1 mail clerk handed me two letters—one from my mom and one marked "SWAK, Tracer."

"I got a letter too," Ski said, holding it up to me. "It's from my . . . sister though. Looks like that lavender letter might be from Tracy."

"Roger, partner. But after she finds out that I've extended my tour, the next one will probably be in a red envelope . . . that is, if there is a next one!" I answered, tucking the letter away and gestering for him to follow me down the hall.

The colonel looked up from his desk as my knuckles hit the door. "Come in," he said flatly.

He stood and reciprocated our salutes without the usual warm greeting and invitation to sit. He paused, waiting for me to speak. I could tell something was troubling him so I got right to the point.

"Sir, I need to get an issue order for about thirty ounces of CS powder. I plan to use it if we encounter any problem from the local dog center north of—"

"Not a problem," he responded, sitting down and pulling a notepad across his desk.

Colonel Kahn had implemented strict CS control after some jilted ARVN soldier took some into town and tossed it into his ex-girlfriend's window.

Tearing the note off the pad with a quick jerk he handed it to me. "This should do. You about ready for launch?"

"Roger, sir. I'm going to give the team about four hours of sleep this afternoon unless you have something for us."

"Sounds okay with me. Do it," he said, standing as if indicating we should leave.

Moving toward the door I turned. "By the way, sir, did you get a chance to visit with Swede?" I asked quickly.

His eyes looked away for a second. "Yes. Yes. I did." He paused. "You might as well know it now. They had to amputate Sergeant Jensen's right arm . . . above the elbow. They did it this morning. I got a call from Iron Oak just a few minutes ago.''

I felt heat surge through me. ''What? The doctor said—''

''I don't know what happened. They didn't mention a goddamn thing about it yesterday while I was there. I'm headed over there now. I'll find out.

''I'll be on hand at 1800 when your team leaves for the airfield. I've got a slick laid-on to put you in the pocket over there.''

''Roger, sir,'' I acknowledged coldly while turning to the door.

''Yancy. Hold it! Sergeant Binkowski, you can wait for Sergeant Yancy in the admin office. Brett, close the door.''

Ski gave me a blank look and quickly exited.

I closed the door and returned to front and center Ivan Kahn. His eyes glared into mine, then relaxed some. ''How you feeling?''

''What do you mean, sir?''

''Don't give me that! You know damn well what I mean!''

My fist gripped the green beret in my left hand. ''Like my best friend's just been raped. That's how I fuckin' feel.''

Kahn turned and walked to a window. With his back to me he spoke loudly. ''When you lost Will Washington I was there to help you carry his body off the LZ, wasn't I?''

''Roger,'' I answered, feeling my jaw tighten.

He turned. ''On your very next mission you went back into Hotel-5, found, and killed the son of a bitch who hit Will. Right?''

''That's right.''

"With complete disregard for your mission, you went into that AO with the primary motivation to hunt down and kill Baldy, that fucking NVA sniper. And you did it, didn't you?"

My eyes darted away from his glare. Up until now I hadn't been aware that Ivan Kahn had pieced together my motive. "That's affirmative," I answered, returning my eyes to his.

"Now, the reason I'm bringing all this to the front of your thick skull is to let you know that I know how you think, Yancy! I don't want you getting wrapped around the axle and flying off the fucking handle because Swede lost his arm.

"Don't go into this mission looking for retribution, because if you do, I want you to know one thing straight out. It's not going to let me down one fucking bit if you blow this operation by going off half cocked and looking for body count.

"You know who it's going to let down? Washington and Jensen, that's who!"

I looked at the angry furrows of dark skin gathered between his eyes and felt the same anguish grip my face.

"I'll see you at 1800. You are dismissed, Sergeant!"

"What did the colonel have to say?" Binkowski questioned, following me out of the S-1 into the crisp morning breeze.

"He wanted to wish me good luck," I said, donning my beret and moving briskly toward the S-4.

"That was nice of him. Gosh, I was sure sorry to hear about Swede."

"Me too!"

Steps later Arnold butted into my quiet thoughts. "Brett,

do you remember what Calvin told us down at the beach yesterday? You know, about what a fine job we're doing?"

"Roger."

"Well, do you think he was just bullshitting, you know, just buttering us up so we would plant that sensor for him?"

"Negative."

"So you think he was being level, I mean, on the level, with us?"

"Roger."

"That didn't sound too convincing. Are you sure—"

"How about if I say it twice, Arnold! Roger, roger. Does that help?"

"Are you mad . . . I mean, angry about something?"

"Negative!"

"Good, because I wanted to ask you how you feel about the CIA. What do you think about them?"

I halted and turned to him. A stout breeze caught the corner of his beret and blew it off. I watched him scurry across the sand chasing the beret as it skimmed along the rippled surface.

Finally he caught it and lumbered back to my position while slapping the beret lightly against his leg before putting it on.

"Sorry 'bout that," he said, grinning.

"Why do you want to know what I think about the Agency?"

"Well . . . well," he muttered, glancing down shyly. "I kind of value your opinion, and well, I know I'd probably never make it, but I kind of thought I might apply for a job with them when I get out.

"You know I only have about sixteen months left in the Army and—"

"Ski, I think the CIA is, for the most part, staffed with

people that are just as dedicated as we are. They work different. They have a different game plan. They're good folks, Calvin included, and they take some high-pucker-factor risks too.''

''So—so if someday I ask you for a recommendation—''

''In a fuckin' heartbeat, partner.''

''Great! And what about Colonel Kahn. Do you think—''

''Absolutely, but I'd think twice about asking him,'' I said, cracking a grin. ''He might recommend that you consider working for the fire department.''

I decided now was a good time to ask him about something I'd been putting off. I narrowed my eyes. ''This is your second mission. How do you feel about it? Primarily, the assassination requirement?''

He took a deep breath and glanced upward before answering. ''To tell you truthfully I've tried not to think about it. I kind of figured you'd be the one to do the actual kill.''

His head tilted slightly but his eyes stayed fixed on mine with a timid, empty look.

''Partner, if it comes down to a choice, I'll do it. But if and when I have to split the team, you're going to be on your own for a while, and . . . well, you need to be ready to handle it.

''There'll be no time for drum rolls and pep talks. You have to do it. Copy?''

He lowered his gaze and nodded. My purpose in planting the reminder in Ski was to keep him aware of mission requirements. In a less subtle way, Ivan Kahn had just instilled the same thing in me—and although I wasn't about to rush out and send him a thank-you card, I understood the colonel's reasoning.

I tapped Ski's shoulder. ''Come on. Let's go give the Cowboys a hand with the rigging.''

Walking onward I felt an uneasy kind of envy about Ski. In his own vague way he'd let me know that he had moral reservations about killing—at least the kind we were now assigned to do. I'd seen Arnold Binkowski laying down high-volume fire in the midst of the fucking mud and the blood and the bullets; he'd performed well and kept his wits about him. The first mission with Binkowski gave me confidence in his combat-grit. As Swede once said, "When your sphincter starts low-crawling up your anal canal even elephant Kotex won't help you get your shit together!"

Chapter 23

The bone-rattling roar of four Hercules C-130 engines hurled us down the runway and high into the dark Asian sky above Da Nang. As the g-force faded I loosened the tight grip of my seat belt and glanced at the luminous glow on my watch: 2310.

The team had been chuted up for over an hour now. I'd conducted a jumpmaster parachute inspection prior to boarding. No one had complained about the hurry-up-and-wait procedure.

During the preflight briefing the pilot had outlined his plan to dogleg northwest over Khe Sanh, then turn and skirt the southern edge of the DMZ eastward to Ben Hoi. At Ben Hoi he'd turn northwest again and vector north on an azimuth of 293 degrees. As we turned toward the Nickle Steel AO he planned to drop immediately to an altitude of five hundred feet AGL, black out running lights, and pour it on. The quick descent would indicate we were twelve minutes out.

At two minutes out he'd bounce up to nine hundred feet AGL and the loadmaster would open the aft jump doors. At one minute off target the pilot would throttle back to 125 knots jump speed. I'd requested a red light on as soon as we crossed the DMZ in order to alert the team. Since we were jumping into a no-light drop zone, I was counting on the navigator to put us in the pocket.

In the afternoon Stapleton had called in and coordinated with the Blackbird crew to let them know of his weather modification operation, but thirty minutes prior to takeoff Air Force radar showed clear skies in the AO.

Now, the soft drone of the engines indicated we'd leveled off at eight grand.

As jumpmaster I occupied the seat nearest the starboard troop door with Rham and Lok seated to my right. I glanced over the team. Ski, Phan, and Tuong were seated on the outboard port side of the dark aircraft. I had Ski positioned to push the stick. I planned to have the team standing up and hooked up four minutes out in order to give me time to conduct a check of the team. I'd put the first men in the doors and ready to rock one minute out.

As soon as we got the green light we'd unass the aircraft in less than five seconds.

My intention to stand the first jumpers in the door only one minute before jump was based on both my conception of human nature and personal experience. I'd been on jumps when the jumpmaster stood me in the door with a five-minute wait. It gave a man too much time to think about what could go wrong. My procedure would reduce that interval of paranoia to a minimum.

Leaning back into the webbed bench seat I smelled the familiar mingled scents of refrigerated air, nylon, and oil. I had jumped C-130s many times at Bragg—I felt comfortable.

Through the dim, cavernous interior I saw the drab silhouette of the stout loadmaster ambling down the starboard isle toward me.

"Pilot says, still no rain in the AO, Sarge," he shouted. I nodded.

"I got butt cans hanging over there if y'all wanna take a final smoke. Piss tubes back there if ya need 'em."

"Roger. Thanks!"

As he moved away I unlocked my seat belt and turned toward the helmeted figures of Rham and Lok and asked if they needed to take a piss. They both smiled and nodded no. I didn't bother to mention smoking. My team SOP didn't allow cigarettes on any mission.

Standing, I felt the cold nose of the Hush Puppy nudge my side. I moved slowly across the troop cabin feeling the strain of the heavy ruck hanging beneath my reserve parachute like an anvil.

I reached down and pulled the leg strap away from my crotch. Nearing Ski's side I yelled, "If y'all need to take a piss now's the time." I pointed rearward.

Ski waved an open palm indicating no.

I smiled and shouted, *"Ho bat coc toi."*

The Yards grinned as he yelled the reply and jutted his arm upward.

I jabbed my extended thumb out to him, then waddled with my swaying ruck to the troop door and peered out the porthole window.

The wingtip strobe light pulsed into the dark night.

I ran my finger around the door facing area checking for any obstructions that could screw up a jumper. None. I reached above my head and tugged on the steel-cable anchor line—taut.

After moving to the other door area I conducted the same check. Looking at the door, my mind keyed on the drone of engines. Strangely the last line of Earhart's poem drifted through my mind: ". . . Mountain heights where bitter joy can hear the sounds of wings."

"Everything okay, Sarge?" the loadmaster shouted from behind me.

Turning, I gave him a nod and a silent thumbs-up response.

He stepped closer and leaned to spit a small glob of chewing tobacco into a butt can. Looking up he drew his knuckles over his lips with a quick sweep of his hand. "Don't worry about being on target, Sarge. The cats flying this bird are second-tour pros from Dover." He grinned. "They spend so much time in the sky they get feathers under their armpits!"

"Roger," I said loudly. It was good to hear his confidence in the crew, but I'd already judged that they had their act together during the preflight session.

I remained standing and moved to center position in the cabin. Moments later I felt the aircraft bank left. My knees tensed as the Blackbird dropped. I steadied myself, holding the center isle seat structure.

On my left side I saw the loadmaster quickly don his intercom headset and plug in. Seconds later he leaned and held out an open hand, fingers spread, in front of my face. We were now rolling northbound twelve minutes out. Red light stabbed the darkness.

Tapping the loadmaster's shoulder, I pointed a thumb to my main parachute. "Pass me my static line!" I shouted.

He fumbled for a moment, freeing the steel mouth of the line from the chute, then passed it to me. I clipped it into my upper reserve handle.

Standing with my legs spread my adrenaline began to pump. I looked left, then right at the dark faces of RT Texas. "Get ready," I yelled, extending my arms outward and raising them upward. "Stand up!"

They unbuckled and struggled to rise from the troop seats as the Blackbird groaned to level off.

I waited for a second giving them a chance to pull the leg straps off their crotches.

"Hook up!" I yelled, forming a crook in my index fingers and moving each hand signal toward the steel cables above their heads.

The Cowboys strained to reach upward, trying to snap the steel static line mouth over the taut cables.

"Shit!" I muttered. I'd failed to anticipate they wouldn't be able to reach the fucking cable. I remembered that the aircraft we'd jumped at Long Tan had been rigged with lowered anchor lines. This one wasn't!

Rham hopped futilely trying to snap his hook over the cable. I stepped quickly forward to him and took his static line hook. I hooked him up and hurriedly inserted the safety wire through the pin hole at the base of the narrow steel hook. After repeating the same quick procedure with Lok, I glanced over and saw Binkowski assisting Tuong and Phan. "Okay," he yelled at me.

I carefully pulled a couple of feet of slack from the yellow static line crisscrossing the back side of Lok's main chute. I routed the thick cord over his right shoulder, then moved back to Rham and gave him some additional slack.

Moving to the other side I inspected all the static line anchor locations for proper safety pin insertion, then slacked and routed Ski's line over his left shoulder.

Glancing his equipment over I noticed the bolt window on his CAR-15 open. I snapped it shut and stepped onward to Phan. "You ready, babysan?" I yelled while hurriedly routing his static line.

"Rogee, Sar Brett!"

Seconds later I'd finished with Tuong and returned to center stage as the loadmaster jerked the sliding troop door upward. Warm wind and engine noise swirled through the dark crimson cabin. The incraft g-force told me the pilot was lofting to jump altitude. When he put the brakes on, decelerated, we'd be on the final slip over the target.

More racket-laden air rushed in as the loadmaster heaved the port troop door upward and locked it into position.

Grabbing the cold steel cable in my left hand, I snapped my static line anchor over it with my right hand, then jammed the retainer pin into the safety pin hole and bent it downward.

I planted my boots wide apart and yelled into the red-tinted faces before me, "Check static lines!"

Hands jerked downward testing the secure grip of steel on steel.

"Check equipment," I yelled, slapping my chest with both hands.

"Sound-off for equipment check!" I shouted, cupping palms behind my ears.

Vigilant eyes scanned their bodies; confident shouts of men bellowed through the blaring engine roar.

"Okay! Okay! Okay! Okay! Okay!"

I stepped quickly to the port side, gripped the steel door facing, and leaned out in the warm prop blast, peering rearward, then down.

Pulling in I half hopped to the starboard door and strained again, leaning into the black, moonless night.

I braced, feeling the quick drop of air speed as the ship slowed. Pulling back inside, a tobacco-laced breath near my face shouted, "One minute!"

"Stand in the door!" Adrenaline pumped as I slid my static line rearward, then leaned to peer out into the blackness above Rham's helmet. My eyes watered from the wind velocity.

I darted a glance to the port side jumper's silhouette. Tuong was poised—ready in the door.

Suddenly—red flicked green. Sucking my lungs full of midnight air I yelled, "Go!"

Chapter 24

The wind-rippled sounds of nylon unfurling in the black-stained night filled my ears just seconds before the opening jerk of a full canopy wrenched through me. I glanced upward at the dark blossomed shroud above, then quickly searched the cool night for other chutes. I counted five parabolic silhouettes, all near me—the exit had been tight. The soft drone of the Hercules faded.

Gazing down, I saw the vast mouth of the drop zone coming up quick—no time to judge lateral drift. Fumbling blindly beneath my reserve I found my quick-release straps, yanked outward, and felt the sharp tug of the felled ruck.

The foul breath of a breeze grazed my face as my boots impacted soft mud. I rolled left, feeling, smelling the squalid textured muck soak into my body. Stout ground wind caught my canopy, dragging me through the mud like a human plow. Grappling madly at the riser cape-well releases I tore away the metal shields and mashed both pressure buttons. My left risers fell away. I stopped, half buried in soft stench, as my canopy flapped, then died in the breeze.

I struggled to my feet and raked globs of mud away

from the rifle tied to my right side. After freeing my CAR-15 I cut my ruck from the drop line and hurriedly put it on.

Peering across the drop zone I saw several of the Yards gathering their equipment.

Moments later I had all the Cowboys present and accounted for, huddled on the northern grassy edge of Ghost Rider. Ski hadn't arrived at the DZ rally point and there'd been no sign of Bacsin.

Just as I started to dispatch two Yards to search for Ski I saw his big silhouette bogging across the DZ.

I waved him into our position and fanned the Yards out into a four-corner security.

Lumbering toward me I was amazed to see Ski clean above the knees.

Nearing me he whispered, "I did a stand-up landing. This was my best jump. What happened to you?" he asked, sniffing me. "You smell like—"

"Take Rham and skirt across this northern edge of the DZ and try to locate Bacsin. I'm going to contact Moonbeam and give them an infil report."

"Roger, but what are we gonna do about the parachutes? We can't leave 'em, can we?"

"Negative, partner. We'll handle that after linkup. Move!"

"I thought Calvin said we'd have rain and you know what else . . ."

"Move out, Arnold."

By 0235 we still hadn't located Mighty-Tight. The Yards cleared the DZ and found a depression near a thicket to cache our helmets and parachutes.

An hour later Tuong and I crept along the southern edge of the DZ in search of our contact when we felt the first droplets. Calvin's delayed promise.

Kneeling near a tree thicket I dug the map from my pocket and tried to locate our position. With no significant terrain features I couldn't be sure we'd hit the right area. I knew it was possible that Bacsin was waiting for us in another area if we'd somehow missed the DZ. But with the clear skies that prevailed during the infil it was doubtful that she hadn't seen the aircraft. She had to have some idea of our location.

We had landed in what appeared to be a huge, vacant rice-paddy zone dissected by dikes and levees and surrounded by low trees and grass. As the storm grew into the King Ranch cattle-pissing version it was obvious that Calvin's weather modification trick needed some calibration. Although the heavy rain obscured our vision as we continued to search, there was one benefit to the rain—if it continued through the night it would blank out the tracks we'd made on the drop zone.

I tucked the map away and whispered to Tuong who was squatted near me. "Put your poncho on, babysan. We go there," I said, pointing west.

"Why you no do same?"

I explained to him that I was going to let the downpour wash some of the stinking mud off me. I was already soaked from the infil, donning a poncho would be useless.

Strong winds lapped through the tall grass along the skirt of the drop zone.

Tuong moved stealthily ahead of me, stopping every few meters to listen. All I could hear was the wind and splatter of rain on his poncho.

After thirty minutes of futile searching we reached the southwest corner.

It was nearing 0400 hours. Now my concern was getting hemmed in to this area when first light yawned over us in less than two hours.

Tuong halted and took a piss near a small grove of trees. Peering into the chilly deluge around us I oriented my view eastward. If we were anywhere near the correct location, then the town of Dong Yen had to be approximately ten klicks east, roughly six miles.

If the rain held up to cloak our movement, it would only take us about an hour to traverse the distance if we kept a rapid pace. The absence of thick vegetation would make movement quick.

I decided to give our collective search another half hour, then move east and try to locate a suitable well-concealed area of observation.

Tuong's whisper brought my attention to him. He grinned and pointed west through the cold shroud toward a levee.

I squinted, seeing what looked like a water buffalo. Seconds later the silhouette was clearer. The buffalo was pulling a big cart along the levee road. A sloped hat peeked above the walls of the cart.

I led out through the swaying grass, motioning Tuong to follow.

We soon moved into a concealed position near the levee and waited.

I tensed as the buffalo plodded slowly closer. I could see the nostril vapor through the rain about twenty meters ahead of us.

Silently I pointed at Tuong and gave him a "talk" signal with my finger. I pointed at the approaching cart, then at my chest and quickly touched the muzzle of my rifle. He smiled and nodded, indicating he understood my signal and that he would move onto the path and issue the challenge while I covered him.

Seconds later I could see the conic-covered head moving slowly from side to side as if scanning the area paralleling the muddy road. No sign of a rifle or other weapon.

I eased my rifle down, reached beneath my wet shirt, and carefully withdrew the Hush Puppy.

With a gentle thumb movement I flipped it off safety and held my left hand palm up at Tuong.

Glancing up at the cart I could see a face through the droplets of water falling off the brim of my bush hat. A hand holding a long cane pole out over the animal was moving, tapping its back with slow rhythm. I decided to let it pass a few feet rather than risk Tuong getting trampled by the animal—if it suddenly bolted. I flicked my open hand, signaling Tuong into action.

The little Montagnard bounded upward, holding his rifle diagonally across his chest as I took point-blank aim on the figure.

"Ho bat coc toi!" he said loudly, jerking his rifle to ready position.

The cane pole raised and the cart halted as if the buffalo had been disconnected.

I held my aim as the figure slowly raised the long pole vertically. *"Troi sap mua,"* a soft voice replied. *"Troi sap mua."*

"Number-focking-one," Tuong muttered.

As I stepped from the roadside the dark figure stood. She had a large plastic bag hanging off her torso as a makeshift raincoat. The thin plastic contoured over her large breasts.

She smiled and repeated the reply.

"So this is Mighty-Tight," I whispered to myself.

Thunder clattered through the pelting rain as RT Texas sat huddled low in the high, jostling confines of the buffalo cart.

I hadn't counted on having transportation to the safe house, and although we could have jogged and walked the distance faster, the cart did provide one advantage: concealment.

During the slow ride to the safe house, I learned from Bacsin that she had two loyal assistants in the AO. They were an elderly Vietnamese couple who'd lost three sons over the past years to the war. The young boys had been conscripted by the NVA and sent into the Tet offensive with virtually no training. The parents were weary of war, aggrieved with the loss of their sons, and now staunchly opposed to the cruel methods of the NVA. I supposed their loyalty was somewhat sweetened by the money Bacsin paid them.

Initially the bold Mariposa trio had ventured to Dong Yen and ate at Bacsin's restaurant. But she'd only seen the three together on that one occasion.

Although she hadn't learned their names, she said they appeared "happy" and boasted that they had escaped the "Pig's War," and were waiting for their "sheep to come in." I assumed Bacsin meant "ship," rather than "sheep," but didn't question her pronunciation. They paid for their meals in North Vietnamese currency.

She added that during the triad visit two of the personnel, a young black man and a blond girl, appeared subservient to a larger white man who was talking the loudest.

The elder Vietnamese friends of Bacsin's had followed them to the town market where they observed them purchase pot and opium.

On two recent occasions only the white male, Defrisco, had dined at Bacsin's Rice Parlor.

Listening to Bacsin talk I was impressed with two things: her English vocabulary was better than I'd expected, and her observations brought out the human characteristics of the people she talked about.

She stood the entire distance, steadily tapping the buffalo with her pole as she talked casually out into the rainy night. I was hunched in the forward corner of the cart gazing up at her. Occasionally she'd glance down at me and say, "No ma far," which I finally decrypted to mean not much farther.

The team had edged away from me and remained silent. Although the rain had melted most of the muck off me, I could tell my deodorant wasn't working.

The safe house turned out to be the safe hut. It was positioned two klicks southwest of town in a sparse coastal forest. The large one-room hut was abutted by a water buffalo corral on one side, and another long combination rice thrashing hut and storage on the other side. There was an additional smaller hut, which the elders used as quarters. The rain obscured the surrounding area, but it looked to be flat and grassy.

After unloading and moving inside the big, plank-floored room, Bacsin lit a candle and left. She returned with the two elders.

They bowed politely, removing their sloped hats as she introduced the couple.

"Dis Papasan Lonwa Tran, an Ba Ngoc Tran."

Rising, the gray-goateed man spoke softly. *"Toi se bao ve anh."* He bowed again and so did his wife. "Da no Englee spek. Da sy, will take care you good."

Lonwa and Ngoc smiled through black-stained teeth.

I turned and introduced the team. The Yards returned a courteous bow but kept quiet. I reasoned that a half century of Vietnamese discrimination had taught them a lesson of cautious response when dealing with Vietnamese. Binkowski stepped forward, bowed, and replied with the only Vietnamese words he was certain of, hello. *"Chao-ong!"*

Ngoc moved near me, touching my mud-stained fatigues while muttering rapid-fire words: *"Coi do ra."*

Bacsin grinned. "She say take off clo. She wash for you."

I bowed. *"Khong,* thank you. Tell her it can wait till morning."

Bacsin never got the words out.

"Coi do ra!" the old woman growled again.

From the timid expression on Bacsin I gathered that age had its priority.

"Her say take off clo, now, so can have in morn."

I glanced around the big room looking for something to stand behind while my audience waited. Nothing in the hut would provide cover.

I didn't have any hang-ups about modesty; it was simply that I never wore underwear to the field.

About the time I saw mamasan drawing in another breath I held my hand up. "Okay! Wait! *Dung lai."*

I grabbed Tuong's poncho that he had laid across a small table and headed for the door. "You wait. *I'll be back.* I'll be back," I muttered, pacing out into the rain.

Chapter 25

When I returned to the hut Papasan Lonwa was laying out woven mats over low piles of straw for the team to bed down on. I handed over my wet fatigues to mamasan. I still didn't know how she planned on drying the fatigues, but didn't ask. Right now there were more important questions to broach with Bacsin.

When the old couple bowed and left, Bacsin remained. I kept my words slow. "When do you have to go back to Dong Yen?" I asked, watching her curious eyes inspect the sleeping area, and the Montagnards as they pulled poncho liners from their rucks.

"I go mornin when sun come," she answered, noticing a puddle of water near a box-framed straw bed in the corner. She took a long stick and jabbed it up into the thatched roofing. After poking at the thatch several times the drip stopped. "You sleeping here, Yon-cee," she said, pointing to the box straw bed.

"Thanks, but no. I sleeping there," I said, pointing to a mat along the wall by the Yards. I never allowed myself to enjoy a privilege that the Yards weren't allowed.

"Where you sleep?" I asked, taking a piece of twine from a ring hanger on the center hut support pole. I quickly tied it around the waist of my poncho to cut off some of the draft blowing up my draped plastic skirt.

Her eyebrows raised. "I'm slip wid old pepo," she said, taking a step closer to me. "You stink! You come."

Bacsin walked to the door, turned, and looked back at me. "You come," she said, making a low waving movement with her hand.

"She's right, Brett," Mr. Stand-up Landing blurted with a smirk.

I glanced at my watch: 0417. "Arnold, we've got a couple of hours till first light. You take watch till 0500. I'll take second watch. Douse that candle."

I followed Bacsin out of the hut and dashed across the rainy courtyard to a long open-sided hut.

She led me to a large rain barrel at the far end of the hut. Water cascaded off the roof and splattered into the full barrel.

Taking my hand in hers, she pulled me to the edge of the barrel and began splashing water over the mud residue on my arms. I saw a trace of her smile in the dim rainy shadows.

"I can do this, you know. You don't—"

"Have custom here. I do," she said, reaching to pull the waist string off my poncho. "Take off poncha."

I remembered Calvin saying she liked Americans. As I complied with her orders I felt like I was being set up for some close-quarters inspection.

Standing naked, with only my boots, bush hat, and holstered Hush Puppy on, I felt a chill ripple down my spine. I removed my weapon and placed it on the soap shelf above the rain barrel.

Using a moistened soapy cloth she washed my shoulders and chest. As her massaging fingers moved down my lower abdomen I watched her face.

She smiled, letting her hand move gently over my hips. Then she folded the cloth over the length of my cock and stroked. "You like," she whispered, darting a glance up, then back down.

Discipline, Yancy, I silently reminded myself while thinking this would be a perfect opportunity to conduct the fabled nipple inspection.

Releasing her grip she said, "You turn, please."

After turning she hurriedly washed my back and buttocks. She pressed her plastic-covered torso against my back, moved her hands around to the front of my hips, then down over my groin.

"I have a custom too."

"Wha custom you have?"

Turning to face her I winked. "My custom is, I always wash the person who washes me."

"You wan wash me?" She giggled.

"Yes," I answered, dipping my hand into the barrel to splash water over my chest and stomach.

She smiled as I reached to pull the plastic bag up and over her head. I laid the bag aside and watched her unbuttoning her black shirt.

Slipping the dark garment over her shoulders and off, my gaze fixed on her prominent breasts.

Her smile broadened. "You like?" she asked, handing the cloth to me.

I dipped the cloth into the barrel, then squeezed the water out before placing my hand onto her chest. "Yes. Very beautiful," I answered, carefully moving the cloth over a nipple. The unobstructed movement confirmed Stapleton's report about the inverted nipples. In the darkness I couldn't determine the "splendid pink" color he'd mentioned, but it was apparent enough—this was the real Mighty-Tight in person.

After washing her shoulders and arms she started to remove her pants.

"Wait. I think that's enough for now. Let's sit and talk," I whispered, handing the shirt back to her.

"You no wan me," she said with a slight pout on her lips.

I'd never met a woman who handled rejection well. For that matter, neither did I, but this was not the time or place to get into a heavy-breathing exercise. I decided "no" was not the right answer. "Yes, of course I want you but . . . well, you see I need to ask you some questions and—"

"I'm understan. You man who think abou job fur, then fun. Yes?"

I couldn't have invented a better excuse if I had a staff of *Playboy* advisers helping me.

"Yes. That's right, Bacsin. We can have fun when I get this mission accomplished, finished. Okay?"

"Yes. I'm be helping you all can. I'm wan focking you good, Yon-cee."

"I want same-same, Bacsin," I replied as I took the Hush Puppy and put it on. She smiled and jostled her breasts at me playfully before putting her shirt on.

After shifting the poncho back over my body we sat on a bench adjacent to the barrel.

Bacsin lit a cigarette and edged forward exhaling the smoke lazily into the cool night. "Befo we talk I'm nee ask you sumting."

"Sure. What?"

"Cal-ven give you breeng gol for me?"

Studying her subtle expression I decided that it wasn't my irresistible charm that motivated Bacsin's sexual interest in me. It now occurred to me that Mighty-Tight never lost a grip on her business interests.

"Roger, I have gold for you," I said, telling her that I

was ordered to give it to her upon our exfiltration. I figured she'd be a little more attentive to our needs if she knew payday was near. "Let's talk about the big American, Donald Defrisco. When and where was the last time you saw him?"

Mighty-Tight and I talked for almost an hour. I asked her leading questions about her mother and Monsieur Pollas, her father, then moved the conversation toward mission-related questions.

The most significant discovery I made was accidental; Bacsin did not know anything about the presence of the Device. When she asked what "the Device" was, I masked an answer and told her it was a large mechanical instrument used to encrypt top-secret data.

It bothered me that Calvin hadn't told me that Bacsin did not know of the SADM. It seemed there was no logical explanation for why he'd failed to tell me that. I reasoned it was natural that the CIA didn't want their agent knowing there was a loose nuclear bomb in the AO, but what prevented Stapleton from sharing that with me?

I learned that during DD's last solo visit to the restaurant he'd talked freely with an NVA officer who was one of Mighty-Tight's "boyfriends." She learned later from the officer that DD had told the NVA that his rank was spec-four, and he'd deserted and made his way to Vinh Son to await a Portuguese ship so he could escape to Europe. It was clever for Defrisco to downplay his rank—it made him a less valuable source of interest to the NVA. Listening to her chronicle of Defrisco it was apparent the NVA considered him little more than a tolerable amusement.

But I thought it strange that Defrisco hadn't mentioned anything about Gordon or Abbey to the NVA officer.

It was Bacsin's belief that Defrisco was staying at a *katch-san,* a small hotel, in Vinh Son. When I asked her if opium was available there, she told me that a *nha-hot,* an opium den, was part of the *katch-san.* She boasted that her restaurant was much better than anything available in Vinh Son and that the reason people would travel the nine-mile distance was to enjoy her famous French cuisine.

The common method of travel between Dong Yen and Vinh Son was taxi, bicycle, or bus. She mentioned that although cover and concealment was sparse along the road, there was one remote area a klick outside the small village of Dai Hoi, where the coastal road turned inland through a thick grove of trees.

Bacsin only shrugged and said, "Who know," when I asked if she had any idea when Defrisco might visit her restaurant again.

As dawn approached she said she needed to return to Dong Yen. Her sleepy eyes indicated she'd prefer to stay.

I asked her to bring some civilian peasant clothes on her return tonight—clothes that would fit my Montagnards.

Chapter 26

Calvin's synthetic storm began to subside into light rain as Bacsin and buffalo ambled slowly along the path. She'd told me that the Trans would be with us and would help in any way we asked.

When I returned to the central hut I found Ski asleep—Tuong had taken up the watch at the door.

"You sure take long bath, Sar Brett. What else you do?" he asked with an insinuative grin.

"I talked, babysan," I said, stepping inside and noticing my fatigues hanging neatly across a bamboo stick. I felt the pants. "How did she dry these?" I muttered to myself.

"Her maybe use fire. I see fire over dare." Tuong pointed out the door toward the small hut. Yellow light flickered beneath the hanging door curtain.

"You wan I make coffee, Sar Brett?"

"Not a bad idea, partner."

After putting on clean, dry fatigues I double-checked our position on the map, then coded a fast situation report for my first scheduled contact with Moonbeam at 0600 hours. I had about ten minutes to spare before contact time.

I woke Ski and told him to get the radio set up and ready.

The contact with Moonbeam was brief. I transmitted my message first and asked if they had traffic for me. None.

I'd deliberately kept the message short in order to limit any RDF. I knew it was likely the NVA scanned our UHF frequency spectrum and if they'd heard any of my signal they'd at least know there was an alien transmitter somewhere in their range. My next contact was at 2100 hours. I planned to keep all contacts short.

As the remainder of the team started to wake, I put on a poncho.

"Where you going, Brett?" Ski asked.

I took a sip of coffee and handed the canteen cup to him. "I'm taking Tuong with me to do a short north-side recon while we still have some low-light conditions.

"I want you to take Rham and do a hundred-meter box recon of the western area. Try to find that abandoned antiaircraft position and make sure it's inactive. Be careful and be back here by 0800."

Bacsin had told me the safe-house area was isolated, several klicks from the main road. I estimated the road was about two klicks east of our location. I wanted to get a look at the surrounding terrain in case we had to move. I hoped to find a suitable first-rally-point to use if we got hit.

I wasn't going to be too bold with my presence during daylight hours; anyone over six feet tall could be spotted at a considerable distance in this area. My eventual plan was to break the Cowboys into two two-man surveillance teams, once I got the clothes I'd ordered from Bacsin. Initially, I'd have them recon the tree grove near Dai Hoi, then skirt the road southward, toward Vinh Son.

My long-shot hope was that we could intercept Defrisco or one of the Mariposa somewhere along the road, capture one or more of them, and get down to some serious questions and answers right away.

As I moved slowly eastward through the fog with Tuong I remembered something Tracy had once told me about myself: "You tend to be an optimist about things, Brett." I'd replied that anything less than optimism was a tree farm for paranoia. Then, to put things in perspective, I quoted a friend of mine who was working with Delta: "Optimism is fine, but just remember, if everything's going great, chances are it's a trap."

"Sar Brett, you look-see," Tuong whispered, pointing through the elephant grass toward the southern road zone.

I wiped the water off my binoculars, rose, and scanned the misty distance.

I could see a large truck stopped in the center of the muddy highway.

Pith-helmeted figures were moving off into the east side of the ditch that paralleled the corridor. Their AKs were at sling arms, which told me whatever they were doing wasn't critical. "No dogs," I whispered.

Crouching, I tucked the field glasses away and motioned Tuong to follow me.

I moved along the grass line toward the truck. I hadn't counted on a squad-sized NVA element being in the area, but I was glad we'd spotted them first.

Nestling myself into a well-concealed grassy area sixty meters ahead of the vacant truck, I took out my map. The area we were in was near the exfil location Calvin had noted in red. With no idea what they were up to, I decided to wait. The salt-scented air of the South China Sea laced through the pale fog as we lay in wait.

Thirty-five minutes later the light fog began to dissipate. It was nearing 0730.

I told Ski to return by 0800 and I knew we needed to be headed back too. What concerned me most about daylight movement was the potential for aerial overflight by Soviet MIGs patrolling the coast. So far we hadn't seen or heard any aircraft, but it would only take one sharp-eyed pilot to bring the world in on us.

Tuong nudged me and whispered that he'd seen movement near the truck.

I pulled the binoculars to my eyes and watched the soldiers stumble up the sandy ditch embankment carrying crates. One dropped his wooden box, spilling some of the contents. I focused on the ground around his feet, hearing the distant loud chatter of the men.

"Fish," I muttered.

"Wha you say?" Tuong whispered.

"Fish. They're loading boxes of fish."

Moments later black diesel smoke bellowed from the truck as it whined past our position. My guess was that they were buying food for the K-9 training center personnel. It appeared that the fishing village Calvin mentioned was located about one hundred or so meters off the road, due east.

The NVA I'd observed were not wearing magazine vests, which indicated the local troops were in a lax attitude.

When we returned to the safe hut Ski and Rham were still out. I sent Lok to post himself sixty meters down the dirt path to provide security along the corridor as an early warning against intrusion. I told him I'd rotate another man into the guard slot every two hours through the remainder of the day.

It was almost 0845 when Ski and Rham returned. They

hadn't located the AA battery, nor had they seen any personnel in the area.

"About all we saw was a daylight version of what we went through last night," Ski remarked.

We heated water with heat-tabs and prepared our LRPRs.

Mamasan Tran came into the hut as we ate.

I thanked her for the one-hour martinizing service. She went about the large room sweeping and re-forming the individual piles of straw, then laid the mats carefully over them.

When she left I conducted a map orientation with the team and explained my night recon plan. I told the Yards they'd be wearing civilian clothes tonight and that I planned to try and locate a static vigil area to observe the road running through the tree grove.

I explained that our ultimate goal was to conduct a kidnaping with a quick hit and run.

I emphasized that if any kills had to be made during the seizure, on extraneous personnel in the area, that it had to be done with the Hush Puppies—either Ski or myself would make the determination.

After plotting a primary and alternate E and E route and the rally points, I made sure the Yards understood it. I told Tuong to explain the plan to Lok when he went to relieve Lok at the pathway vigil position.

"Brett, are you aware that if the Yards are caught wearing civilian clothes they can be shot as spies?" Ski asked matter-of-factly.

Tuong tapped Binkowski and spoke before I could answer. "Hey, that no big deal, Skee. We caugh, we die anyho."

I nodded at Ski. "He's right, partner. The NVA don't care if they're wearing tuxedos or tiger stripes."

• • •

The remainder of day one was blanketed with more heavy rain and boredom. By zero-dark-thirty Bacsin hadn't returned.

When I'd sent Rham, the third shift guard, out to relieve Tuong, I also sent one of our two radios with him. I cautioned Rham not to use verbal commo unless he felt it was critical. I told him we would monitor the common frequency and that he was to break squelch three times if Bacsin came into view. If anybody but Bacsin came along the path I instructed him to break squelch "like his hand was on fire."

As we waited Ski busied himself writing a letter to Megan. I didn't know where he planned on mailing it, but he seemed consoled in the moment.

Phan was seated beneath the porch overhang with the radio hand receiver pressed to his ear. I was anxious for Bacsin's return so we could get the Yards suited up and to conduct our night recon on the tree grove. On the initial trip I planned to take Rham and Lok with me and have Ski remain at the hut to make the 2100 contact with Moonbeam.

"Sar Brett," Phan said, raising his free hand. "I'm hear *mot hai, ba*!"

"Good," I said, grabbing my poncho. I put it on and stepped outside to watch Bacsin approach.

Moments later she arrived. I took a large box out of the cart and carried it inside with her following.

"I'm bring same-same here for you to, Yon-cee," she said, cheerfully pointing to the plastic sack raincoat she had on.

"Great, thank you."

After opening the box I distributed the Goodwill clothing to the Yards and told Rham and Lok to make a quick change and get ready to move out with me.

Removing her rain cover Bacsin sat on the edge of the box bed.

The candlelight glittered off her soft features as she spoke. "I'm have good new for you, maybe."

She explained that she'd heard of a fire in Vinh Son at the opium den. The fire had supposedly damaged the little hotel area where Defrisco was hanging his hat these days. It was Bacsin's feeling that the Mariposa would likely move to Dong Yen since the small town of Vinh Son didn't have another hotel.

I wasn't sure how encouraging Bacsin's news was but at least it was intel. It was also the first indication that she was trying to provide me with timely information.

I knew she'd received her news secondhand, but if the Mariposa was now out on the streets so to speak, and if Bacsin's guesswork was correct, it wouldn't take long for them to travel to Dong Yen for accommodations.

Suddenly I wished I were lying in ambush along the road with a good area of observation right now.

I struck a match and held it to her cigarette while speaking. "You know they could be taking a taxi to Dong Yen tonight. If that happens we'll miss—"

"No do tonigh," she said, blowing a stream of smoke into the air.

"Why's that?" Ski asked quickly.

"Becau, law say no truk, no car go nigh."

"Why?" Ski asked again.

Glaring at Arnold she said, "You no lis-in. I'm say becau law say no trabel nigh!"

"She's telling us the NVA don't allow vehicular traffic along that road at night," I explained.

"Oh, I see," he said, studying Bacsin's chest.

I yanked the map from my pocket and opened it on the tabletop. Studying the coastline I asked, "What's to keep them from moving south toward—toward Hoa Thuong?"

Bacsin walked to the table and slipped her arm around my waist as she looked down at the map. "See here," she said, pointing at the map and pecking her finger along the coastline around the area near Hoa Thuong.

"Sumtime many bum fall here. They no go where bum go."

"You mean bombs fall there, right?"

"That wa I'm say. Bum fall!"

I remembered Calvin telling me that the area of operation in which Bacsin was located was exempted from bombing runs. Evidently anything south of Vinh Son was open season. Her reasoning seemed valid because even if Defrisco didn't know of the bombing he'd find out quick from any local he tried to hire to take him there.

I slipped away from Bacsin's waist grip, turned, and leaned against the table facing her at eye level. "So you think they'll be coming to Dong Yen tomorrow sometime?"

"Yes. I tink yes becau we having *katch-san* in Dong Yen and him liking my foo. And I'm also tink da come morning."

I winked. "Well, darlin', there's a lot of what-ifs about all this, but I'll throw in one more.

"If they're coming north tomorrow by road, we'll be waiting with our best smile!"

I walked to the door and turned back to Mighty-Tight. "Did you ever have a flat tire on your water buffalo?"

She giggled. "Fla tire? Buff-lo no have tire."

Chapter 27

Although I knew it was possible that DD and company could take a boat ride up the coast to Dong Yen I'd decided not to crowd another what-if into the scenario. Right now I was going to let my optimism run half throttle and hope that Bacsin knew what she was talking about.

Before departing with Rham and Lok I instructed Ski on how to code a short message.

The message I gave him was simple: continuing mission. Negative contact.

I told Binkowski we planned to recon the tree grove location to determine if it was a suitable ambush/kidnap zone, then skirt the highway south for a ways, then head back in.

We'd return by 0130 hours via the cart road and bring our guard in with us. I wanted the team, and Bacsin, to get at least four to five hours' sleep before we crept out at first light to begin our monitor of the road.

As we left, Bacsin asked if I needed her to come with us. Since I really didn't anticipate any problem finding the grove I told her to get some sleep. Looking down into her concerned eyes I said, ''Darlin', you rest, because tomorrow you are going to experience your first flat tire on a water buffalo.''

By 2230 hours we were still moving steadily northeast toward the area where I hoped to see the silhouette of trees rising out of the grassy fields.

Rham kept a quick pace through the windy night. The rain had stopped shortly after we departed. The terrain we crossed on our northern trek was mostly dormant rice paddies overgrown with weeds.

Rham and Lok both wore civilian clothes with the standard plastic-bag raincoats and carried their CAR-15s. My reasoning for putting them in local costume was to free them up for inconspicuous movement if I encountered something that needed a closer inspection.

If close recon proved necessary, I'd have them leave their weapons with me and I would cover them from a distance. Before leaving the hut I borrowed Ski's Hush Puppy and gave it to Rham.

Moving through the desolate fields the stout breeze whipped over the plastic sacks the Yards had on, giving a crackling sound in the darkness.

We maintained a compass azimuth of 010 degrees for several hundred meters.

We crossed two east–west oriented footpaths before reaching the main road.

We hadn't seen the grove as we crept closer to the highway.

Right now it boiled down to a choice—left or right. I decided to stay in position and send Rham left and Lok right along the road. I told them to go no more than two hundred meters each, then return.

"Leave rifles here," I whispered, pulling my Hush Puppy out. I handed the pistol to Lok, showing him the safety was off.

They both grinned, nodded, and departed their separate directions.

Using the road I knew they would make good time. I knew it was unlikely they'd encounter anyone this time of night.

I settled into a wet, grassy spot behind a knoll at the road's edge and waited. If they didn't find the trees while skirting a span totaling four hundred meters, then either I needed a refresher course in land navigation or Bacsin needed glasses.

I pulled a red-filter flashlight off my web harness and studied the map. If Mighty-Tight's information was correct, it would more likely be Rham who discovered the elusive bend-in-the-road tree grove.

Suddenly I became alert to the rapidly approaching sound of boots splattering against water and mud.

I killed the light and hugged wet earth. A second later the small figure of Lok sprinted into view. He dove headfirst over the knoll and scrambled to my side.

"Truck . . . come," he whispered.

Through a labored breath I heard the strain of an engine, then saw the dull yellow glow of headlights.

"Did they see you?"

"Don't tink see."

We stayed low as the NVA version of a dark three-quarter-ton truck rounded the bend in low gear.

The profiles of two men were visible in the cab. The bed was covered with a canvas—so much for the no-vehicles-at-night story, I thought to myself.

The vehicle was moving slow, about five miles per hour. I was hopeful that Rham would hear the diesel before the headlights caught him.

The thought of ambushing the truck dribbled across my mind like a slow-motion basketball. I'd rush the truck and be on the running board pouring Super-val lead into them before they could say fucking Ho Chi Minh. I could put Rham and Lok in the NVA uniforms and elevate us to mobile status.

Then I remembered a Special Forces rule of thumb about targets of opportunity: "Let sleeping alligators lie unless you know the swamp well."

Right now I didn't "know the swamp" at all. It was possible there was another truck following at a distance. And I hadn't been able to determine if there were troops in the covered section. As the vehicle passed our position I could hear chatter and laughter coming from the cab. They sounded drunk.

We maintained our position for several minutes after the vehicle disappeared.

Easing out onto the muddy road I decided to follow the direction the truck was heading.

Lok and I took up a quick pace staying in the vehicle's tracks. About eighty meters later the road curved right; steps father on, we saw the dim, animated silhouette of tall trees swaying in the wind. They weren't sequoias but they'd do. The thick lofty branches would provide concealment from air observation. The curve in the road was almost hairpin—any Tijuana taxi rounding the corner would have to slow down to make the curve.

Turning to Lok I whispered, "See that thicket?"

"Rog-ee."

"In morning I put you and Ski there with radio to watch road. You remember this place. Okay?"

"Okay."

It was beginning to bother me that we hadn't seen or heard from Rham. We walked the forty-meter distance through the tree-shrouded road to the clear end. Not a peep from Rham.

Returning back through the center of the corridor I felt something strike my back.

Turning, I saw Lok grinning and pointing up at a tree branch. Rham was squatted on the low limb waving at us.

During our return to the hut area it occurred to me that I'd discovered another Montagnard talent. I decided to tailor my roadway ambush plan and put Rham up in a tree to watch for approaching vehicles.

When he spotted something I'd have him drop a stone into Ski and Lok's radio site. They could immediately alert me at the intercept zone near the center of the grove.

It was 2317 when Rham, Lok, Phan, and I returned to the hut area. We'd pulled Phan off the road guard position during our reentry. The rain and wind had subsided leaving the night etched with only the soft sound of water dripping into puddles beneath the roof's edge.

As we entered the hut the dim candlelight revealed Tuong squatted near the far end of the room with his back to us. He turned and smiled while holding a slender bamboo stick in his hand.

"What you do, babysan?" I asked, slipping my rifle carrying strap over my head.

"I'm try kill rat. He down dare," Tuong answered, pointing the stick into a wide space between the planks.

Rham and Lok began wiping down their weapons and the Hush Puppies while Phan did the same to the PRC-25.

"Where's Ski?"

"Him take walk," Tuong answered.

"Take walk . . . where's Bacsin?"

"Her walk wid Ski. Be gone maybe one hour."

I draped my poncho over a low crossbeam and removed my web gear. "Y'all get ready to hit the rack. We have early day tomorrow. I take the first watch, then Ski, Phan, Lok, Rham, and babysan.''

Tuong went back to his rat hunt surveillance. I walked to his side and looked down. He held the pointed stick above the plank opening as if he planned to spear the rodent when it came into view. ''Dis rat try bite me tonigh. I'm kill.''

I turned and walked outside looking for Ski. A moment later I found him sitting with Bacsin near the rain barrel. Seeing me approach he quickly handed a lighted cigarette to her.

''Oh, hi, Brett,'' he said, standing abruptly. ''How did the recon go?''

Binkowski had that freshly fucked look all over his face. ''Went good. Did you make contact with Moonbeam?'' I asked while casting a courteous nod to Bacsin. She smiled and remained seated.

''Uh, roger. They didn't have any traffic for us, partner,'' he answered, shoving his hands in his pockets and looking out into the night. ''Rain stopped.''

''Yeah, I noticed that too. Bacsin, I'm going to have the team up at 0400. Can you be at the hut about then? I want to go over my plan with everybody.''

She dropped her cigarette and stood crushing it beneath her foot. ''Yes, I be wid you like say. I say good nigh and go sleep now.''

After bidding Bacsin good night I turned back to Arnold. ''Your shirt is buttoned up lopsided, partner.''

''Oh,'' he said, looking down. ''I washed off . . . a while ago and guess I—''

''Did Bacsin give you a hand washing?''

''Well . . . yeah, you know she said it was a habit, a social—''

''Custom?''

"Yeah, custom. That's it! And you know what else?" he said, keeping his attention on his fingers as he rebuttoned his shirt.

I leaned against a wooden support post. "No, what else?"

"Well, well, you see, I could kind of tell, she was attracted to me, and well, I figured it was a perfect time to, I mean, check out her—her . . . her—"

"Her nipples?" I assisted.

"Roger, you know," he muttered, nodding his head at me with a dramatic frown, "like Calvin told us. I was keeping my mind on the mission, Brett," he said proudly. "And Bacsin is definitely Mighty-Tight!"

I took a piece of ration chewing gum from my pocket and put it in my mouth. "Well, that's great, buddy. But I wish I'd told you earlier. . . . I made that determination last night. Gosh, I could have saved you the trouble."

"What . . . you mean? You mean . . . I was, sec . . . second?"

I grinned. "Well, after all. You are the One-One, Arnold." I tapped him on the shoulder. "Thanks for your effort, partner. Now I've got some ambush site info you need to know about."

Chapter 28

"And remember, gang, no rifle fire unless the shit is clogging the fan," I emphasized, shifting a quiet stare to everyone gathered around the small candle-lit table. "If any hits have to be made it will be done by me or Ski, with these." I held a black Hush Puppy vertically in my grip, then slid it down into my shoulder holster.

I folded the map, placed it into my shirt pocket, and tossed a question to Rham. "What's your job?"

"I stay twee look for v-call come. When see v-call come I drop rock on Ski to tell v-call come."

"You don't have to drop the rock directly on me, Rham, okay? I mean, don't try and knock me out," Binkowski responded.

"Okay, no knock out Skee when drop rock," Rham echoed.

"All right, what's next?"

I pointed to Ski; he took a deep breath. "I tap Lok who will give you three squelch breaks on the radio to notify you. Then I, as you say, glue my binoculars on the road and try to see if there is a big-looking American in the car. If I determine that either Defrisco, a blond female, or black male is in the car, I hold five fingers up to Lok,

who will break squelch five times. When they pass my
position I will have Lok give you another three squelch
breaks. If, for some reason, I can't see who is in the vehicle, I give you one squelch break. At no time will I
initiate verbal commo unless the situation is critical."

"Roger. Perfect. Now, Lok, what happens if we see a
vehicle approaching from our end, from north?"

Lok grinned. "You gibbing five sqa bak to me and I'm
tell Skee."

"Roger. And remember that y'all need to stay well concealed, hidden, until the vehicle gets on past you."

Ten minutes later I was convinced that everyone knew
their actions at the objective. In the interest of time I decided not to try to conduct a rehearsal. I estimated first
light at 0545; that gave us about one hour to move to the
ambush location and get into position. I instructed all of
the Yards, except Tuong, to wear civilian clothes. I wanted
him, Ski, and myself in full battledress.

Turning to Bacsin, I asked, "Do you understand what
to do?"

"Yes. I'm understan."

"Do you have any questions?"

"Yes pleasing, one. Maybe, can Skee ride me in cart?"

Bacsin's disjointed question was probably closer to what
she really had in mind than she intended for it to be. She'd
stood near Ski during my entire early morning briefing and
given him that I'm-wan-focking-you-good look several
times.

I kept my tone objective. "No, Bacsin, Ski needs to
move to the target with us. You know, in case we get hit."

I didn't have any heartburn about Binkowski's previous
amorous civil-action performance with Bacsin. But I knew
if I let Ski ride with her, nature would likely take its course
again—intercourse—somewhere along the way. I didn't

want them arriving late for the show; and exhausted before the curtain went up.

My plan required Mighty-Tight to take her cart down the road and hook north as if she were on her normal route back to Dong Yen.

RT Texas would move cross-country and be in position when she came around the curve. I'd then intercept Bacsin and position her and her buffalo cart off to the side of the road, and wait. When, and if, I got five squelch breaks, I'd move her into a center road lateral position as a block to the vehicle. The vehicle would have to slow to make the hairpin curve. When the driver saw Buffalo Bacsin in his path and stopped, I'd move with Tuong covering me. I'd then nail the driver and seize any or all of the Mariposa at gunpoint. I was aware that my act would have to be swift.

I expected Defrisco, and perhaps the others, to be armed. But these dopers were not instant-action combat troops—they were garrison-type bureaucrats, like so many others in this war. I was counting on the element of surprise, combined with the horror of the driver-kill, to rattle their bones into quivering-lipped submission.

If I met with resistance from any of them my hit priorities were simple: Kill the puppets and keep the puppet master.

Once I'd gained control I'd signal Bacsin homeward. I planned to drive the vehicle back to the safe area and park it under the long thrashing hut. If I left it on or anywhere near the road, it would be a red flag.

There were three what-if holes in my plan—one, if any other vehicle came along while we were "conducting business" it had to be eliminated. And then I inherited the immediate problem of disposing of the vehicle. Two, if by some chance DD and company had hitched a ride north in a covered military vehicle it was very likely Ski could not determine Mariposa's presence. If that occurred the vehicle would still have to stop—I'd then have to make a decision about moving in based on the number, if any, of armed NVA on board.

The third hole was the big one—a Mariposa no-show. All I could do was hope that Murphy's proverbial law didn't get that far into our act.

An SF instructor had once posed the question to me during an ambush class: "What do you do if you set up an ambush and nobody comes?"

"Wait," I'd answered.

"Wrong! You move out quietly and don't even think about using the same site again."

As we gathered our gear to move out I glanced around the room. "If anybody needs to take a shit do it before we leave."

A pale curtain of first light crept through the dank, tangled shadows of our concealed position. Bacsin hadn't arrived yet. I checked my watch: 0558.

Tuong lay silent beside me studying the muddy road to our front.

Phan was positioned twenty meters to our left to observe the flat north stretch of road. He'd just given me an in-position arm wave.

I kept the radio receiver clipped to the shoulder harness. I'd placed the radio between Tuong and me. I'd decided to miss the 0600 contact with Moonbeam. The absence of one contact wasn't going to bother our monitor aircraft— two would.

It was Sunday morning in Southeast Asia. Bacsin had told me that traffic along the road would be sparse, "little bit" until late morning. If heavy rain came she estimated there would be virtually no traffic because of the already muddy conditions of the road.

The sharp murmur of one squelch break intruded. I'd instructed Ski to notify me when Bacsin came into view with one single break.

Moments later the black, horned silhouette of the buffalo ambled lazily down the road with Bacsin's pole tapping lightly over the animal's back. I handed the receiver to Tuong. "You stay," I said, pushing up from the wet, matted ground and moving out into the road. Using an arm signal I guided her into an area thirty meters beyond the curve and off to the right side.

Picking up a long branch I broke it in half and walked to a spot about ten meters to the left front of the animal. I placed the sticks in an X configuration in the middle of the road and mashed them into the mud with my boot.

I pointed down at the sticks while glancing at Bacsin.

Pacing to the side of the cart I looked up at her. "Will you have any trouble getting your buffalo in that spot when I give you the signal?" I asked quietly.

"Spot? Wha is spot?"

"That place. That X," I answered, holding my crossed fingers up to her.

Her eyebrows raised. "Oh, yes I'm do now."

"No, Bacsin. Wait until I do this," I said, exaggerating the waving arm signal I planned to use. "You move there when I do this. Understand, darlin'?"

She smiled. "Is gud. I'm understan."

I winked. "Okay. It could be hours until they get here. Try to stay awake," I said encouragingly.

"Yon-cee."

"Yes, what is it?"

"When you fini here I'm go Dong Yen. Rih?"

"Right."

"When I'm come tonigh you wan I breeng sum foo for you tim? I having *beaucoup* good foo."

I glanced down the tree-shrouded road, then back up at her. "Thanks but no, Bacsin. Maybe later, okay?"

"Okay."

The thought of eating something other than a rice and fish heads LRPR was tempting, but I didn't want to chance any skeptical eyes seeing her load food into her cart and following her. As I eased back into my vigil position beside Tuong I made myself a silent promise to take the team into Da Nang when we got back, for a good store-bought meal.

It was nearing 0900 hours and the morning sun's heat was beginning to penetrate the tree grove. So far we'd had a total of one southbound pedestrian pushing a bicycle and one small northbound bus through the zone. The pedestrian stopped and asked Bacsin what was wrong.

As near as I could understand, listening from the distance, she told the man her buffalo was tired and she was giving the animal a break. The man laughed and patted his empty bicycle seat indicating, it seemed, that she should trade her buffalo cart in on a bike.

I was starting to feel tired, bored, and hungry. My team was probably feeling about the same—we'd skipped morning chow. Now, the thought of Bacsin's French food was becoming more tempting.

During the first hour Bacsin had stood faithfully in her cart. The second hour found her sitting, and now I could see her starting to nod off. I knew Rham had to be getting tired of his tree-perch position.

By 1010 hours there had been no additional traffic.

Tuong nudged my arm. I looked and followed his pointed finger upward to a long green viper crawling through the branches just above our heads. It was moving

toward us at a too-close-for-comfort range. I gently pulled
my HP and took aim.

Tuong touched my pistol hand. "Sar Brett," he whispered. "That good snake. He like eat rat. No kill." He
smiled.

"No poison?" I questioned in a whisper.

"No po-sin. Good snake." He nodded.

"Okay. You get snake put here," I said, reaching to tap
the right side cargo pocket of his fatigues.

Tuong reached slowly upward, then jabbed his hand into
the branches, grabbing the thick reptile near the head. He
jerked his hand several times yanking the snake loose from
its wrapped grip on the limb. As he wrestled the writhing
viper to the ground the long body slapped across my face.

The snake quickly coiled around Tuong's arm. He held
its head down into his pocket while I gripped the tail and
began to unwind the snake from its spiral grasp. I shoved
a wad of the tail into Tuong's pocket. Tuong released the
head and pushed the remainder of the snake in, then fas-
tened both flap buttons on the pocket.

"Why you wan snake? You hungry?" he said, rolling
back to his prone position.

I peered back to make a check of the road. "That's
right, babysan. I'm hungry."

At 1100 the Asian sun thermostat was rising. The hu-
midity was bringing out some of the special stinks that I
thought were only found in Laos.

I decided it was time to head in and dig out the drawing
board again. I hoped that when Bacsin returned that night
she'd have news about whether the Mariposa had made it
in to Dong Yen. It was possible that her theory about them
not moving south was wrong.

We'd been in position over five long hours and all we
had to show for it was one three-foot green snake. The

good news was that the lack of military traffic on the road and the absence of aircraft in the area indicated we'd slipped into Nickle Steel without detection.

"Tuong, you go down there and get Phan," I said, shifting my arms into the radio pack straps. "I'm going to call Ski and tell him we're moving out."

I noticed Bacsin asleep. "Wake her and the buffalo up while you're out there," I said, pointing to the cart.

"Rogee, Sar Brett."

Suddenly three distinct noises whispered from the handset.

"Bacsin!" I blurted in a loud whisper. "Bacsin! Wake up, darlin'."

Tuong and I dropped back into our spot. I kept the handset pressed tightly to the side of my head.

Seconds later five squelch breaks caressed my ear— Mariposa was inbound.

Chapter 29

Mighty-Tight extended her long pole out to the buffalo's head and began tapping his right ear. Slowly the big animal sauntered to the left and moved out over the X. Her pole lifted.

I waved a clenched-fist signal to Phan, indicating he should halt any vehicle or other intrusion from the north end. I anticipated that he could handle anything but a truckload of NVA during the brief moments it would take to spring my snatch trap.

Three quick breaks flashed on the handset. The vehicle had passed Ski's position. I freed my arms from the pack straps and prepared to move. My eyes scanned the approach, then glanced up to Bacsin. She was standing in the cart with her eyes fixed on the approach.

I waved for her to get down. Reluctantly she knelt behind the cart walls.

I could hear the vehicle before I could see it. The noise sounded like the muffler was perforated.

The small black sedan chugged around the curve slowly, straining through the mud.

Through the branches I could see two personnel bouncing slightly in the front seat. The driver was clearly shorter

241

than the passenger. He appeared to be wearing a dark green uniform. No headgear.

The car skidded to a slow stop near the cart. The shrill horn blasted sporadically.

Gripping my pistol I lurched out of the shadows bounding toward the driver's open side window.

Seeing me, the driver quickly yanked a pistol into vertical view, then jabbed the barrel at me.

My tense grip triggered two thudding point-blank rounds into his head, hurling him into a bloody sprawl over the passenger.

"Oh, no! Oh, no no! God no! Ohhh, please no! Fuck! Please, God—"

"Out!" I yelled, yanking the driver's door open and jabbing my pistol at the big man. "Out!" I darted a glance at the limp NVA. Dark paths of blood streamed over the red lapel trim of his coat.

The passenger scrambled, prying himself away from the dead body humped over his legs.

"Tuong, get this communist bastard out!" I shouted, stepping back, then hurrying around the nose of the car.

The splattered residue of exploded blood trickled off the face of the hysterical man as he screamed and hopped wildly with his arms stretched above his head. "Oh, God, oh, God, please—"

"On the ground, puke!"

He dropped to his knees—quivering, molding his hands into a praying grip.

"On your back!" I shouted while turning to see Bacsin standing—petrified.

"Move out," I motioned to her with my pistol. "Now!"

"Phan, *lai day*!" I shouted to the north. I looked down at the supine figure shivering in the mud, still praying up to me.

I glanced at Tuong. He was pulling the dead NVA out of the front seat. "You and Phan get that body loaded in the back seat *le mau!*"

"Please . . . sir, I'm not, I'm not the en—the enemy. Please God, don't ki-kill me. I'm Lieutenant De-Defrisco. Please God, I'm an Amer—"

I dropped, ramming a solid knee into his chest. "I'm not God and you are not an American, asshole!" I yelled, thrusting black steel into his big gape. "The only fucking thing American about you is gonna be my lead pumping into your ugly scum-suckin' skull if you don't tell me right now—*right fuckin' now!*—where the Saydem is!"

A quivering stream of wet snot spilled over the thick rod jammed in his mouth.

"Right fuckin' now!" I screamed, shoving the steel against his gullet.

His eyes shuttered as his gut heaved violently under my knee. Yellow puke belched over the barrel.

I jerked the dripping steel away and grabbed a fistful of his greasy hair with my left hand. Yanking his writhing head toward me I leaned over, whispering loudly, "You're drowning, Donald. What's the matter—vomit got your tongue?"

Blood and puke spewed over my face as he gasped, trying to talk. "It's in . . ." he gulped, jabbing a hand toward the car. "It's in—in the . . . back," his gagging voice sputtered.

Releasing him, I stood and nudged him with my foot. "Roll over, anus!" I knelt and quickly ran my hand over his torso, buttocks, and legs feeling for a weapon. I found a small leg-holstered revolver. "Don't get up!" I said, standing and tucking his pistol into my belt.

He squirmed clawing at the mud, belching more vomit.

I hurried to the car and scanned the back seat area.

Tuong and Phan were struggling to bend the NVA's legs upward so they could get the rear door closed. There was nothing in the rear passenger area except a small duffel bag.

I reached out and grabbed the ignition keys, then hurried to the rear of the sedan.

"Brett, Brett," Ski's labored voice shouted.

I glanced back and saw Binkowski jogging toward me.

"We heard yelling. . . . I thought . . . I—I better come and—"

"Get up front and take charge of Defrisco! He's on the ground up there."

"What are you doing with—"

"Do like I said!"

"Okay, okay."

Two quick tries later I found the trunk-lid key. I tensed, feeling the key turn right, then heard a muffled click.

I knelt at eye level to the rear edge of the deck lid before easing it upward. If Defrisco was telling the truth about the SADM being in here, I knew he could have omitted the fact it was booby-trapped.

Inching the lid upward I squinted, trying to see any wire or cord attached to the inside rim of the trunk lid. None. I slowly ran my fingers beneath the curved edge of the metal. Nothing.

Carefully opening the lid I peered into the small cavern. A dark blanket was contoured over a large circular object. Two large blocks of wood were chocked at the lower inward portion of the object as if to prevent it from rolling. I reached to gently pull the blanket away and gazed, half awed, at the blunt nose of five-zero-one.

"What dat, Sar Brett?" Tuong's voice whispered.

I glanced around, seeing him and Phan standing beside me.

"Never mind, gang," I said, looking down at them. "I want you to get your eyes glued on that fucking road. Tell me if anything comes."

As they departed I reached to pull the chocks away. I gripped the cold gray surface and turned it slowly 180 degrees to see the flat steel heart face. The locking cover was missing.

Leaning my head downward for a closer look I stopped. My stunned eyes blinked. Red pierced my eye like a tracer round. I shifted my eyes to the arming well—loaded.

I took a deep breath to steady my senses and leaned closer to scan the timer setting. The dark interior obscured my view of the small window. I fumbled for the flashlight, then flipped it on holding the bright red filter light near my eyes.

"Zero-nine-two-four," I said softly. Suddenly the right side minute window clicked to the number three.

"Brett, I've tied his hands. What do you want me to do with—"

"Bring him here!"

Ski led the stumbling dirt-splotched figure of Defrisco to the rear of the car. A large puke-stained peace symbol hung from his neck. His eyes got big seeing me.

"He'll never fit in there—he's too—"

Arnold's shocked eyes fixed on the SADM. "What the fuck is . . . is that it, it, the—"

"That's it, partner."

Defrisco avoided my glare. I reached to grasp his thick leather necklace and tugged him to my face. "Your toy here is armed and running, cool breeze. We are going for a ride and when we stop you're going to disarm it."

He sucked air. "Ah, I—I—"

I gripped tighter on the leather cord. "No, don't talk, cool breeze. Silence is golden."

We placed Defrisco in a contorted prone position lying across the blood-spattered NVA in the back seat.

I instructed Ski to gather the radios, and the team, and move posthaste back to the safe house.

With Tuong in the right seat monitoring DD I backed the sedan up and drove south to the cart road and turned west.

Fifteen minutes later, as I pulled under the long thrashing hut, DD was still reverently quiet.

Chapter 30

We bound DD's waist in a seated position to the bench
beside the rain barrel with his hands tied in front. I stood
back and looked at him. "Did you ever see that nifty little
sign that says, 'Today is the first day of the rest of your
life,' cool breeze?"

"Ah, yes, I did. Yes," he answered.

He placed his tied hands down on his lap and cringed
as I slapped cold water out of the open barrel top and over
his vomit-crusted face and chest.

"Well," I continued while splashing more water over
him. "We have a sign that hangs over the bar back at my
recon camp. You want to know what it says, Donald?"

He coughed. "No . . . ah, I mean yeah. Yes."

"It says, 'Today may be the last day in the short remainder of your life. Drink up.'

"And at times it's been right, Donald, because a lot of
my friends have died over here."

I glanced at Phan who was squatted, watching, smiling.

I nodded, indicating for Phan to follow me. "Be right
back, Donald."

Walking with Phan a slight distance from the hut I gave

him some instructions, then returned to the front of the car, which was pulled up near where DD was seated.

I washed my face and arms in the barrel, then stepped back, leaning against the car fender.

"You know a lady named Megan Blair?"

His head raised up with squinted eyes. "Yeah," he grunted.

"She says you're a charming and charismatic guy, Donald. You don't seem like that to me. At least not right now.

"But, anyhow, Megan is a great gal. She gave my partner and me some technical training on this Saydem you ran off with." I jerked a nod toward the rear of the car.

Glancing at my watch, I explained to DD that I estimated we had a little over eight hours until detonation. I told him that I was aware that all I had to do was set a thermite on it, ignite the grenade, and a few smoldering minutes later a big part of my mission was accomplished.

My next sentence was a bald-faced lie. "The other part of my mission is finding and bringing back you and your cronies, Donald." I shrugged.

"I already have you, but I need Gordon and Abbey. So you are going to tell me where they are, aren't you?"

He looked at me with just one eye squinted. "They went to Hanoi. They're going to—to an interview with Hanoi Hanna."

"Why didn't you tag along, Donald?"

When Ski and the team returned I coded a long message and requested exfil of nine personnel at 2300. I was a little premature in saying "mission accomplished" but I knew that the SADM was the main concern with MACV— Mariposa neutralization was just so much icing on the cake.

I put the Yards out on a 360-watch and had Ski set up

our radio on the emergency guard freq. After transmitting my message in the blind twice to Sunburst, the day SOG monitor aircraft, Ski and I returned to Defrisco's location with a small box. DD was asleep, leaning his head back against the wall.

I'd instructed Phan to have Tuong take our friendly reptile and tape the mouth with electrical tape and place it in a radio battery box.

I'd already prepped Ski on his role in my charade. I opened the box, gently reached in, and grabbed the snake by its narrow head. Tuong had taped the long finger-shaped mouth well.

Without waking Defrisco I pulled the long snake out and dangled him in front of DD. "Wake up, asshole!" I yelled.

He blinked, raising his head slowly until his nose touched the snake scales. "Oh, no! No!" he screamed, jerking backward, banging his head loudly against the wall and calling me God again several times.

I pulled the snake away, keeping its taped head in my grasp.

"Okay, Donald, let me tell you about my little friend here.

"Did you ever hear of the famed green mamba of South Africa?"

He nodded with eyes as wide as porthole windows.

"Well this little fellow is the mamba's Asian cousin. It's called a greendink—neurotoxic venom, Donald! Bad shit, buddy! Know what I mean?"

He gave me the porthole nod again.

I explained to DD that I didn't feel any real danger because my life was going well. "Donald, I've got an exfil on the way. Plenty of time on the clock over there, and . . ." I paused, smiling at the snake, then looked back at my petrified prisoner. "Well, they'll probably give Ski and me a medal when we get back.

"But you, asshole, are in deep do-do." I raised my voice. "Because I need some fuckin' answers!" I moved closer and let greendink wrap about two feet of length around Defrisco's neck. "And if I don't get 'em I'm taking the tape off greendink here and dropping him down your shirt!

"We'll just load your limp carcass on the chopper and tell MACV you died of multiple snake bites. Now that I've sorta got your attention, anus, let me ask you something important, may I!" I said loudly, holding the snake's head to his face.

"Oh, oh, yes! Fuck yes!"

"Are you gonna play ball with me?" I whispered.

"Yes, yes, sir. Anything. Please, God."

I unraveled greendink from DD.

"First off, Donald, I don't believe your bullshit Hanoi Hanna story. Second, I want to know why you were bounding along the fuckin' highway with an NVA chauffeur in front and an armed Saydem in the fuckin' trunk."

By mid-afternoon I finally pieced together that Donald Defrisco had killed his puppets in order to keep his forthcoming ransom all for himself. For some strange reason I felt a kind of sadness for Abbey and Gordon—they'd really believed in the lieutenant's "ideals."

I learned that the reason DD was northbound was because he'd made plans to give the SADM to the NVA and become a hometown hero with the hippie cult. He'd still have his ransom and grab a little slice of fame at the same time.

The officer was an NVA captain he'd met at Bacsin's. Nugyen Van Nuclear was probably planning to put a feather in his pith helmet by taking Defrisco to Hanoi personally. The reason Defrisco had armed the SADM was to make sure his NVA chauffeur didn't get tricky and try to double-cross him on the way. With the bomb activated the host had to deliver.

Bacsin returned to our location at 1930. We'd already got a confirmation on exfil from our SOG monitor aircraft at 1700.

I took Bacsin and the elder couple into the empty main hooch. I still had the Cowboys on guard and Ski was watching Defrisco.

I set the box of sterile gold on the table in front of them and opened it.

"Bacsin," I said with a concerned tone. "My recommendation is that you take this money and you and the Trans exfil with me. This area is going to get hot after they discover that officer MIA and particularly after our Jolly Green swoops in here tonight."

All three politely declined my offer.

Bacsin smiled and said, "My friend Cal-van say me something one time I say to you now. I can fake the hea."

I interpreted her words easily. "Fade the heat," I said, smiling.

She departed at 2040 hours at my request and took the Trans into town with her.

As Ski and I sat watching the white-hot glow of my thermite burn slowly into the SADM he looked over at me, then glanced at the hut where we'd left Defrisco tied.

"Brett," he said, glancing at his watch. "You said we were moving out to the exfil LZ in about an hour. Who's—who's going to do the . . . job, the, you know, on De-Defrisco before we go?"

"Nobody, partner," I said, pulling the Pen-EE from my pocket. "In about ten minutes we're going to walk DD down to the main road and turn him loose. I told Bacsin to tell the local NVA that she saw a big white male yesterday in the tree grove with a stalled vehicle.

"They'll probably figure out he did it. Do you know the method of capital punishment in North Vietnam?"

I reached and dropped the Pen-EE into the big white-hot hole in the top of the thermite.

"No, I don't know," Ski answered softly.

"Hanging, partner. Hanging."

Author's note: Readers' comments about this story and other Command and Control novels are appreciated. Comments may be addressed to: James Mitchell P.O. Box 1885 Hurst, TX 76053.